THE LADY AND THE UNICORN

TRACY CHEVALIER was born and grew up in Washington, DC. She moved to England in 1984 and worked as a reference book editor. In 1993 she took an MA in Creative Writing at the University of East Anglia and her first novel, *The Virgin Blue*, was published in 1997. She is the author of three further books: *Girl with a Pearl Earring, Falling Angels* and *The Lady and the Unicorn*. She is currently researching and writing her fifth novel, which will be about the painter and poet William Blake. Tracy Chevalier lives in London with her husband and their son.

THE TAPESTRIES

Little is known about the Lady and the Unicorn tapestries. They were woven in c.1500, probably in Flanders. In 1841, they were rediscovered in very poor condition in Boussac. They were purchased and restored in 1882 by the French government for the Museé de Cluny in Paris (now the Museé National du Moyen-Age), where they still hang today. Among other things, the tapestries represent the five senses. Each tapestry is usually referred to by the sense it depicts: Taste, Touch, Smell, Sound and Sight. The sixth – which either introduces or concludes the series – is known as Á Mon Seul Désir (To My One Desire), for the words woven into it.

The illustrations show Á Mon Seul Désir, L'Odorat, L'Ouie, Le Goût, La Vue, Le Toucher all from *The Lady and the Unicorn*, wool and silk tapestry, late 15th century. Photograph © RMN/Museé National du Moyen-Age, Cluny.

THE LADY
AND
THE UNICORN

Tracy Chevalier

HarperCollinsPublishers

HarperCollins*Publishers*
77–85 Fulham Palace Road,
Hammersmith, London W6 8JB

www.harpercollins.co.uk

This paperback edition 2004
5

The verse quoted on pages 179–80 and 193 is from the motet
'Joliement, en douce desirree / Quant voi la florete / Je sui joliete /
Aptatur' published in *The Montpellier Codex*, edited by Hans Tischler,
Recent Researches in the Music of the Middle Ages and Early Renaissance,
vols. 2–8 (Madison, Wisconsin: A–R Editions, Inc., 1978). The passage is
reprinted from Part 4 (vol. 8): *Texts and Translations*, p. 11. Translations by
Susan Stakel and Joel C. Relihan. Used with permission.

A catalogue record for this book
is available from the British Library

ISBN 0 00 714091 6

Set in Postscript Linotype Giovanni with Spectrum display by
Rowland Phototypesetting Ltd, Bury St Edmunds, Suffolk

Printed and bound in Great Britain by Clays Ltd, St Ives plc

I
PARIS

Lent–Eastertide 1490

NICOLAS DES INNOCENTS

The messenger said I was to come at once. That's how Jean Le Viste is – he expects everyone to do what he says immediately.

And I did. I followed the messenger, stopping just briefly to clean my brushes. Commissions from Jean Le Viste can mean food on the table for weeks. Only the King says no to Jean Le Viste, and I am certainly no king.

On the other hand, how many times have I rushed across the Seine to the rue du Four, only to come back again with no commission? It's not that Jean Le Viste is a fickle man – on the contrary, he is as sober and hard as his beloved Louis XI once was. Humourless too. I never jest with him. It's a relief to escape his house to the nearest tavern for a drink and a laugh and a grope to restore my spirits.

He knows what he wants. But sometimes when I come to discuss yet another coat of arms to decorate the chimney, or to paint on his wife's carriage door, or to work into a bit of stained glass for the chapel – people say the Le Viste arms are as common as horse dung – he'll stop suddenly, shake his head and say with a frown, 'This is not needed. I should not be thinking about such common-place matters. Go.' And I do, feeling guilty, as if I am to blame for bringing a carriage's decoration to his attention, when it was he who called for me.

I'd been to the rue du Four house half a dozen times before. It is not a place that impresses. Even with all the fields around it, it is built as if it were in the middle of the city, with the rooms long and narrow, the walls too dark, the stables too close – the house always smells of horses. It is the sort of house a family that has bought its way into the Court would live in – grand enough but poorly placed. Jean Le Viste probably thinks he has done well to be given such a place to live, while the Court laughs behind his back. He should be living close to the King and Notre Dame, not outside the city walls in the swampy fields around Saint-Germain-des-Prés.

When I arrived the steward took me not to Jean Le Viste's private chamber, a map-lined room where he performs duties for Court and King alongside family matters, but to the Grande Salle, where the Le Vistes receive visitors and entertain. I had never been there. It was a long room with a large hearth at the opposite end from the door and an oak table down the centre. Apart from a stone coat of arms that hung on the chimneybreast and another painted over the door, it was unadorned – though the ceiling was panelled with handsome carved wood.

Not so grand, I thought as I looked around. Although shutters were open, the fire hadn't been lit and the room was chilly with its bare walls.

4

'Wait here for my master,' the steward said, glaring at me. In this house people either respected artists or showed their contempt.

I turned my back on him and gazed out of a narrow window where there was a clear view of the towers of Saint-Germain-des-Prés. Some say Jean Le Viste took this house so that his pious wife could step across to the church easily and often.

The door opened behind me and I turned, prepared to bow. It was only a servant girl, who smirked as she caught me half-bent. I straightened and watched as she moved across the room, banging a pail against her leg. She knelt and began to clear the fireplace of ashes.

Was she the one? I tried to remember – it had been dark that night behind the stables. She was fatter than I recalled, and sullen with her heavy brow, but her face was sweet enough. It was worth a word.

'Stay a moment,' I said when she had pulled herself up clumsily and made her way to the door. 'Sit and rest your feet. I'll tell you a story.'

The girl stopped with a jolt. 'You mean the story of the unicorn?'

She was the one. I opened my mouth to answer, but the girl jumped in before me. 'Does the story go on to say that the woman grows big with child and may lose her place? Is that what happens?'

So that was why she was fat. I turned back to the window. 'You should have taken more care.'

'I shouldn't have listened to you, is what I should have done. I should have shoved your tongue right up your arse.'

'Out you go now, there's a good girl. Here.' I dug into my pocket, pulled out a few coins and threw them onto the table. 'To help with the baby.'

The girl stepped across the room and spat in my face. By the time I'd wiped the spittle from my eyes she was gone. So were the coins.

Jean Le Viste came in soon after, followed by Léon Le Vieux. Most patrons use a merchant like Léon to act as middleman, haggling over terms, drawing up the contract, providing initial money and materials, making sure the work gets done. I'd already had dealings with the old merchant over coats of arms painted for a chimneybreast, an Annunciation for the chamber of Jean Le Viste's wife, and some stained glass for the chapel in their château near Lyons.

Léon is much favoured by the Le Vistes. I have respect for him but I cannot like him. He is from a family that were once Jews. He makes no secret of it, but has used it to his advantage, for Jean Le Viste is also from a family much changed over time. That is why he prefers Léon – they are both outsiders who have made their way in. Of course Léon is careful to attend Mass two or three times a week at Notre Dame, where many will see him, just as Jean Le Viste takes care to act the true noble, commissioning works for his house, entertaining lavishly, bowing and scraping to his King.

Léon was looking at me, smiling through his beard as if he had spotted a monkey on my back. I turned to Jean Le Viste. '*Bonjour*, Monseigneur. You wished to see me.' I bowed so low my head throbbed. It never hurt to bow low.

Jean Le Viste's jaw is like a hatchet, his eyes like knife blades. They flicked around the room now, then rested on the window over my shoulder. 'I want to discuss a commission with you, Nicolas des Innocents,' he said, pulling at the sleeves of his robe, which was trimmed with rabbit fur and dyed the deep red lawyers wear. 'For this room.'

I glanced around the room, keeping my face clear of thoughts. It was best to be so with Jean Le Viste. 'What did you have in mind, Monseigneur?'

'Tapestries.'

I noted the plural. 'Perhaps a set of your coat of arms to hang either side of the door?'

Jean Le Viste grimaced. I wished I hadn't spoken.

'I want tapestries to cover all of the walls.'

'All of them?'

'Yes.'

I looked around the room once again, more carefully this time. The Grande Salle was at least ten paces long and five wide. Its walls were very thick, the local stone rough and grey. Three windows were cut into one of the long walls, and the hearth took up half of one of the end walls. Tapestries to line the room could take a weaver several years.

'What would you have as the subject, Monseigneur?' I had designed one tapestry for Jean Le Viste – a coat of arms, of course. It had been simple enough, scaling up the coat of arms to tapestry size and designing a bit of background greenery around it.

Jean Le Viste folded his arms over his chest. 'Last year I was made President of the Cour des Aides.'

The position meant nothing to me but I knew what I should say. 'Yes, Monseigneur. That is a great honour to you and your family.'

Léon rolled his eyes to the carved ceiling, while Jean Le Viste waved his hand as if he were ridding the room of smoke. Everything I said seemed to annoy him.

'I want to celebrate the achievement with a set of tapestries. I've been saving this room for a special occasion.'

This time I waited.

'Of course it is essential that the family coat of arms be displayed.'

'Of course, Monseigneur.'

Then Jean Le Viste surprised me. 'But not on its own. There are already many examples of the coat of arms alone, here as well as in the rest of the house.' He gestured at the arms over the door and hearth, and to some carved in the ceiling beams that I hadn't noticed before. 'No, I want it to be part of a larger scene, to reflect my place at the heart of the Court.'

'A procession, perhaps?'

'A battle.'

'A battle?'

'Yes. The Battle of Nancy.'

I kept my face thoughtful. I even smiled a little. But in truth I knew little of battles, and nothing of this one at Nancy, of who had been there, who had been killed and who had won. I'd seen paintings of battles but never done one myself. Horses, I thought. I would need to paint at least twenty horses to cover these walls, tangled with men's arms and legs and armour. I wondered then what had made Jean Le Viste – or Léon, more likely – choose me for this work. My reputation at the Court is as a miniaturist, painter of tiny portraits of ladies that they give men to carry. Praised for their delicacy, the miniatures are much in demand. I paint shields and ladies' carriage doors for drink money, but my true skill is in making a face the size of my thumb, using a few boar bristles and colour mixed with egg white. It needs a steady hand, and that I have, even after a long night of drinking at Le Coq d'Or. But the thought of painting twenty huge horses – I began to sweat, though the room was chilly.

'You are sure that you want the Battle of Nancy, Monseigneur,' I said. It was not quite a question.

Jean Le Viste frowned. 'Why would I not be sure?'

'No reason, Monseigneur,' I answered quickly. 'But they will be important works and you must be sure you have chosen what you want.' I cursed myself for my clumsy words.

Jean Le Viste snorted. 'I always know what I want. I wonder at you, though – you don't seem so keen on this work. Perhaps I should find another artist who is happier to do it.'

I bowed low again. 'Oh no, Monseigneur, of course I am most honoured and grateful to be asked to design such a glorious work. I am sure I am not worthy of your kindness in thinking of me. You may have no fear that I'll put my heart and blood into these tapestries.'

Jean Le Viste nodded, as if such grovelling were his due. 'I'll leave you here with Léon to discuss details and to measure the walls,' he said as he turned to go. 'I will expect to see preliminary drawings just before Easter – by Maundy Thursday, with paintings by the Ascension.'

When we were alone Léon Le Vieux chuckled. 'What a fool you are.'

With Léon it's best to come straight to the point and ignore his gibes. 'My fee is ten *livres tournois* – four now, three when I finish the drawings, and three when the paintings are done.'

'Four *livres parisis*,' he responded quickly. 'Half when you finish the drawings, the rest when you deliver the paintings and they're to Monseigneur's satisfaction.'

'Absolutely not. I can't work with no pay at the start. And my terms are in *livres tournois*.' It was just like Léon to try to confuse me by using Paris *livres*.

Léon shrugged, his eyes merry. 'We are in Paris, *n'est-ce pas*? Shouldn't we use *livres parisis*? That is what I prefer.'

'Eight *livres tournois*, with three now, then three and two.'

'Seven. I will give you two tomorrow, then two and three at the end.'

I changed the subject – it is always best to let the merchant wait a little. 'Where will the tapestries be made?'

'North. Probably Brussels. They do the best work there.'

North? I shuddered. I once had business in Tournai and hated the flat light and suspicious people so much I vowed never to go north of Paris again. At least I wouldn't have to do more than paint designs, and that I could do in Paris. Once they were done I would have no more to do with the making of the tapestries.

'So, what do you know about the battle at Nancy?' Léon asked.

I shrugged. 'What does it matter? All battles are the same, *non*?'

'That's like saying that all women are the same.'

I smiled. 'I repeat – all battles are the same.'

Léon shook his head. 'I pity your wife one day. Now tell me, what will you have in your tapestries?'

'Horses, men in armour, standards, pikes, swords, shields, blood.'

'What will Louis XI be wearing?'

'Armour, of course. Perhaps a special plume in his helmet. I don't know, in truth, but I know people who can tell me that sort of thing. Someone will carry the royal standard, I expect.'

'I hope your friends are cleverer than you and will tell you that Louis XI was not at the Battle of Nancy.'

'Oh.' This was Léon Le Vieux's way – to make a fool of all around him, excepting his patron. You did not make a fool of Jean Le Viste.

'*Bon*.' Léon took out some papers from his pocket and laid them on the table. 'I've already discussed the contents of the tapestries with Monseigneur and done some measuring. You'll need to do them more precisely, of course. Here.' He pointed to six rectangles he had roughly sketched. 'There's space for two long ones here and here, and four smaller. Here is the sequence of the battle.' He explained the battle carefully, suggesting scenes for each of the tapestries – the grouping of the two camps, the initial strike, two scenes of battle chaos, then the death of Charles the Bold and the triumphant procession of the victors. Though I listened and made sketches of my own on the paper, part of me stood apart and wondered at what I was agreeing to do. There would be no women in these tapestries, nothing miniature and delicate, nothing that would be easy for me to paint. I would earn my fee with sweat and long hours.

'Once you've made the paintings,' Léon reminded me, 'your work is done. I'll take them north to the weaver, and his cartoonist will enlarge them to use for the weaving.'

I should have been pleased that I wouldn't have to paint the horses large. Instead, however, I became protective of my work. 'How do I know that this cartoonist is a proper artist? I don't want him making a mess of my designs.'

'He won't change what Jean Le Viste has decided on – only changes that will help the design and making of the tapestries. You haven't done many tapestries, have you, Nicolas? Only a coat of arms, I believe.'

'Which I scaled up myself – I had no need of a cartoonist. Surely I'm capable of doing so on this commission.'

'These tapestries are a very different matter from a coat of arms. They will need a proper cartoonist. *Tiens*, there's one thing I forgot to mention. You'll need to be sure there are Le Viste coats of arms throughout the tapestries. Monseigneur will insist on that.'

'Did Monseigneur actually fight there?'

Léon laughed. 'Undoubtedly Jean Le Viste was on the other side of France during the Battle of Nancy, working for the King. That doesn't matter – just put his coat of arms on flags and shields that others carry. You may want to see some pictures of that battle and others. Go to Gérard the printer on the rue Vieille du Temple – he has a book he can show you of engravings of the Battle of Nancy. I'll tell him to expect you. Now, I'll leave you to your measurements. If you have problems, come and see me. And bring the drawings to me by Palm Sunday – if I want changes you'll need enough time to get them done before Monseigneur sees them.'

Clearly Léon Le Vieux was Jean Le Viste's eyes. I had to please him, and if he liked what he saw, Jean Le Viste would too.

I couldn't resist a last question. 'Why did you choose me for this commission?'

Léon gathered his plain brown robe about him – no fur trim for him. 'I didn't. If it were my choice I would have someone who has done more tapestries, or go direct to the weaver – they have designs in hand and can work from those. It's cheaper and they are good at the designs.' Léon was always frank.

'Why did Jean Le Viste choose me, then?'

'You'll find out soon enough. *Alors*, come to me tomorrow and I'll have the papers for you to sign, and the money.'

'I haven't agreed to the terms yet.'

'Oh, I think you have. There are some commissions an artist doesn't say no to. This is one of them, Nicolas des Innocents.' He gave me a look as he left.

He was right. I had been talking as if I were going to do them. Still, the terms were not bad. In fact, Léon had not haggled very hard. I wondered suddenly if his terms were still in Paris *livres* after all.

I turned my eyes to the walls I was to dress so sumptuously. Two months to draw and paint twenty horses and their riders! I stood at one end of the room and walked to the other, counting twelve paces, then walked across, counting six paces. Pulling a chair to one wall, I stood on it, but even reaching as high as I could, I was far from touching the ceiling. I pulled the chair back and, after hesitating a moment, stepped up onto the oak table. I reached up but was still at least my height again from the ceiling.

I was wondering where I could find a long pole to use for measuring when I heard humming behind me and turned around. A girl stood in the entrance watching me. A lovely girl – she had pale skin, a high forehead, a long nose, hair the colour of honey, clear eyes. I'd not seen such a girl before. For a moment I couldn't say anything.

'Hello, beauty,' I managed at last.

The girl laughed and hopped from one foot to the other. She was wearing a simple blue dress, with a tight bodice, a square neck and narrow sleeves. It was cut well and the wool was fine, but it was not ornate. She wore a plain scarf too, her long hair falling almost to her waist. Compared to the servant who had cleaned the fireplace, she was clearly too fine to be a maid. Perhaps a lady-in-waiting?

'The mistress of the house wishes to see you,' she said, then turned and ran away, still laughing.

I didn't move. I've learned from years of experience that dogs and falcons and ladies come back to you if you stay where you are. I could hear her feet slap across the floor of the next room, then stop. After a moment the steps began again and she reappeared at the door. 'Are you coming?' She was still smiling.

'I will, beauty, if you will walk with me and not hurry ahead as if I were a dragon you had to flee.'

The girl laughed. 'Come,' she beckoned, and this time I hopped down from the table. I had to step quickly to keep up with her as she ran from room to room. Her skirt flapped, as if she were blown along by a secret wind. Up close she smelled of something sweet and spicy, underlined with sweat. Her mouth moved as if she were chewing something.

'What do you have in your mouth, beauty?'

'Toothache.' The girl stuck out her tongue – on its pink tip lay a clove. The sight of her tongue made me hard. I wanted to plough her.

'Ah, that must hurt.' I will suck it better. 'Now, why does your mistress want to see me?'

The girl looked at me, amused. 'I expect she'll tell you herself.'

I slowed down. 'Why rush? She won't mind, will she, if you and I have a little chat along the way?'

'What do you want to talk about?' The girl turned up a round staircase.

I leapt onto the stair in front of her to stop her from climbing. 'What sorts of animals do you like?'

'Animals?'

'I don't want you to think of me as a dragon. I'd rather you thought of me as something else. Something you prefer.'

The girl thought. 'A parakeet, perhaps. I do like parakeets.

I have four. They eat from my hand.' She ran around me to stand on the stairs above me. She didn't go higher. Yes, I thought. I've set out my wares and she's coming for a look. Come closer, my dear, and see my plums. Squeeze them.

'Not a parakeet,' I said. 'Surely you don't think of me as a squawker and an imitator.'

'My parakeets make no noise. But anyway, you are an artist, *non*? Isn't that what you do – imitate life?'

'I make things more beautiful than they are – though there are some things, my girl, that cannot be improved upon with paint.' I stepped around her and stood three steps above. I wanted to see if she would come to me.

She did. Her eyes remained clear and wide, but her mouth was twisted into a knowing smile. With her tongue she moved the clove from one cheek to the other.

I will have you, I thought. I will.

'Perhaps you're a fox instead,' she said. 'Your hair has a little red in among the brown.'

I pouted. 'How can you be so cruel? Do I look devious? Would I cheat a man? Do I run sideways and never straight? Rather I'm a dog who lays himself at his mistress's feet and is loyal to her forever.'

'Dogs want too much attention', the girl said, 'and they jump up and muddy my skirts with their paws.' She stepped around me and did not stop this time. 'Come – my mistress waits. We must not keep her.'

I would have to hurry – I'd wasted too much time on other animals. 'I know which animal I want to be,' I panted, running after her.

'What's that?'

'A unicorn. Do you know of the unicorn?'

The girl snorted. She'd reached the top of the stairs and was opening the door to another room. 'I know it likes to lay its head in maidens' laps. Is that what you like to do?'

'Ah, don't think of me so coarsely. The unicorn does something far greater than that. His horn has a special power, you see. Did you know that?'

The girl slowed down to look at me. 'What does it do?'

'If a well is poisoned –'

'There's a well!' The girl stopped and pointed out of a window to the courtyard. A younger girl was leaning over the edge of a well and looking down into it, the sun bathing her hair in gold light.

'Jeanne always does that,' the girl said. 'She likes to look at her reflection.' As we watched the girl spat into the well.

'If your well there was poisoned, beauty, or sullied such as Jeanne has just done, a unicorn could come along and dip his horn into it and it would become pure again. What do you think of that?'

The girl moved the clove around with her tongue. 'What do you want me to think of it?'

'I want you to think of me as your unicorn. There are times when you're sullied, yes, even you, beauty. Every woman is. That is Eve's punishment. But you can be made pure again, every month, if you will only let me tend to you.' Plough you again and again until you laugh and cry. 'Every month you will go back to Eden.' It was that last line that never failed when I was hunting a woman – the idea of that simple paradise seemed to snare them. They always opened their legs to me in the hope that they would find it. Perhaps some of them did.

The girl laughed, raucously this time. She was ready. I reached out to squeeze her and seal our exchange.

'Claude? Is that you? What's taken you so long?' A door across from us had opened and a woman stood staring at us, her arms folded across her chest. I dropped my hand.

'*Pardon*, Maman. Here he is.' Claude stepped back and gestured at me. I bowed.

'What's in your mouth?' the woman asked.

Claude swallowed. 'Clove. For my tooth.'

'You should be chewing mint – that's much better for toothache.'

'Yes, Maman.' Claude laughed again – probably at the look on my face. She turned and ran from the room, banging the door behind her. The room echoed with her steps.

I shuddered. I had just tried to seduce Jean Le Viste's daughter.

In the times I'd been to the house on the rue du Four I had only ever seen the three Le Viste girls from afar – running across the courtyard, leaving on horses, walking with a group of ladies to Saint-Germain-des-Prés. Of course the girl by the well was one of them too – if I'd been paying attention I would have understood when I saw her hair and how she held herself that she and Claude were sisters. Then I would have guessed who they were and never have told Claude the story of the unicorn. But I had not been thinking about who she was – I'd been thinking about how to bed her.

Claude had only to repeat to her father what I'd said and I would be thrown out, the commission taken from me. And I would never see Claude again.

I wanted her more than ever, and not just for bedding. I wanted to lie with her at my side and talk to her, touch that mouth and hair and make her laugh. I wondered where she had run to in the house. I would never be allowed in there – not a Paris artist with a nobleman's daughter.

I stood very still, thinking of these things. Perhaps I did so for a moment too long. The woman in the doorway moved so that the rosary hanging at her waist clicked against the buttons on her sleeve, and I stepped back from my thoughts. She was looking at me as if she'd guessed all that was going through my head. She said nothing, though, but pushed the door open and went back in. I followed.

I had painted miniatures in many ladies' chambers – this one was not so different. There was a bed made of chestnut and hung with curtains of blue and yellow silk. There were oak chairs in a semicircle, padded with embroidered cushions. There was a side table covered with bottles and a casket for jewels and several chests for dresses. An open window framed a view of Saint-Germain-des-Prés. Gathered in the corner were her ladies-in-waiting, working on embroidery. They smiled at me as if they were one person rather than five, and I chided myself for ever thinking Claude could be one of them.

Geneviève de Nanterre – wife of Jean Le Viste and mistress of the house – sat down by the window. She had clearly once been as beautiful as her daughter. She was still a handsome woman, with a wide forehead and a delicate chin, but where Claude's face was heart-shaped, hers had become triangular. Fifteen years as Jean Le Viste's wife had straightened the curves, set the jaw, lined the brow. Her eyes were dark currants to Claude's clear quinces.

In one way, at least, she outshone her daughter. Her dress was richer – cream and green brocade, intricately patterned with flowers and leaves. She wore fine jewels at her throat and her hair was braided with silk and pearls. She would never be mistaken for a lady-in-waiting – she was clearly dressed to be attended to.

'You have just been with my husband in the Grande Salle,' she said. 'Discussing tapestries.'

'Yes, Madame.'

'I suppose he wants a battle.'

'Yes, Madame. The Battle of Nancy.'

'And what scenes will the tapestries display?'

'I am not sure, Madame. Monseigneur has only just told me of the tapestries. I need to sit down and sketch before I can say for certain.'

'Will there be men?'

'Certainly, Madame.'

'Horses?'

'Yes.'

'Blood?'

'*Pardon*, Madame?'

Geneviève de Nanterre waved her hand. 'This is a battle. Will there be blood flowing from wounds?'

'I expect so, Madame. Charles the Bold will be killed, of course.'

'Have you ever been in a battle, Nicolas des Innocents?'

'No, Madame.'

'I want you to think for a moment that you are a soldier.'

'But I am a miniaturist for the Court, Madame.'

'I know that, but for a moment you are a soldier who has fought in the Battle of Nancy. You lost your arm in that battle. You are sitting in the Grande Salle as a guest of my husband and myself. Beside you is your wife, your pretty young wife who helps you with the little difficulties that arise from not having two hands – breaking bread, buckling on your sword, mounting your horse.' Geneviève de Nanterre spoke rhythmically, as if she were singing a lullaby. I began to feel I was floating down a river with no idea where I was going.

Is she a little mad? I thought.

Geneviève de Nanterre crossed her arms and turned her head to one side. 'As you eat you look at the tapestries of the battle that has cost you your arm. You recognize Charles the Bold being slaughtered, your wife sees the blood spurting from his wounds. Everywhere you see Le Viste banners. But where is Jean Le Viste?'

I tried to remember what Léon had said. 'Monseigneur is at the King's side, Madame.'

'Yes. During the battle my husband and the King were snug at Court in Paris, far from Nancy. Now, as this soldier, how would you feel, knowing that Jean Le Viste was never at the Battle of Nancy, yet seeing his banners everywhere in the tapestries?'

21

'I would think that Monseigneur is an important man to be at the King's side, Madame. His counsel is more important than his skills in battle.'

'Ah, that is very diplomatic of you, Nicolas. You are far more of a diplomat than my husband. But I'm afraid that is not the right answer. I want you to think carefully and tell me in truth what such a soldier would think.'

I knew now where the river of words I floated on was heading. I didn't know what would happen once I moored.

'He would be offended, Madame. And his wife.'

Geneviève de Nanterre nodded. 'Yes. There it is.'

'But that's no reason –'

'*De plus*, I don't want my daughters to look at bloody carnage while entertaining at a feast. You've met Claude – would you want her to stare at some gash in a horse's side or a man with his head cut off while she's eating?'

'No, Madame.'

'She shall not.'

In their corner the ladies-in-waiting were smirking at me. Geneviève de Nanterre had led me to just where she'd wanted. She was cleverer than most of the noblewomen I'd painted. Because of that I found I wanted to please her. That could be dangerous.

'I can't go against Monseigneur's wishes, Madame.'

Geneviève de Nanterre sat back in her chair. 'Tell me, Nicolas – do you know who chose you to design these tapestries?'

'No, Madame.'

'I did.'

I stared at her. 'Why, Madame?'

'I've seen the miniatures you do of ladies in the Court. There is something about them that you capture which pleases me.'

'What is that, Madame?'

'Their spiritual nature.'

I bowed, surprised. 'Thank you, Madame.'

'Claude could do with more examples of that spiritual nature. I try, but she doesn't listen to her mother.'

There was a pause. I shifted from one foot to the other. 'What – what would you have me paint instead of a battle, Madame?'

Geneviève de Nanterre's eyes gleamed. 'A unicorn.'

I froze.

'A lady and a unicorn,' she added.

She must have heard me with Claude. She must have heard me or she wouldn't have suggested it. Had she heard me seducing her daughter? I tried to guess from her face. She seemed pleased with herself, mischievous even. If she did know, she could tell Jean Le Viste about my attempt to seduce their daughter – if Claude hadn't done so already – and the commission would be lost. Not only that – with a word Geneviève de Nanterre could ruin my reputation at Court and I would never paint another miniature.

I had no choice but to try to sweeten her. 'Are you fond of unicorns, Madame?'

One of the ladies-in-waiting giggled. Geneviève de Nanterre frowned and the girl stopped. 'I've never seen one, so how would I know? No, it's Claude I am thinking of. She likes them, and it is she as the eldest child who will inherit the tapestries one day. She may as well have something she likes.'

I'd heard talk of the family *sans* heir, of how it must rankle Jean Le Viste not to have a son to pass on his beloved coat of arms to. The blame for having three daughters must lie heavily upon his wife. I looked at her a little more kindly.

'What would you have the unicorn do, Madame?'

Geneviève de Nanterre waved a hand. 'Suggest to me what he might do.'

'He could be hunted. Monseigneur might like that.'

She shook her head. 'I don't want horses and blood. And Claude wouldn't be pleased if the unicorn were killed.'

I couldn't risk suggesting the story of the unicorn's magic horn. I would have to repeat Claude's idea. 'The Lady might seduce the unicorn. Each tapestry could be a scene of her in the woods, tempting him with music and food and flowers, and at the end he lays his head in her lap. That is a popular story.'

'Perhaps. Of course Claude would like that. She is a girl at the beginning of her life. Yes, the virgin taming the unicorn might be the thing. Though it may pain me as much to sit among that as to be amidst a battle scene.' She said the last words almost to herself.

'Why, Madame?'

'I will be surrounded by seduction, youth, love. What is all that to me?' She tried to sound dismissive of these things, but she seemed wistful.

She doesn't share her husband's bed, I thought. She has had her daughters and has done her part. Not well, either

– no sons. Now she is shut off from him and there is nothing left for her. I was not in the habit of pitying noblewomen, with their warm fires and full bellies and their ladies to attend them. But at that moment I felt sorry for Geneviève de Nanterre. For I had a sudden vision of myself in ten years' time – after long journeys, harsh winters, illnesses – alone in a cold bed, limbs aching, hands crabbed and unable to hold a paintbrush. At the end of my own usefulness, what would become of me? Death would be welcome then. I wondered if she thought that.

She was looking at me with her sad, clever eyes.

Something in these tapestries will be hers, I thought in a rush. They will not only be about a seduction in a forest, but about something else as well, not just a virgin but a woman who would be a virgin again, so that the tapestries are about the whole of a woman's life, its beginning and its end. All of her choices, all in one, wound together. That was what I would do. I smiled at her.

A bell rang in the tower of Saint-Germain-des-Prés.

'Sext, ma Dame,' said one of the ladies.

'I will go to that,' Geneviève de Nanterre said. 'We've missed the other offices, and I can't go to Vespers this evening – I'm expected at Court with my lord.' She rose from her chair as another lady brought over the casket. She reached up, undid the clasp of her necklace, and took it off, allowing the jewels to lie glistening in her hands for a moment before they tumbled into the casket to be locked away. Her lady held out a cross dotted with pearls on a long chain, and when Geneviève de Nanterre nodded she slipped it over her mistress's head. The other ladies began

25

putting away their sewing and gathering their things. I knew I would be dismissed.

'*Pardon*, Madame, but will Monseigneur agree to unicorns rather than battles?'

Geneviève de Nanterre was rearranging the corded belt at her waist while one of the ladies unpinned her dark red overskirt so that its folds fell to the floor and covered the green and white leaves and flowers. 'You will have to convince him.'

'But – surely you should tell him yourself, Madame. After all, you were able to get him to agree to have me do the designs.'

'Ah, that was easy – he cares nothing about people. One artist or another means little to him, as long as they are accepted at Court. But the subject of the commission is between him and you – I am meant to have nothing to do with it. So it is best if he hears from you.'

'Perhaps Léon Le Vieux should speak to him.'

Geneviève de Nanterre snorted. 'Léon would not go against my husband's wishes. He protects himself. He is clever but not cunning – and what is needed to convince Jean is cunning.'

I frowned at the floor. The dazzle of the designs I would make had blinded me, but now the difficulty of my place was sinking in. I would prefer to design a lady and a unicorn over a battle with its many horses, but I did not like to go against Jean Le Viste's wishes either. Yet it seemed I had no choice. I'd been caught in a web woven between Jean Le Viste and his wife and daughter, and I didn't know how to escape. These tapestries will bring me to grief, I thought.

'I have a cunning idea, Madame.' The lady-in-waiting who spoke was the plainest but had lively eyes that moved back and forth as she thought. 'In fact, it's a punning idea. You know how Monseigneur likes puns.'

'So he does,' Geneviève de Nanterre agreed.

'Visté means speed. The unicorn is visté, n'est-ce pas? No animal runs faster. So when we see a unicorn we think of Viste.'

'Béatrice, you're so clever – if your idea works with my husband you may marry this Nicolas des Innocents. I will give you my blessing.'

I jerked my head. Béatrice laughed, and all the women joined her. I smiled politely. I had no idea if Geneviève de Nanterre was joking.

Still laughing, Geneviève de Nanterre led her ladies out, leaving me alone.

I stood still in the quiet room. I should find a long pole and go back to the Grande Salle to begin measuring again. But it was a pleasure to stay here, with no ladies smirking at me. I could think in this room.

I looked around. There were two tapestries hanging on the walls, with the Annunciation I had painted for the room next to them. I studied the tapestries. These were of grape harvesters, men cutting the vines while women stamped on the grapes, skirts tucked high to reveal their spattered calves. They were much bigger than the painting, and with less depth. The weave made them look rough, and less fleshy and immediate than the Virgin in my painting. But they kept the room warm, and filled more of it with their vivid reds and blues.

27

A whole room full of these – it would be like making a little world, and one full of women rather than the horses and men of a battle. I would much prefer that, no matter how hard it would be to convince Jean Le Viste.

I glanced out of the window. Geneviève de Nanterre and Claude Le Viste were walking with their ladies towards the church, their skirts blowing about them. The sun was so bright that my eyes watered and I had to blink. When I could see again they were gone, replaced by the servant girl who carried my child. She held a basket and was plodding in the other direction.

Why did that lady-in-waiting laugh so hard at the thought of marrying me? Though I had not yet given much thought to marrying, I'd assumed I would one day have a wife to look after me when I was old. I had a good standing in the Court, steady commissions, and now these tapestries to keep me and any wife. There was no grey in my hair, I had all but two of my teeth, and I could plough thrice a night when the need arose. It was true that I was an artist and not a squire or rich merchant. But I wasn't a blacksmith or cobbler or farmer. My hands were clean, my nails trim. Why should she laugh so?

I decided first to finish measuring the room, whatever I was to design for its walls. I needed a pole, and found the steward in the storerooms, counting out candles. He was as sour with me as before, but directed me to the stables. 'You watch out with that pole,' he ordered. 'Don't go doing any damage with it.'

I smirked. 'I didn't take you for a bawd,' I said.

The steward frowned. 'That's not what I meant. But I'm

28

not surprised that's how you took it, you who can't control your own rod.'

'What do you mean?'

'You know what I mean. What you done to Marie-Céleste.'

Marie-Céleste – the name meant nothing.

When the steward saw my blank look he snarled, 'The maid you got with child, pisspot.'

'Ah, her. She should have been more careful.'

'So should you. She's a good girl – she deserves better than you.'

'It's a pity about Marie-Céleste, but I've given her money and she'll be all right. Now, I must get that pole.'

The steward grunted. As I turned to go, he muttered, 'You watch your back, pisspot.'

I found a pole in the stables and was carrying it across the courtyard when Jean Le Viste himself came striding out of the house. He swept by without even looking at me – he must have thought I was just another servant – and I called out, 'Monseigneur! A moment, please!' If I didn't say something now I might never get another chance alone with him.

Jean Le Viste turned to see who was calling, then grunted and kept walking. I ran to catch up with him. 'Please, Monseigneur, I would like to discuss the tapestries further.'

'You should talk to Léon, not me.'

'Yes, Monseigneur, but I felt that for something as important as these tapestries you should be consulted directly.' As I hurried after him, the end of the pole dipped and caught on a stone, tumbling from my hands and clattering to the ground. The whole courtyard rang with the sound. Jean Le Viste stopped and glared at me.

'I am concerned, Monseigneur,' I said hastily. 'Concerned that you should have hung on your walls what others would expect from such a prominent member of Court. From a President of the Cour des Aides, no less.' I was making up words as I went along.

'What's your point? I am busy here.'

'I have seen designs for a number of tapestries this past year commissioned by noble families from my fellow artists. All of these tapestries have one thing in common – a *millefleur* background.' This much was true – backgrounds of a dense pattern of flowers were popular now, particularly as weavers in the north perfected the technique.

'Flowers?' Jean Le Viste repeated, looking down at his feet as if he had just trampled upon some.

'Yes, Monseigneur.'

'There are no flowers in battles.'

'No, Monseigneur. They have not been weaving battles. Several of my colleagues have designed scenes with – with unicorns in them, Monseigneur.'

'Unicorns?'

'Yes, Monseigneur.'

Jean Le Viste looked so sceptical that I quickly added another lie that I could only hope he wouldn't discover. 'Several noble families are having them made – Jean d'Alençon, Charles de St Émilion, Philippe de Chartres.' I tried to name families Jean Le Viste was unlikely to visit – they either lived too far away, or were too noble for the Le Vistes, or not noble enough.

'They are not having battles made,' Jean Le Viste repeated.

'No, Monseigneur.'

'Unicorns.'

'Yes, Monseigneur. They are *à la mode* now. And it did occur to me that a unicorn might be appropriate for your family.' I described Béatrice's pun.

Jean Le Viste didn't change expression, but he nodded, and that was enough. 'Do you know what to have this unicorn do?'

'Yes, Monseigneur, I do.'

'All right, then. Tell Léon. And bring me the drawings before Easter.' Jean Le Viste turned to cross the courtyard. I bowed to his back.

It hadn't been so hard to convince him as I'd thought. I had been right that Jean Le Viste would want what he thought everyone else had. But then, that is nobility without the generations of blood behind it – they imitate rather than invent. It didn't occur to Jean Le Viste that he might gain more respect by commissioning battle tapestries when no one else had. As sure of himself as he seemed, he wouldn't strike out on his own. As long as he didn't find out that there were no other unicorn tapestries, I would be safe. Of course I would have to design the finest tapestries possible – tapestries that would make other families want their own, and make Jean Le Viste proud to have been the first to own such a thing.

It wasn't just him I wanted to please, though, but his wife and daughter too. I wasn't sure which mattered more to me – Claude's lovely face or Geneviève's sad one.

Perhaps there was room for both in the unicorn's wood.

That night I drank at Le Coq d'Or to celebrate the commission, and afterwards slept poorly. I dreamt of unicorns and ladies surrounded by flowers, a girl chewing on a clove, another gazing at herself in a well, a lady holding jewels by a small casket, a girl feeding a falcon. It was all in a jumble that I could not set straight. It was not a nightmare, though, but a longing.

When I woke the next morning, my head was clear and I was ready to make the dreams real.

CLAUDE LE VISTE

Maman asked Papa about the tapestries after Mass on Easter Sunday, and that was when I heard the artist was coming back. We were all walking back to the rue du Four, and Jeanne and Petite Geneviève wanted me to run ahead with them and jump over puddles, but I stayed back to listen. I am good at listening when I'm not meant to.

Maman is always careful not to bother Papa, but he seemed to be in good spirits – probably glad like me to be out in the sun after such a long Mass! When she asked he said that he already had the drawings and that Nicolas des Innocents would be coming soon to discuss them. Until now he has said little about the tapestries. Even admitting that much seemed to irritate him. I think he regrets changing the battle into a unicorn – Papa loves his battles and his King. He left us abruptly then, saying he had to speak to the steward. I caught Béatrice's eye and we both giggled, making Maman frown at us.

Thank Heaven for Béatrice! She has told me everything – the switch from battle to unicorn, her own clever pun on *Viste*, and best of all, Nicolas' name. Maman would never tell me any of it, and the door of her room is too thick – I couldn't hear a thing when he was in with her, except for Béatrice's laugh. Luckily Béatrice tells me things – soon I will have her for my own lady-in-waiting. Maman can spare her, and she would much rather be with me – she will have much more fun.

Maman is so tedious these days – all she wants to do is to pray. She insists on going to Mass twice a day now. Sometimes I have dancing lessons during Terce or Sext, but she does take me to Vespers for the music, and I get so restless I want to scream. When I sit in Saint-Germain-des-Prés my foot starts to jiggle and the women on my pew can feel it but don't know where it's from – except for Béatrice, who places her hand on my leg to calm me. The first time she did that I jumped and shrieked, I was so surprised. Maman leaned over and glared at me, and the priest turned around too. I had to stuff my sleeve in my mouth to keep from laughing.

I seem to irritate Maman now, though I don't know what bothers her so. She irritates me too – she's always telling me I'm laughing too much or walking too fast, or that my dress is dusty or my head-dress is not straight. She treats me like a girl yet expects me to be a woman too. She won't let me go out when I want – she says I'm too old to play at the Fair at Saint-Germain-des-Prés during the day and too young for it at night. I'm not too young – other girls of fourteen go to the fair to see the *jongleurs* at night. Many are already betrothed. When I ask, Maman tells me I'm disrespectful and must wait for Papa to decide when and what man I shall marry. I grow so frustrated. If I am to be a woman, where is my man?

Yesterday I tried to listen to Maman's confession at Saint-Germain-des-Prés to find out if she felt bad about being so spiteful to me. I hid behind a pillar near the pew where she sat with the priest but her voice was so low that I had to creep quite close. All I heard was '*Ça c'est mon seul désir*' before one of the priests saw me and chased me away. '*Mon seul désir*,' I murmured to myself. My one desire. The phrase is so bewitching that I repeat it to myself all day long.

Once I was sure that Nicolas would be coming I knew I had to see him. *C'est mon seul désir*. Hah! There is my man. I've thought about him every hour of every day since I met him. Of course I've said nothing to anyone, except for Béatrice, who to my surprise was not very kind about him. That is her one fault. I was describing his eyes – how they are brown as chestnuts and pinched at the corners so that he looks a little sad even when he clearly is not. 'He's not worthy of you,' Béatrice interrupted. 'He's just an artist, and not trustworthy at that. You should be thinking of lords instead.'

'If he were untrustworthy, my father would never have hired him,' I retorted. 'Oncle Léon wouldn't have allowed it.' Léon is not really my uncle, but an old merchant who looks after my father's business. He treats me like a niece – until recently he chucked me under the chin and brought me sweetmeats, but now he tells me to stand straight and comb my hair. 'Tell me what sort of husband you'd like and I'll see if there's one ripe at market,' he likes to say. Wouldn't he be surprised if I described Nicolas! He doesn't think much of the artist, I'm sure – I overheard him with Papa, trying to undo Nicolas' unicorns, saying they wouldn't be right for the Grande Salle. Papa's door is not so thick, and if I put my ear right up to the keyhole I can hear him. Papa won't change his mind again, though. I could have told Léon that. To change once was bad enough, but to switch back now would be unthinkable.

Once I knew that Nicolas would be coming to the rue du Four, I went straight to the steward to find out exactly when. As usual, the steward was in the stores, counting things. He is always worried we are being robbed. He looked even more horrified than Béatrice when I said Nicolas' name. 'You don't want anything to do with that lot, Mademoiselle,' he said.

'I'm simply asking when he is coming.' I smiled sweetly. 'If you don't tell me I shall just have to go to Papa and say that you have not been helpful to me.'

The steward grimaced. 'Thursday at Sext,' he muttered. 'Him and Léon too.'

'You see, that wasn't so bad. You should always tell me what I want to know, and I'll be happy.'

The steward bowed but kept looking at me as I turned to go. It seemed he was about to say something, but then he didn't. That struck me as comical and I laughed as I ran away.

Thursday I was meant to go with Maman and my sisters to grandmother's at Nanterre for the night, but I pretended to have a bellyache so that I could stay at home. When Jeanne heard I wasn't going she wanted to pretend along with me, even though she didn't know why I was really staying behind. I couldn't tell her about Nicolas – she is too young to understand. She hung about until I had to say nasty things to her, which made her cry and run off. Afterwards I felt awful – I shouldn't treat my sister so. She and I have been close all our lives. Until recently we shared the same bed, and Jeanne cried then too when I said I wanted to begin sleeping alone. But I am so restless at night now. I kick off the covers and roll about, and even the thought of having another body in the bed – apart from Nicolas' – annoys me.

Now Jeanne has to be more with Petite Geneviève, who is sweet but only seven, and Jeanne has always preferred to be with older girls. Also Petite Geneviève is Maman's favourite, and that is irritating to Jeanne. Of course she has Maman's lovely name, while Jeanne and I have names that remind us we are not the boys Papa wanted.

Maman had Béatrice stay back to look after me, and she and my sisters finally left for Nanterre. I then sent Béatrice out to buy some honeyed orange peel I have a liking for, saying it would settle my stomach. I insisted that she go all the way to a stall near Notre Dame for it. She rolled her eyes at me but she went. When she was gone I let out a big sigh and ran to my room. My nipples were rubbing against my underdress and I lay on my bed and pushed a pillow between my legs, longing for an answer to my body's question. I felt like a prayer sung at Mass that is interrupted and left unfinished.

Finally I got up, straightened my clothes and head-dress, and ran to my father's private chamber. The door was open and I peeked in. Only Marie-Céleste was there, crouching at the hearth to light the fire. When I was younger and we were at the Château d'Arcy for the summer, Marie-Céleste used to take me and Jeanne and Petite Geneviève down to the river and sing us bawdy songs while she washed clothes. I wanted to tell her now about Nicolas des Innocents, about where I wanted his hands to go and what I would do with my tongue. After all, it had been her songs and stories that taught me about such things. But something stopped me. She had been my friend when I was a girl, but now I am growing up, soon to have a lady-in-waiting and prepare for a husband, and it was not right to speak of such things with her.

'Why are you lighting the fire, Marie-Céleste?' I asked instead, even though I knew already.

She looked up at me. There was a smudge of ash on her forehead, as if it were still Ash Wednesday. She always was a messy girl. 'Visitors coming, Mademoiselle,' she answered. 'For your father.'

The wood was beginning to smoke, with flames licking here and there. Marie-Céleste grabbed onto a chair and hauled herself to her feet with a grunt. Her face looked fatter than before. In fact – I gazed at her body in growing horror. 'Marie-Céleste, are you with child?'

The girl hung her head. It was strange – all those songs she had sung about maids getting caught, and she must never have thought it would happen to her. Of course every woman wants a child, but not like that, with no husband.

'You silly thing!' I scolded. 'Who is he?'

Marie-Céleste waved her hand as if batting away the question.

'Does he work here?'

She shook her head.

'*Alors*, will he marry you?'

Marie-Céleste scowled. 'No.'

'But what will you do?'

'Don't know, Mademoiselle.'

'Maman will be furious. Has she seen you?'

'I keep away from her, Mademoiselle.'

'She'll find out soon enough. You should wear a cloak at least to hide it.'

'Maids don't wear cloaks, Mademoiselle – can't work in a cloak.'

'You won't be able to work soon anyway, by the look of you. You'll have to go back to your family. *Attends*, you must tell Maman something. I know – tell her your mother's ill and you must tend to her. Then you can come back after the baby's born.'

'Can't go to the mistress looking like this, Mademoiselle – she'll know straight away what's wrong.'

'I'll tell her, then, when she comes back from Nanterre.' I did feel sorry for Marie-Céleste and wanted to help her.

Marie-Céleste brightened. 'Oh, thank you, Mademoiselle. That is good of you!'

'You'd best be off as soon as you can.'

'Thank you, Mademoiselle. Thank you. I'll see you when I come back.' She turned to go, then turned back again. 'If it's a girl I'll name her after you.'

'That would be nice. If it's a boy will you name it after the father?'

Marie-Céleste narrowed her eyes. 'Never,' she sneered.

'He don't want nothing to do with it, so I don't want nothing to do with him!'

After she left I had a look around Papa's chamber. It is not a comfortable room. The oak chairs have no cushions on them, and they creak when you shift about. I think Papa has them made like that so no one will meet with him for long. I've noticed that Oncle Léon always stands when he comes to see Papa. The walls are lined with maps of his properties – the Château d'Arcy, our house on the rue du Four, the Le Viste family house in Lyons – as well as maps of disputes Papa is working on for the King. The books he owns are kept here in a locked case.

There are two tables in the room – one that Papa writes at, and a bigger one where he spreads maps and papers for meetings. Usually that table is bare, but today some large sheets of paper had been left there. I looked down at the top one and stepped back in surprise. It was a drawing, and it was of me. I was standing between a lion and a unicorn, holding a parakeet on my gloved finger. I was wearing a beautiful dress and necklace, with a simple headscarf that left my hair loose. I was glancing sideways at the unicorn and smiling as if I were thinking of a secret. The unicorn was handsome, plump and white and rearing up on his hind legs, with a long spiralling horn. He had turned his head from me, as if trying not to become spellbound by my beauty. He was wearing a little cloak with the Le Viste arms on it, and the wind seem to whip through the drawing, blowing out his cloak and the roaring lion's as well, and my headscarf and the Le Viste standard held by the lion.

I gazed at the drawing for a long time. I couldn't take

my eyes from it or move it to see the drawings underneath. He had drawn me. He was thinking of me as I was of him. My breasts tingled. *Mon seul désir*.

Then I heard voices in the hall. The door swung open and all I could think to do was drop to the floor and scramble under the table. It was dark under there, and strange to be on the cold stone floor alone. Normally I would hide in such a place with my sisters, and we would giggle so much we would be found out immediately. I sat with my arms wrapped round my knees, praying that I couldn't be seen.

Two men entered and came straight over to the table. One wore the long brown robes of a merchant, and must be Oncle Léon. The other wore a grey tunic to his knees and dark blue hose. His calves were shapely, and I knew even before he spoke that it was Nicolas. I had not just spent so many days thinking of him for naught. All of my thoughts had filled in the details of him – the width of his shoulders, the curls of his hair brushing his neck, his bottom like two cherries, and the taut line of his calves.

My thoughts would have to fill in more details now, for as the men began to speak I could see nothing of them but their legs. I could only imagine the looks on Nicolas' face – his smooth brow crinkling, his pinched eyes staring at me in the drawing, his long fingers tracing the rough drawing paper. All this I filled in as I sat in near-darkness, listening to them.

'Monseigneur will be along in a moment,' Oncle Léon said. 'Let us consider a few things while we wait.' I could hear paper rustling.

'Did he like the designs?' Nicolas asked. 'Was he full of

praise?' The sound of his confident voice went straight to my maidenhead, as if he had touched me there.

Léon didn't answer, and Nicolas became insistent. 'He must have said something. Surely you can see that these are superior drawings. He must be overjoyed with them.'

Léon chuckled. 'It is not in his nature for Monseigneur Le Viste to be overjoyed by anything.'

'But he must have approved of them.'

'You are getting ahead of yourself, Nicolas. In this business you wait for the patron to give his opinion. *Alors*, you must prepare yourself to meet Monseigneur. The first thing you must understand is that he hasn't looked at the drawings.'

'But he's had them for a week!'

'Yes, and he will say he has studied them carefully, but he hasn't looked at them.'

'Why not, in the name of the Notre Dame?'

'Monseigneur Le Viste is very busy now. He does not consider something until he needs to. Then he makes a quick decision and expects to be obeyed without question.'

Nicolas snorted. 'This is how a nobleman like him does business for such an important commission? I wonder if a man of true noble blood would work this way.'

Oncle Léon lowered his voice. 'Jean Le Viste is only too aware of such opinions of him.' I could hear the frown in his voice. 'He uses hard work and loyalty to his King to compensate for the lack of respect even artists like you who work for him have.'

'My respect is not so slight that I am not willing to work for him,' Nicolas said rather hastily.

'Of course not. One must be practical. A *sou* is a *sou*, whether from a nobleman or a beggar.'

Both men laughed. I tossed my head, almost knocking it against the tabletop. I did not like their laughter. I'm not close to Papa – he is a cold man with me as with everyone – but I didn't like his name and reputation thrown about like a stick for a dog to fetch. And Oncle Léon – I hadn't thought he could be disloyal. I would be sure to tread on his foot next time I saw him. Or worse.

'I won't deny the designs are promising – ' he said now.

'Promising! They're more than promising!'

'If you would keep quiet for a moment, I'll help you to make these tapestries far better than they are – better than even you could imagine them to be. You're too close to your own creation to see what will make it better. You need another eye to look and see the flaws.'

'What flaws?' Nicolas echoed what I thought. What could possibly make the drawing of me better than it was?

'There are two things I have thought on looking at the designs, and doubtless Jean Le Viste will have other suggestions.'

'What two things?'

'There are to be six tapestries lining the walls of the Grande Salle, *n'est-ce pas*? Two large ones, four slightly smaller.'

'Yes.'

'And they're following the Lady's seduction of the unicorn, *n'est-ce pas*?'

'As I agreed with Monseigneur.'

'The seduction is clear enough, but I wondered if you

43

have not concealed something else within the designs. Another way of looking at them.'

Nicolas' feet shifted about. 'What do you mean?'

'There seem to me to be here suggestions of the five senses.' Léon tapped on one of the drawings, the sound drumming close to my ear. 'The Lady playing the organ for the unicorn, suggesting Sound, for instance. And holding the unicorn by the horn is surely Touch. Here –' he tapped the table again – 'the Lady weaves carnations into a crown for Smell, though that is perhaps not as obvious.'

'Brides wear crowns of carnations,' Nicolas explained. 'The Lady is tempting the unicorn with the idea of marriage and the marriage bed. It's not meant to mean Smell.'

'Ah. Well, I suppose you're not that clever. The senses are an accident, then.'

'I –'

'But do you see that you could easily weave in the senses? Have the unicorn sniff the carnation. Or another animal. And in the tapestry where the unicorn lies in the Lady's lap, you could have her show him a mirror, for Sight.'

'But that would make the unicorn seem vain, wouldn't it?'

'So? The unicorn does look a bit vain.'

Nicolas didn't answer. Perhaps he heard me under the table, snorting with laughter at him and his unicorn.

'Now, you have the Lady holding the unicorn's horn, that is Touch. Playing the organ, that is Sound. The carnations, that is Smell. The mirror, that is Sight. What is left? Taste. We have two tapestries left – those of Claude and Dame Geneviève.'

Maman? What did Léon mean?

Nicolas made a funny sound, like a snort and a cry together. 'What do you mean, Claude and Dame Geneviève?'

'Come, you know exactly what I mean. That was my other suggestion. The likenesses are too apparent. Jean Le Viste won't like that. I know you are used to painting portraits, but in the final paintings you must make them look more like the other ladies.'

'Why?'

'Jean Le Viste wanted battle tapestries. Instead you have given him his wife and daughter to look at. There is no comparison.'

'He agreed to the unicorn tapestries.'

'But you don't have to give him an ode to his wife and daughter. Now, I do have sympathy for Dame Geneviève. Jean Le Viste is not an easy man. But you know that she and Claude are thorns in his side. He wouldn't want them depicted in something as valuable as the tapestries.'

'Oh!' I cried, and this time I did knock my head against the tabletop. It hurt.

There were surprised grunts, then two faces appeared beneath the table. Léon was glaring, but Nicolas smiled when he saw it was me. He held out his hand and helped me up.

'Thank you,' I said when I was standing. Nicolas bowed over my hand, but I pulled my hand away before he could kiss it, and made a show of straightening my dress. I wasn't quite ready to forgive him the rude things he had said about my father.

'What were you doing there, you naughty girl?' Oncle

Léon said. For a moment I thought he was going to swat me as if I were the same age as Petite Geneviève, but he seemed to remember himself and didn't. 'Your father would be very angry if he knew you had been spying on us.'

'My father would be very angry if he knew what you said about him, Oncle Léon. And you, Monsieur,' I added, glancing at Nicolas.

There was a silence. I could see both men thinking back to their earlier words, trying to remember what would be offensive to Papa. They looked so worried that I couldn't help laughing.

Oncle Léon frowned at me. 'Claude, you really are a very naughty girl.' He sounded less stern this time – more as if he were trying to placate a little lapdog.

'Oh, I know. And what about you, Monsieur – do you think I'm a very naughty girl?' I said to Nicolas. It was wonderful to be able to see his handsome face.

I didn't know how he would answer, but he delighted me by saying, 'You are certainly the naughtiest girl I know, Mademoiselle.' For a second time his voice touched my maidenhead, and I felt wet there.

Oncle Léon snorted. 'That's enough. Claude, you must go now. Your father will be here soon.'

'No, I want to see the picture of my mother. Where is it?' I turned to the drawings and pushed them about the table. They were a jumble of ladies and Le Viste banners and lions and unicorns.

'Claude, please.'

I ignored Oncle Léon and turned to Nicolas. 'Which one is it, Monsieur? I would like to see.'

Without a word he pulled a drawing from across the table to me.

I was relieved to see that Maman was not so pretty as me in the drawing. Nor was her dress so fine as mine, but much plainer. And the wind wasn't blowing through the drawing – the banner wasn't rippling, and the lion and unicorn sat tamely rather than standing rampant as they did in mine. In fact, everything in it was very still, except that Maman was pulling a necklace from a casket held by one of her ladies-in-waiting. I didn't mind now that Maman was in the tapestries as well – the comparison favoured me.

But if Oncle Léon had his way neither of our faces would remain. I would have to do something. What, though? Although I had threatened Léon with repeating his words to my father, in truth I knew that Papa wouldn't listen to me. It was terrible to hear Maman and me referred to as thorns, but Léon was right – Maman had not produced an heir, for my sisters and I were not boys. Every time Papa looked at us he was reminded that all of his wealth would one day go to my husband and son, who would not carry the Le Viste name or coat of arms. Knowing this had made him even colder with us. I knew too from Béatrice that Papa did not share Maman's bed.

Nicolas tried to save Maman and me. 'I will only change their faces if Monseigneur asks me to,' he declared. 'Not if you do. I make changes for the patron, not the patron's merchant.'

Oncle Léon glared at him, but before he could respond we heard footsteps in the hallway. 'Go!' Léon hissed, but it was too late for me to escape. Nicolas put his hand on my head and gently pushed me down so that I was kneeling. For a moment my face was close to his bulging groin. I looked up and saw him smiling. Then he shoved me under the table.

It felt even colder and harder and darker under the table this time, but I wouldn't have to endure it for long. Papa's feet came straight to the table, where he stood next to Léon, with Nicolas to one side. I sat looking at Nicolas' legs. He seemed to be standing differently now that he knew I was there, though I could not say what exactly was different. It was as if his legs had eyes and were watching me.

Papa's legs were like himself – straight and indifferent as a chair's. 'Now, the designs,' he said.

Someone was scrabbling among the drawings, moving them around the table. 'Here they are, Monseigneur,' Nicolas said. 'As you see, you can look at them in this order. First the Lady dons her necklace for the seduction of the unicorn. In the next she plays the organ to get the unicorn's attention. And here she is – feeding a parakeet – and the unicorn has moved closer, though he is rampant and his head is still turned away. He is almost seduced, but needs more temptation.'

I noted the pause before Nicolas said 'feeding'. So, I have become Taste, I thought. Then taste me.

'Then the Lady weaves a crown of carnations in preparation for a wedding. Her own wedding. As you can see, the unicorn is now sitting calmly. At last – ' Nicolas tapped the table – 'the unicorn lies in her lap and they look at

48

each other. And in the final tapestry she has tamed him – she holds him by the horn. You can see that the animals in the background are now in chains – they have become the slaves of love.'

When Nicolas finished there was a silence, as if he expected my father to speak. But Papa said nothing. He often does that, keeping quiet to make people unsure of themselves. It worked this time too, for after a moment Nicolas began to speak again, sounding nervous.

'You can see, Monseigneur, that throughout the unicorn is accompanied by the lion, who represents nobility, strength and courage as a complement to the unicorn's purity and wildness. The lion is an example of noble savagery tamed.'

'Of course the background will be filled with *millefleurs*, Monseigneur,' Léon added. 'The Brussels weavers will design that themselves – that is their speciality. Nicolas has only hinted at it here.'

There was another pause. I found I was holding my breath, waiting to see if Papa would remark on the drawings of Maman and me. 'There are not enough coats of arms,' he said at last.

'The unicorn and lion hold Le Viste banners and standards throughout,' Nicolas said. He sounded annoyed. I reached over and nudged his leg to remind him not to use such a tone with my father. Nicolas shuffled his feet.

'In two of the drawings there is only a banner,' Papa said.

'I could add shields for the lion and unicorn to carry,

Monseigneur.' Nicolas must have taken my hint, for he sounded calmer. I began to stroke his calf.

'The standard and banner poles should be spiked,' Papa declared. 'Not the round ends you have drawn.'

'But – spikes are for battles, Monseigneur.' Nicolas spoke as if someone were strangling him. I giggled and moved my hand up to his thigh.

'I want spikes on the poles,' Papa repeated. 'There are too many women and flowers in these tapestries. There should be battle poles, and something else to remind us of war. What happens to the unicorn when the Lady has caught him?'

Luckily Nicolas didn't have to answer, as he couldn't have spoken. I had placed my hand on his bulge, which was as hard as a tree branch. I had never touched one before. 'Doesn't the Lady lead him to the hunter who kills him?' Papa continued. He likes to answer his own questions. 'You should add another tapestry to complete the story.'

'I believe there is no room in the Grande Salle for another tapestry,' Oncle Léon said.

'Then replace one of these women. The one with the carnations, or the one feeding the bird.'

I dropped my hand.

'That is a very good idea, Monseigneur,' Oncle Léon said. I gasped. Luckily Nicolas made a noise too, so I don't think Papa heard me.

Then Oncle Léon showed just why he is so good at business. 'It is a fine idea,' he repeated. 'Of course the boldness of the kill will contrast well with the more subtle hints of the battle poles. One would not want to be too cunning at the end, would one?'

'What do you mean, too cunning?'

'Well, for instance, one might simply imply the hunt – or the battle, if you like – with the spiked poles (a fine touch, Monseigneur, I must say), the battle shields Nicolas has suggested adding, and perhaps something else. Let me think. What about a tent – the kind set up in battles for the King? That would also remind one of the King as well as the battle. But then again, perhaps that would be too subtle. Perhaps a hunter killing the unicorn would be better.'

'No, I want the King's tent.'

I sat back on my heels in wonder at Oncle Léon. He had hooked Papa like a fish, without Papa even noticing, and brought him to land just where he pleased.

'The tent would be quite large and so should go on one of the larger tapestries,' Léon said briskly, to keep Papa from changing his mind. 'The Lady with the jewels or the Lady with the parakeet. Which would you prefer, Monseigneur?'

Nicolas began to speak but Papa interrupted. 'The jewels – she is more regal than the other.'

Before I could cry out again, Nicolas reached under the table with his foot and pressed my own foot. I kept quiet and he left his foot there, tapping mine.

'All right, Nicolas, add a tent to this one,' Oncle Léon said.

'Of course, Monseigneur. Would Monseigneur like a special design on the tent?'

'A coat of arms.'

51

'That goes without saying, Monseigneur. But I was thinking more of a motto for a battle. Something to indicate that it is a battle for love.'

'I know nothing of love,' Papa growled. 'What would you have? I suspect you are familiar with it.'

I had an idea, and tapped Nicolas' leg. After a moment one of the drawings floated to the floor. 'Oh! *Pardon*, Monseigneur. I am so clumsy.' Nicolas crouched down to retrieve the drawing. I leaned over and whispered in his ear, '*C'est mon seul désir.*' Then I bit him.

Nicolas stood up.

'Is your ear bleeding?' Papa said.

'*Pardon*, Monseigneur. I knocked it against the table leg. But I have had a thought. What about "*À mon seul désir*"? It means –'

'That will do,' Papa cut him off. I knew that tone – it meant that the meeting had gone on for too long. 'Show your changes to Léon and bring the finished paintings here a fortnight after May Day. No later, as we leave for Château d'Arcy by Ascension Day.'

'Yes, Monseigneur.'

Papa's legs moved away from the table. 'Léon, come with me – I have things to discuss with you. You can accompany me as far as the Conciergerie.'

Léon's robes swayed as he began to move, then stopped. 'Perhaps we should remain here, Monseigneur. It's more comfortable for discussing business. And Nicolas is just going, aren't you, Nicolas?'

'Yes, certainly, as soon as I collect the drawings, Monseigneur.'

'No, I'm in a hurry. Come along.' And Papa was gone.

Oncle Léon still hesitated. He didn't want to leave me alone with Nicolas.

'Go,' I hissed.

He went.

I did not come out from under the table, but remained there on my knees. After a moment Nicolas climbed in to me. We gazed at each other. '*Bonjour*, Mademoiselle,' he said.

I smiled. He was nothing like the kind of man my parents intended for me. I was glad. 'Are you going to kiss me, then?'

He had me on my back and was on top of me before I could think. Then his tongue was deep in my mouth and his hands were squeezing my breasts. It was a strange thing. I had been dreaming of this moment ever since meeting him, but now that there was a body on top of me, a bulge grinding hard into my belly, a wet tongue in my ear, I was surprised by how different it felt from what I had dreamed.

Part of me liked it – wanted the bulge to push even harder, and not through so many layers of clothes. My hands wanted to touch every part of him – squeeze his cherry bum and measure his broad back. My mouth met his as if it were biting into a fig.

But it was a shock to have someone's wet, thrusting tongue in my mouth, to have so much weight squeezing the breath from me, to have his hands touch parts of me no man had ever touched. And I had not expected to think so much when a man was with me. With Nicolas I found words accompanying everything we did – 'Why is he doing that? His tongue is so wet in my ear,' and 'His belt is jabbing into my side,' and 'Does that feel good?'

I was thinking too of my father – of being under the table in his chamber, and of the value he placed on my maidenhead. Could I really throw it away in a moment, as someone like Marie-Céleste had? Perhaps that more than anything stopped me from truly enjoying myself. 'Should we be doing this?' I whispered when Nicolas had begun biting my breasts through the cloth of my dress.

'I know, we're mad. But we may never have another chance.' Nicolas began pulling at my skirt. 'They never leave you alone – not the daughter of Jean Le Viste with a mere painter.' He lifted up my skirt and underdress and ran his hand up my thigh. 'Now this, beauty, this is *mon seul désir.*' With that he touched my maidenhead, and the surge of pleasure I felt was so strong that I was ready to give it up to him.

'Claude!'

I looked behind me and saw Béatrice's face upside down, glaring at us.

Nicolas pulled his hand from under my skirt, but he did not immediately jump off me. That pleased me. He looked at Béatrice, and then he kissed me deeply before slowly sitting back on his knees.

'For this,' Béatrice said, 'I really will marry you, Nicolas des Innocents. I swear I will!'

GENEVIÈVE DE NANTERRE

Béatrice has told me the bodices of my dresses have become too loose. 'Either you eat more, Madame, or we must call in the tailor.'

'Send for the tailor.'

That was not the answer she wanted, and she kept her big dog-brown eyes on me until I turned from her and began playing with my rosary. I'd had the same look from my mother – though her eyes are shrewder than Béatrice's – when I took the girls to visit her at Nanterre. I told her that Claude did not come with us because of a stomach ache that I suffered from as well. She didn't believe me, just as I hadn't believed Claude when she made her excuses to me. Perhaps it is always thus, that daughters lie to their mothers and their mothers let them.

I was just as glad that Claude didn't go with us, though the girls begged her to. Claude and I are like two cats around each other, our fur always ruffled. She is sullen with me, and her sideways looks are critical. I know she is comparing herself to me and thinking that she does not want to be like me.

I do not want her to be like me either.

I went to see Père Hugo after I got back from Nanterre. As I sat down on a pew next to him he said, '*Vraiment, mon enfant*, you cannot have sinned so much in three days that you need to confess again already.' Though his words were kind his tone was sour. In truth he despairs of me, as I despair of myself.

I repeated the words I had used the other morning, staring at the scratched pew in front of us.'It is my one desire to join the convent at Chelles,' I said. '*Mon seul désir*. My grandmother joined before she died, and my mother is sure to as well.'

'You are not about to die, *mon enfant*. Nor is your husband. Your grandmother was a widow when she took the veil.'

'Do you think my faith is not strong enough? Shall I prove it to you?'

'It is not your faith that is so strong, but your desire to be rid of your life that is. It troubles me. I am sure enough of your faith, but you need to want to surrender yourself to Christ –'

'But I do!'

'– surrender yourself to Christ without thought of yourself and your worldly life. The world of the convent should not be an escape from a life you hate –'

'A life I detest!' I bit my tongue.

Père Hugo waited a moment, then said, 'The best nuns are often those who have been happy outside, and are happy inside.'

I sat silent, my head bowed. I knew now that I had been wrong to speak like this. I should have been more patient

56

– taken months, a year, two years to plant the seed with Père Hugo, soften him, make him agreeable. Instead I'd spoken to the priest suddenly and desperately. Of course, Père Hugo did not decide who entered Chelles – only the Abbess Catherine de Lignières had that power. But I would need my husband's consent to become a nun, and must get powerful men to argue on my behalf. Père Hugo was one of those men.

There was one thing that might still sway Père Hugo. I smoothed my skirt and cleared my throat. 'My dowry was substantial,' I said in a low voice. 'I'm sure that if I became a bride of Christ I would be able to give a portion of it to Saint-Germain-des-Prés, in thanks for the succour it has given me. If only you would speak to my husband . . .' I let my voice trail away.

It was Père Hugo's turn to be silent. While I waited I ran my finger along one of the scratches on the pew. When he spoke at last there was true regret in his voice – but whether for what he said or for the money just out of his grasp was not clear. 'Geneviève, you know Jean Le Viste will never give his consent for you to enter a convent. He wants a wife, not a nun.'

'You could talk to him, tell him how it would suit me to enter Chelles.'

'Have you talked to him yourself, as I suggested the other day?'

'No, because he doesn't listen to me. But he would to you, I'm sure of it. What you think matters to him.'

Père Hugo snorted. 'Your slate is clean at the moment, *mon enfant*. Don't go telling lies now.'

'He does care about the Church!'

'The Church has not had as much influence on him as you and I might wish,' Père Hugo said carefully. I was silent, chastened by my husband's indifference. Would he burn in Hell for it?

'Go home, Geneviève,' Père Hugo said then, and did sound kind. 'You have three lovely daughters, a fine house and a husband who is close to the King. These are blessings many women would be content with. Be a wife and mother, say your prayers, and may Our Lady smile down on you.'

'And on my cold bed – will She smile on that as well?'

'Go in peace, *mon enfant*.' Père Hugo was already getting to his feet.

I didn't leave immediately. I didn't want to go back to the rue du Four, to Claude's judging eyes or Jean's that would not meet mine. Better to stay in the church that had become my shelter.

Saint-Germain-des-Prés is the oldest church in Paris, and I was glad when we moved so close. Its cloisters are beautiful and quiet, and the view from the church is very fine – when you stand outside it on the river side you can see straight across to the Louvre. Before the rue du Four we lived nearer to Notre Dame de Paris, but that place is too big for me – it makes me dizzy to look up. Of course Jean liked it, as he would any place grand where the King is likely to come. Now, though, we live so close to Saint-Germain-des-Prés that I don't even need a groom to escort me to it.

My favourite place in the church is the Chapel of Sainte

Geneviève, patron of Paris, who came from Nanterre and whom I am named after. It is off the apse and I went there now, after my confession to Père Hugo, telling my ladies as I knelt to leave me alone. They sat on the low step leading up to the chapel, a little way from me, and kept whispering until I turned and said, 'You would do well to remember that this is God's house, not a corner for gossip. Either pray or go.' They all ducked their heads, though Béatrice fixed me with those brown eyes for a moment. I stared at her until she too bowed her head and closed her eyes. When I saw her lips move at last to form a prayer I turned back around.

I myself did not pray, but looked up at the two windows of stained glass with their scenes from the life of the Virgin. I don't see as well as I once did, and couldn't make out the figures but saw only the colours, the blues and reds and greens and browns. I found myself counting the yellow flowers that lined the edge of the glass and wondering what they were.

Jean has not come to my bed for months. He has always been formal with me in front of others, as befits our status. But he was once warm in bed. After Petite Geneviève was born he began to visit even more frequently, looking at last to make a son and heir. I was with child a few times but lost it early on. These last two years there has been no sign of a baby. Indeed my courses ran dry, though I did not tell him. He found out somehow, from Marie-Céleste or one of my ladies – maybe even Béatrice. No one knows what loyalty is in this house. He came to see me one night with this new knowledge, saying I had failed in the one thing expected of a wife and that he wouldn't touch me again.

He was right. I had failed. I could see it in the faces of others – in Béatrice and my ladies, in my mother, in the people we entertained, even in Claude who is part of the failing. I remember that when she was seven years old, she came into my room after I had given birth to Petite Geneviève. She gazed down at the swaddled baby in my arms, and when she heard it wasn't a boy she sniffed and turned on her heel. Of course she loves Petite Geneviève now but she would prefer a brother and a satisfied father.

I feel like a bird who has been wounded with an arrow and now cannot fly.

It would be a mercy to let me enter a convent. But Jean is not a merciful man. And he still needs me. Even if he despises me, he wants me next to him when he dines at home, and when we entertain or go to Court to attend the King. It would not look right for the place next to him to be empty. Besides, they would laugh at him at Court – the man whose wife runs off to a nunnery. No, I knew Père Hugo was right – Jean might not want me, but he would have me at his side still. Most men would be like that – older women joining convents are usually widows, not wives. Only a few husbands will let them go, no matter their sins.

Sometimes when I walk over to the Seine to look across at the Louvre, I think about throwing myself in. That is why the ladies keep close to me. They know. I heard one of them just now, huffing behind me from boredom. For a moment I felt sorry for them, stuck with me.

On the other hand, they have fine dresses and food and a good fire in the evenings because they are with me. Their cakes have more sugar in them, and the cook is generous with the spices – the cinnamon and nutmeg and mace and ginger – because he is cooking for nobles.

I let my rosary drop to the floor. 'Béatrice,' I called, 'pick up my beads.'

Two ladies helped me to my feet as Béatrice knelt to fetch the rosary. 'I would have a word with you, Madame,' she said in a low voice as she handed them back to me. 'Alone.'

It was probably something about Claude. She no longer needed a nurse to look after her like Jeanne and Petite Geneviève, but a proper lady-in-waiting. I had been lending her Béatrice to see how they got on. And I could spare her – my needs were simpler now. A woman at the start of her life has far more need of a good lady like Béatrice than I do. Béatrice still told me everything about Claude, to help me prepare her for womanhood and keep her from mischief. But one day Béatrice would go over to her new mistress and not come back.

I waited until we had gone outside and around to the great door of the monastery. As we passed through the gate and out into the street I said, 'I fancy a stroll down to the river. Béatrice, come with me – you others may go back. If you see my daughters tell them to come to my chamber after. I want to speak to them.'

Before the ladies could say more I pulled Béatrice by the arm and turned left down the road leading to the river. The ladies had to turn right to go home. Though they tutted a bit, they must have obeyed because I didn't hear them follow.

Passers-by on the rue de Seine stared to see a noble-woman without her entourage. For me it was a relief not to have my ladies flapping about me like a flock of mag-pies. They can be noisy and tiresome at times, especially when I'm looking for peace. They wouldn't last a day in a convent. I never take them when I visit Chelles – except Béatrice, of course.

A man passing along the other side with his scribe bowed so low when he saw me that I could not guess who he was by the crown of his hat. Only when he straightened did I recognize him as Michel d'Orléans, who knows Jean at Court and has dined with us. 'Dame Geneviève, I am at your command,' he said now. 'Tell me where I may escort you. I would never forgive myself for allowing you to walk the streets of Paris on your own. What would Jean Le Viste think of me if I were to do such a thing?' He gazed into my eyes for as long as he dared. At one time he had made it clear that we might be lovers if I wished it. I did not, but on the rare occasions when we meet his eyes still hold that question.

I have never taken a lover, though many women do. I don't want to give Jean a stick to beat me with. If I were to commit adultery he could choose to marry someone else, to try for a son. I'm not so desperate for company in my bed that I would throw away my title.

'Thank you, Monsieur,' I said, smiling kindly, 'but I'm not alone – I have my woman here to walk with me to the river. We like to look at the boats.'

'Then I will come with you.'

'No, no, you're too kind. With your scribe with you, you're clearly on your way to important business. I would not keep you.'

'Dame Geneviève, nothing is more important than being at your side.'

Once again I smiled, though more firmly and less kindly. 'Monsieur, if my husband were to find that you neglected work for King and Court in order to walk with me, he would be very displeased with me. I'm sure you don't want him to be angry with me?'

At this thought Michel d'Orléans stepped back, crest-fallen. When he had apologized several times and gone on his way, Béatrice and I began to giggle. We hadn't laughed like that in some time, and I was reminded of how she and I used to laugh all the time when we were both younger. I would miss her when she became Claude's lady. She would go to her and remain, unless Claude allowed her to marry and leave service.

The river was busy with boats moving up and down it. Men were unloading sacks of flour on the opposite bank, destined for the Louvre's many kitchens. We watched them for a time. I have always liked to look at the Seine – it holds out the promise of escape.

'I have something to tell you about Claude,' Béatrice said then. 'She's been very foolish.'

I sighed. I didn't want to know, but I was her mother and was meant to. 'What did she do?'

'Do you remember that artist – Nicolas des Innocents – who is designing the tapestries for the Grande Salle?'

I kept my eyes on a little patch of sunlight on the water. 'I remember him.'

'While you were away she was with him, alone, under a table!'

'Under a table? Where?'

She hesitated, her big eyes fearful. Béatrice dresses well, as do all of my ladies. But even fine silk woven with gilt thread and dotted with jewels can't make her face anything but plain. Her eyes may be lively, but she has hollow cheeks, a snub nose, and skin that goes red at the slightest upset. She was red now.

'In her chamber?' I suggested.

'No.'

'In the Grande Salle?'

'No.' My suggestions were annoying her, even as her hesitation annoyed me. I turned and looked at the river again, stifling my desire to shout at her. It's always better to be patient with Béatrice.

Two men were fishing in a boat not far from us. Their lines were slack but they didn't seem bothered – they were chatting and laughing about something. They hadn't seen us and I was glad, for they would have bowed and moved away if they had known we were there. There is something cheering about seeing an ordinary man happy.

'It was in your husband's chamber,' Béatrice whispered, even though there was no one to hear but me.

'Sainte Vierge!' I crossed myself. 'How long was she alone with him?'

'I don't know. Just a few minutes, I think. But they were – ' Béatrice stopped. I really did want to shake her.

'They were?'

'Not quite – '

'Where in Heaven's name were *you*? You were meant to be keeping an eye on her!' I had left Béatrice behind with Claude to keep her out of such mischief.

'I was! She gave me the slip, the silly thing. She asked me to fetch her – ' Béatrice rattled her rosary – 'oh, it doesn't matter. But she didn't lose her maidenhead, Madame.'

'Are you sure?'

'Yes. He was not – not yet undressed.'

'But she was?'

'Only partly.'

As angry as I was, part of me wanted to laugh at Claude's brazenness. If Jean had caught them – I couldn't bear to think of it. 'What did you do?'

'I sent him running! I did.'

She hadn't – I could see it in her face. Nicolas des Innocents had probably laughed at Béatrice and taken his time leaving.

'What are you going to do, Madame?' Béatrice said.

'What did you do when he left? What did you say to Claude?'

'I told her you would be sure to speak to her about it.'

'Did she beg you not to tell me?'

Béatrice frowned. 'No. She laughed in my face and ran off.'

I gritted my teeth. Claude knows only too well how valuable her maidenhead is to the Le Vistes – she must be intact for a worthy man to marry her. Her husband will inherit the Le Viste wealth one day, if not the name. The house on the rue du Four, the Château d'Arcy, the furniture, the jewels, even the tapestries Jean is having made – all will go to Claude's husband. Jean will have chosen him carefully, and the husband in turn will expect Claude to be pious, respectful, admired, and a virgin, of course. If her father had caught her – I shivered.

'I will speak to her,' I said, no longer angry at Béatrice but furious at Claude for risking so much for so little. 'I will speak to her now.'

The ladies had already gathered my daughters in my chamber when Béatrice and I returned. Petite Geneviève and Jeanne ran to greet me as I came in, but Claude sat at the window playing with a little dog in her lap and would not look at me.

I had forgotten why I'd had the other girls called to my chamber. But the two of them – especially Petite Geneviève – were so eager to see me that I had to make up something quickly.

'Girls, you know that the roads will soon be clear of mud and we'll go down to Château d'Arcy for the summer.'

Jeanne clapped her hands. Of the three she most liked our stay each year at the château. She ran wild there with children from the nearby farms, and hardly wore shoes the whole summer.

Claude sighed heavily as she cupped the lapdog's face in her hands. 'I want to stay in Paris,' she muttered.

'I have decided that we will have a May Day feast before we go,' I continued. 'You may wear your new dresses.' I always had new dresses made for the girls and my ladies at Easter.

The ladies began chattering at once, except for Béatrice.

'Now, Claude, come with me – I want to look at your dress. I'm not sure of the neckline.' I walked to the door and turned to wait for her. 'Just us,' I added as the ladies began to stir. 'We won't be long.'

Claude pursed her lips and didn't move, but continued to play with her dog, flopping its ears back and forth.

'You will come with me or I'll rip that dress apart with my own hands,' I said sharply.

The ladies all murmured. Béatrice stared at me. 'Maman!' Jeanne cried.

Claude's eyes widened and a look of fury crossed her face. Then she got up, pushing the dog from her lap so roughly that it yelped. She walked past me and through the door without a glance. I followed her rigid back through the rooms separating hers from mine.

Her room is smaller than mine, with less furniture. Of course she doesn't have five ladies with her for much of the day. My ladies need chairs and a table. They need cushions and footstools and fires, tapestries on the walls and jugs of wine. Claude's room simply has a bed dressed in red and yellow silk, a chair and small table, and a chest for her dresses. Her window looks onto the courtyard rather than towards the church as mine does.

Claude went straight to her chest, pulled out the new dress, then threw it on the bed. For a moment we both gazed on it. It was a lovely thing, made of black and yellow silk in a pomegranate pattern, with a pale yellow overdress. My new dress used the same pattern, though as the under-dress, with a deep red silk covering it. We would look striking together at the feast – though now that I thought on it, I wished we would be wearing completely different dresses so that there would be no comparisons.

'There's nothing wrong with this neckline,' I said. 'That's not what I want to speak to you about.'

'What, then?' Claude went and stood by the window.

'If you continue to be rude I'll send you to live with your grandmother,' I said. 'She'll soon remind you to respect your mother.' My mother would not hesitate to take the whip to Claude, heiress to Jean Le Viste or no.

After a moment Claude muttered, '*Pardon*, Maman.'

'Look at me, Claude.'

She did at last, her green eyes more confused than angry.

'Béatrice told me what happened with the artist.'

Claude rolled her eyes. 'Béatrice is disloyal.'

'*Au contraire*, she did exactly as she should. She is still my woman, and her loyalty is to me. But never mind about her. What ever were you thinking? And in your father's chamber?'

'I want him, Maman.' Claude's face cleared as if there had been a storm there and now the clouds had been blown away.

I snorted. 'Don't be absurd. Of course you don't. You don't even know what that means.'

The storm returned. 'What do you know of me?'

'I know that you're not to mix with the likes of him. An artist is little better than a peasant!'

'That's not true!'

'You know too well that you will marry the man your father chooses. A noble match for a nobleman's daughter.

You aren't to go ruining that with an artist, or with anyone.'

Claude glared at me, her face full of spite. 'Just because you and Papa don't share a bed doesn't mean I too must be dry and hard as a shrivelled old pear!'

For a moment I thought I would hit her across her plump red mouth so that it bled. I took a deep breath. '*Ma fille*, it's clearly you who knows nothing of me.' I opened the door. 'Béatrice!' I bellowed so loudly it carried throughout the house. The steward must have heard it in his storerooms, the cook in his kitchen, the grooms in the stables, the maids on the stairs. If Jean were in he would certainly hear it in his chamber.

There was a short silence, like the pause between the lightning and the thunder. Then the door to the next room burst open and Béatrice came running through, the ladies behind her. She slowed when she saw me standing in the doorway. The ladies stopped at intervals in the room, like pearls on a string. Jeanne and Petite Geneviève remained in the doorway to my chamber, peeking out.

I reached for Claude's arm and pulled her roughly to the door so that she was facing Béatrice. 'Béatrice, you are now my daughter's lady-in-waiting. You are to remain with her at all hours of the day and night. You will go with her to Mass, to market, to visits, to the tailor's, to her dancing lessons. You will eat with her, ride with her, sleep with her – not in the closet nearby but in her bed. You will never leave her side. You will stand by her when she pisses in the pot.' One of the ladies gasped. 'If she sneezes, you will know it. If she belches or farts, you will smell it.'

Claude was crying now. 'You will know when her hair needs combing, when her courses run, when she cries.

'At the May Day feast it will be your task, Béatrice, and all my ladies, to see that Claude comes close to no man there, either to speak to him or dance with him or even to stand next to him, for she cannot be trusted. Let her have a miserable evening.

'First, though, the most important lesson my daughter must learn is respect for her parents. To that end you are to take her immediately to my mother's at Nanterre for a week – I will send a messenger to tell her she may be quick with the whip if she needs to.'

'Maman,' Claude whispered, 'please don't – '

'Quiet!' I looked hard at Béatrice. 'Béatrice, come in and get her packed.'

Béatrice bit her lips. 'Yes, Madame,' she said, lowering her eyes. '*Bien sûr.*' She slipped between me and Claude and went over to the chest full of dresses.

I stepped from Claude's room and strode towards my chamber. As I passed each lady she fell in line behind me until I was like a mother duck leading her four ducklings. When I reached my door my other daughters were standing together, heads bowed. They too followed me when I passed. One of the ladies shut the door. I turned around. 'Let us pray that Claude's soul may yet be saved,' I said to their solemn faces. We knelt.

II
BRUSSELS

Whitsuntide 1490

GEORGES DE LA CHAPELLE

I knew the moment I saw him that I wouldn't like him. I don't normally judge so quickly – I leave that to my wife. But when he walked in with Léon Le Vieux he looked around my workshop as if it were some slummy Paris street rather than the rue Haute off the Plâce de la Chapelle – respectable enough for a *lissier*. Then he didn't bother to meet my eye but watched Christine and Aliénor as they moved about the room, him with his well-cut tunic and tight Paris hose. This one is too sure of himself, I thought. He'll be nothing but trouble.

I was surprised he had come at all. I've been weaving thirty years and never had an artist travel all the way from Paris to see me. There's no need for it – all I want are the artist's designs and a good cartoonist like Philippe de la Tour to draw them large. Artists are no help to a *lissier*.

Léon hadn't warned me he would be bringing with him this Nicolas des Innocents, and they came earlier than expected. We were all in the workshop, preparing for the cutting-off of the tapestry we had been weaving. I had detached the cartoon from under the tapestry and was rolling it up to store with the other tapestry designs I own. Georges Le Jeune was removing the last of the bobbins. Luc was sweeping a place clear on the floor where we would lay out the tapestry when we had cut it from the loom. Christine and Aliénor were sewing shut the last slits in the tapestry left between the colours. Philippe de la Tour stood by, rethreading Aliénor's needle, looking for it when she dropped it, finding more slits in the tapestry for her to sew. He wasn't needed at the workshop, but he knew today was the cutting-off and found reasons to stay.

When Léon Le Vieux appeared at one of the workshop windows that open onto the street, my wife and I jumped up, and she ran to open the door for him. We were surprised that a stranger followed him in, but once Léon had introduced Nicolas as the artist who made the designs for the new tapestries, I nodded and said, 'You are welcome, gentlemen. My wife will bring you food and drink.' Christine hurried through the doorway connecting the workshop and the house at the back. We have two houses together, one where we eat and sleep, the other the workshop. Both have windows and doors opening into the street at the front and the garden at the back, to give the weavers clear light to work by.

Aliénor got to her feet to follow her mother. 'Tell your mother to bring in some cheese, some oysters,' I said quietly as she slipped away. 'Send Madeleine to buy some sweet cakes. And serve them double beer, not small.' I turned back to the men. 'Have you just come to Brussels?' I asked Léon. 'I was expecting you next week at the Feast of Corpus Christi.'

'We arrived yesterday,' Léon said. 'The roads were not bad – very dry, in fact.'

'Is Brussels always so quiet?' Nicolas said, picking bits of wool off his tunic. He would give that up soon if he stayed here long – wool clings to everyone in the workshop.

'Some say it is already too lively,' I answered coolly, annoyed that his first words were spoken with such a sneer. 'Though it is quieter here than by the Grand-Place. We don't need to be so close to the centre for our work. I expect you're used to different down in Paris. We get reports of the doings there.'

'Paris is the finest city in the world. When I go back I shall never leave it again.'

'If you like it so much, why did you come here?' Georges Le Jeune demanded. I shook my head at my plain spoken son, though I couldn't really blame him for speaking so. I wanted to ask it myself. When a man is rude I want to be rude back.

'Nicolas has come with me because of the importance of this commission,' Léon cut in smoothly. 'When you see the designs you will understand that they are very special indeed, and may require some supervision.'

Georges Le Jeune snorted. 'We don't need minders.'

'This is my son, Georges Le Jeune,' I said. 'And my apprentice Luc, who has two years training yet with us, but does fine *millefleurs*. This is Philippe de la Tour, who makes the cartoons from artists' designs.'

Nicolas glared openly at Philippe, whose pale face went red. 'I am not in the habit of having other men change my work,' Nicolas sneered. 'That's why I've come to this loathsome city – to be sure that my designs stay as I made them.'

I had never heard an artist so keen on his own work. He should know better – first designs always change when cartoonists make them into the large paintings on cloth or paper that weavers follow as they make the tapestries. It is the nature of the thing that what looks fine small doesn't when made large. There are gaps to be filled – figures must be added, or trees or animals or flowers. That is what a cartoonist like Philippe does well – when he draws large he fills the empty space so that the tapestry will be full and lively.

'You must be used to designing for tapestries and the changes that must be made to them,' I said. I did not address him as Monsieur – he might be a Parisian artist, but I ran a good workshop in Brussels. I had no reason to grovel.

Nicolas frowned. 'I am known at Court for – '

'Nicolas has a fine reputation at Court,' Léon interrupted, 'and Jean Le Viste has been content with his designs.' Léon said this too quickly, and I wondered what Nicolas was really known for at Court. I would have to send Georges Le Jeune to find out at the painters' guild. Someone must have heard of him.

By the time the women returned with the fare, we were ready to cut off the tapestry. The cutting-off is a good day for a weaver, when a piece you have worked on for so long – this time eight months on the one tapestry – is ready to be taken off the loom. Since we are always working on just a strip of tapestry the size of a hand's length, which is then rolled inside itself onto a wooden beam, we never see the tapestry whole until it is done. We also work on it from the back and don't see the finished side unless we slide a mirror underneath to check our work. Only when we cut the tapestry off the loom and lay it face-up on the floor do we get to see the whole work. Then we stand silent and look at what we have made.

That moment is like eating fresh spring radishes after months of old turnips. Sometimes – when the patron won't pay upfront and the dyers, the wool and silk merchants, the gilt wire sellers begin demanding payments I can't make, or when the weavers I've brought in refuse to work unless they see money first, or when Christine says nothing but the soup gets thinner – on those days only knowing that one day the moment of silence will come keeps me working.

I would have preferred that Léon and Nicolas weren't there for the cutting-off. They hadn't broken their backs over the loom for all those months, or cut criss-crosses into their fingers while handling the gilt wire, or had headaches from looking so hard at the warp and weft. But of course I couldn't ask them to go, or let them see that I was annoyed. A *lissier* does not show such things to the merchant he is to haggle with.

'Please eat,' I said, waving at the plates Christine and Aliénor had brought in. 'We'll take this tapestry off the loom and then we can discuss the commission from Monseigneur Le Viste.'

Léon nodded, but Nicolas muttered, 'Brussels fare, eh?

Who can be bothered?' Nonetheless, he wandered over to the plates, picked up an oyster, tipped his head back, and slurped it down. Then he licked his lips and smiled at Aliénor, who stepped around him to fetch a stool for Léon. I chuckled to myself – eventually she would surprise him, but not yet. He was not so clever after all.

Before the cutting-off we knelt to say a prayer to St Maurice, patron saint of weavers. Then Georges Le Jeune handed me the pair of scissors. I took up a handful of warp threads, held them taut and snipped through them. Christine sighed at that first cut, but no one made a sound as I cut through the rest.

When I was done, Georges Le Jeune and Luc rolled the tapestry off the bottom beam. They had the honour of cutting through the other end of the warp before they brought the tapestry over to the cleared space on the floor and laid it down. I nodded, and they unrolled it so that the tapestry was facing up. Then we all stood still and looked – save Aliénor, who went back into the house to fetch beer for the boys.

The scene in the tapestry was of the Adoration of the Magi. The Hamburg patron who commissioned it had paid handsomely. We had used both silver and gilt wire among the wool and silk, and where possible had dovetailed the colours, with plenty of hachure for the shading. These techniques made its weaving take longer, but I knew the patron would find it had been worth the cost. The tapestry was glorious, even if it was the *lissier* saying so.

I had expected Nicolas merely to glance at it, or to sneer and say the design was poor or the workmanship shoddy compared to Parisian workshops. Instead he kept his mouth shut and studied it, which put me in a better humour with him.

Georges Le Jeune broke the silence first. 'The Virgin's robe is very fine,' he said. 'I could swear it was velvet.'

'Not half so fine as the red hachure creeping up and down the young king's green hose,' Luc replied. 'Very striking, the red and green together.'

The hachure was indeed very fine. I'd allowed Georges Le Jeune to weave it himself, and he had made a good job of it. It is not easy to weave thin lines of one colour into another without blurring the two. The beads of colour must be accurate – just one out of place will be noticed, and the shading effect ruined.

Georges Le Jeune and Luc make a habit of praising each other's work. Afterwards they will find each other's faults, of course, but they try first to see the good in the other. It was generous of my son to praise an apprentice when he could just as easily order him to sweep the floor or fetch a hank of wool. But they work side by side for months, and if there's ill feeling between them the tapestries suffer, as do we all. Young Luc may be still learning, but he has the makings of a weaver in him.

'Wasn't there an Adoration of the Magi made in Brussels for Charles de Bourbon a few years ago?' Léon said. 'I saw it in his house in Paris. The young king wore green hose in that tapestry as well, as I recall.'

Aliénor was passing through the workshop with mugs of beer. She halted at his words, and in the sudden silence that fell we could all hear the slopping of beer to the floor.

79

I opened my mouth to speak, but closed it again. Léon had caught me out, and with very little cunning.

The Adoration of the Magi he spoke of had been woven at another Brussels workshop, but the cartoon design had been bought by Charles de Bourbon so that the tapestry would not be copied. I had admired the king's green hose in it and had used them in this work, assuming that Charles de Bourbon's family were unlikely to see the Hamburg patron's tapestry. I knew the other *lissier* well, and could bribe the Guild to keep quiet about my borrowing. We may steal each other's business, but in some matters we Brussels *lissiers* are loyal to each other.

But I had forgotten about Léon Le Vieux. He sees most work that goes in and out of Paris, and he never forgets details, especially a memorable one like green hose marked with red hachure. I had broken a rule in copying them, and now Léon could use that in the haggling – he could demand whatever he liked for the Le Viste tapestries, and I would have to agree. Otherwise he could tell the Bourbons their design had been copied and I would be heavily fined.

'Will you have an oyster, Monsieur?' Christine held out a plate to Léon, bless her. She is a clever wife. Although she couldn't repair the damage done, she could at least distract him from it.

Léon Le Vieux gazed at her. 'Oysters don't agree with me, Madame, but thank you all the same. Perhaps a cake instead.'

Christine bit her lip. It was Léon's way to make even Christine feel wrong-footed in her own house and yet be so pleasant about it. It was impossible either to like him or despise him. I've worked with him before – he admires the workshop's *millefleurs* and has brought us several commissions – but I could not call him a friend. He keeps to himself.

'Come into the house where we can spread out the designs,' I said to him and Nicolas, gesturing to Philippe as well – I wanted him to see the designs too. Georges Le Jeune made to follow us. I shook my head. 'You and Luc stay here and begin undressing the loom. Clear the rollers of the remains of the warp. I'll be along later.'

Georges Le Jeune slumped his shoulders and turned back to the loom. Christine followed him with her eyes, then frowned at me. I frowned back. She had something on her mind. Later she would tell me what it was – she always does.

Just then Nicolas des Innocents said, 'What is she doing?' He was watching Aliénor, who had crouched by the tapestry and was running her hands over it.

'Checking her work,' Philippe answered, going red in the face again. He is protective of Aliénor, as a brother might be.

I led the men inside to where Christine and Madeleine had set on trestles the long table where we eat. It was darker and smokier in the house, but I wanted the boys to get on with their work without being distracted by the new commission. Léon began to unroll the canvases, and Christine got out heavy crocks and tankards to weigh down the corners. As she placed them I could see her glancing at the designs. She would have her say later, when we were alone.

'*Attendez* – that's not how you should look at them,'

Nicolas said, and began rearranging the paintings. I didn't like to look while he was fussing about, so I turned my back on the glimpses of red and blue I'd had and looked around the room instead, trying to see it as these Parisians must. I expect they are used to more luxury – a bigger hearth, indeed a separate room for cooking, more carved wood, more cushions on the chairs, more silver plates for show rather than pewter, more tapestries on the wall. It's odd – I make tapestries for others but have none of my own. They cost too much – a *lissier* does well enough but still we cannot afford our own work.

Perhaps Nicolas expects my wife and daughter to dress in fine clothes and wear jewels in their hair and have their servants hand them everything. But we don't flaunt our wealth as Parisians do. My wife does have jewels but those are locked away. Our servant Madeleine is useful but Christine and Aliénor like to do things for themselves, especially Aliénor, who is always keen to show that she doesn't need help. If they wanted, Christine and Aliénor could choose not to sew the tapestries. They could keep their fingers smooth and let someone else bear the needle pricks. But they prefer to help in the workshop. Christine knows how to dress a loom, and has the strong arms to stretch warp threads as well as a man. If I am short of a weaver she can fill in on the easier parts, though the Guild will not allow it for more than a day or two.

'That's done,' Nicolas said. I turned around and went to stand next to Philippe.

The first words to say when negotiating with the patron's man are not praise. I never let them know what I think of designs. I always start with the problems. Philippe is also careful with his words. He is a good lad – he has learned much from me about haggling.

We looked for a time. When I finally spoke I kept the surprise from my tone. That I would speak of later, with Christine. Instead I sounded indignant. 'He's not designed tapestries before, has he? These are paintings, not designs. There is no story within each tapestry, and not enough figures – instead we look to the Lady in the centre, as we do with paintings of the Virgin and Child, rather than all along the tapestry.'

Nicolas began to say something, but Léon interrupted. 'Is that all you can say about them? Look once more, Georges. You may not see the likes of such designs again.'

'What is it, then? What is meant to be the story?'

Aliénor appeared in the doorway between the kitchen and the workshop, an empty mug in each hand.

'The Lady's seduction of the unicorn,' Nicolas said, shifting from one foot to the other so that he was turned towards Aliénor. The fool. 'Also there are the five senses – ' he pointed – 'Smell, Sound, Taste, Sight, Touch.'

Aliénor crossed to the barrel in the corner.

We looked for longer. 'There are too few figures,' I said. 'Once they're the size of the tapestries there'll be much space to fill. We would have to design a field full of *mille-fleurs*.'

'Which is what you are known for, and why I chose you for the commission,' Léon replied. 'It should be simple for you.'

'It isn't that simple. We'll have to add other things.'

83

'What things?' Nicolas demanded.

I looked at Philippe, expecting him to speak, for it would be his work to make these designs usable, to fill the empty space. He said nothing. He's a shy boy and takes his time about speaking. I thought he was sensible, but now the silly lad had a strange look on his face and was gazing at the paintings as if he were looking on the most beautiful woman in Brussels.

Mind you, the women in the tapestries were – I shook my head to clear it. I would not let them seduce me. 'More people, more animals, more plants,' I said. 'Eh, Philippe?'

Philippe tore his eyes from the designs. '*Bien sûr.*'

'What would you add to them, apart from people and animals?'

'Oh. Er, trees, perhaps, to give it structure. Or a trellis of roses.'

'I won't have these designs touched,' Nicolas said. 'They're perfect as they are.'

There was a loud clatter as Christine dropped a plate of oysters. She didn't pick it up, but glared at Nicolas. 'I won't have such blasphemy spoken in this house! No man can design anything perfect – it's only in God's power to do that. You and your designs are as full of flaws as anyone.'

I smiled to myself. It had not taken Nicolas long to feel my wife's temper. After a moment he bowed. 'I'm sorry, Madame. I didn't mean to offend.'

'You should demand God's pardon, not mine.'

'All right, Christine,' I said. 'You'd best go and start sewing the hem of the Adoration. We'll need to bring it to the Guild soon.'

The hemming could have waited, but if she stayed with us she might force Nicolas des Innocents to his knees to say his prayers in front of her. Though that would entertain us, it would not help with the haggling.

Christine glared at me, but she obeyed. Aliénor crouched where her mother had dropped the plate and began feeling about for the oyster shells. Philippe made a move to join her but I squeezed his elbow to stop him. His eyes darted between her and the designs. He lives near, and often helps Aliénor when he is here – he has looked out for her since they were children. Now he often works with me on designs. I forget sometimes that he is not my son.

'Tell me the size of the tapestries,' I said to Léon Le Vieux.

Léon went through them while I added up in my head. 'What about gilt or silver thread? Silk from Venice? English wool? How many figures in each? How dense the *millefleurs*? How much blue? How much red? Dovetailing or not? Hachure?' As Léon answered each question, I altered the time and cost of the work.

'I can do them in three years,' I said at last. 'It will cost 400 *livres tournois*, and I keep the designs.'

'Monseigneur wants them finished by Palm Sunday 1492,' Léon responded quickly. He always answers quickly, as if he is several steps ahead in his thoughts. 'He will pay 300 *livres tournois* for them and for the designs, which he will keep – he wants fully painted cartoons he can hang in the place of the tapestries if he takes those with him somewhere.'

'Impossible,' I said. 'You know that's impossible, Léon.

That's in less than two years. I can't possibly weave them so fast, for so little. In fact, your offer is insulting. You'd best take it elsewhere.' It was indeed insulting – I should take my chances with the green hose rather than work for such wages.

Aliénor was getting to her feet with the plate of oysters. She shook her head slightly at me. She's like her mother, I thought, watching out for me. Though without the temper. She can't afford to have a temper.

Nicolas des Innocents was still making eyes at her. Of course she didn't notice.

'You can take on twice the men and make them in half the time,' Léon said.

'It's not so simple. The workshop will only fit two horizontal looms at best, and even with twice the men there's only me to look after them. A work like this can't be rushed. Then there are other jobs I agreed to long before you told me about this one.'

Léon waved his hand to dismiss my feeble arguments. 'Give up the other jobs. You will manage. Look at them, Georges.' He held his hand out to the designs. 'You can see that this is an important commission, perhaps the most important this workshop has ever been offered. You don't want a little detail like how long they will take to stop you from agreeing to this one.'

Nicolas looked pleased. Compliments from Léon were rare.

'What I see,' I said, 'are designs made by a man who knows nothing about tapestries. We will have to make many changes to them.'

Léon spoke smoothly over Nicolas' sputters. 'Perhaps a few changes will make the terms more appealing.'

I hesitated. The terms offered were so bad that I wasn't sure I could even haggle. If I took on such a job it might ruin us.

'What about the gilt thread?' Philippe suggested. 'The Lady is not royal, nor is she the Virgin, even if she and the unicorn remind us of Our Lady and Her Son. Her dress doesn't have to be gilted.'

I gave him a sharp look. Now he was speaking when I didn't want him to. I was meant to haggle, not him. Still, he could be right. 'Yes,' I said. 'The gilt is costly and hard to use. Weaving with it takes longer.'

Léon shrugged. 'So we leave off the gilt. What does that save?'

'The dovetailing too,' I added. 'It is not such an easy technique to interweave colours, and the weaving takes longer, though it is finer work in the end. If we don't dovetail but sew the colours together we'll save some time. If Monseigneur Le Viste truly wants the best, he'll have to pay more and allow more time.'

'There isn't more time,' Léon said. 'He wants them for Easter 1492, for an important occasion. And he isn't a patient man – he would never accept your paltry excuses.'

'Then he can't have gilt thread or dovetailed weaving. That is your choice.'

I watched Léon as he thought. He has a closed face – it's hard to see what he is thinking. That is why he is good at what he does – he hides his thoughts until they are clear, and when he speaks it is hard to disagree.

'All right,' he said.

'I have not agreed to take it on,' I said. 'There's more to discuss. Philippe, you and Nicolas take the designs into the workshop. I'll join you later. Aliénor, go and help your mother to sew the hem.'

Aliénor made a face. She likes to listen to the haggling. 'Go,' I repeated.

With the room clear, I poured us more beer, and Léon and I sat back to drink. Now that the others weren't hanging over our necks, I could think seriously about Léon's offer.

That evening Christine and I went for a walk in the Grand-Place. As we entered the square we stopped to admire the Hôtel de Ville, with its thin tower that Georges Le Jeune and Luc like to climb up for the view. They've been making that building all through my life, yet it still surprises me when I see it. It makes me proud to live in Brussels, however much Nicolas des Innocents may sneer.

We strolled past the guildhouses lining the square – the tailors, the painters, the bakers and tallow-makers and carpenters, the archers, the boatmen. The houses were busy, of an evening. Business doesn't stop when daylight fades. We nodded and smiled to friends and neighbours, and idled in front of L'Arbre d'Or, which houses the weavers' guild. Several *lissiers* gathered around me to ask about Léon Le Vieux's visit, about the designs, the terms, and why Nicolas des Innocents had come. I dodged their questions like a boy playing tag.

At last we moved on – Christine fancied seeing the Church of St Michel and St Gudule in the twilight. As we walked along the rue de la Montagne she said what I knew had been ready on her lips all afternoon. 'You should have let Georges Le Jeune hear the business between you and Léon.'

Another wife might have asked it as a timid question. Not mine – she speaks her mind. When I didn't answer she spoke it some more. 'Georges Le Jeune is a good lad and a good weaver. You've trained him well in that. But if he is to take over the workshop he needs to know about the business side as well – the haggling, the terms agreed. Why do you keep him from that?'

I shrugged. 'I'll be the *lissier* a long time yet. There is no hurry.'

Christine pursed her lips. 'Georges, your hair is going grey. Your son is a man and could marry if he wanted. One day the workshop will be his. Do you want him to ruin it and destroy all you've built up? You have to –'

'That's enough, Christine.' I have never hit my wife, though I know of men who would if she were theirs.

Christine clamped her mouth shut. I would think on what she said – I would have to, for she was sure to bring it up again. Some men don't listen to their wives, but I do listen to her. I would be a fool not to – Christine was brought up a weaver's daughter near Notre Dame du Sablon, and knows almost as much about the running of a workshop as I do.

We walked in silence until the church's twin towers loomed up before us in the growing dark. 'How did

Brussels and Paris get on with the designs?' I asked, to make things better between us.

Christine snorted. 'That Nicolas des Innocents thinks much of himself. Philippe has his hands full convincing him that we'll have to make changes to the designs. I had to step in once or twice – Philippe is a good lad but he's no match for a Paris rooster.'

I chuckled. 'I should go. They're waiting for me at Le Vieux Chien to drink to the cutting-off.'

'*Attends*, George,' Christine said. 'What did you decide, you and Léon Le Vieux? Did you take the work?'

I kicked at a bit of dung. 'I've not said yes, I've not said no. I may have no choice, what with the problem of the green hose. Léon could go to the Bourbon family to say I copied their design.'

'You didn't copy, you only borrowed one detail. The Guild will back you.' She stopped in her tracks, her skirt swaying. 'Tell me – are we to make these tapestries or not?'

I should not make them. All of my experience as a *lissier* told me not to – the money was poor, the workshop would be overstretched, I would lose other work and strain to finish them on time. If I weren't careful, the workshop would be ruined.

'Yes,' I said, my gut knotting. 'We will make them. Yes. For I have never seen designs so fair.' There, I thought. I have let the Ladies seduce me.

Christine laughed then, a sharp sound like a knife clattering to the floor. I think she was relieved. 'They will be the making of us,' she said. 'You'll see.'

PHILIPPE DE LA TOUR

No one was in the workshop when I arrived in the morning. I was glad, for I could look at the designs alone, without Nicolas des Innocents boasting or Christine butting in or Aliénor cocking her head and smiling as she sewed. Now I could look and think in peace.

It was a bright day, with light streaming in at the windows. Luc had swept the floor clean and cleared away the hanks of wool left over from the Adoration of the Magi tapestry. The loom had been stripped as well and sat empty, waiting for the next warp threads to be laid across it. The wood creaked occasionally, making me think of a horse shifting in its stall.

Nicolas' designs had been rolled up and stored in a chest with other tapestry designs. I knew where Georges kept the key, and got them out now, spreading them on the floor as they had been the evening before. When Nicolas and I had been talking about them then, he'd kept looking over at Aliénor as she sat with her mother, sewing on the tapestry that had just been cut off. He had turned himself this way and that, thinking it was for her benefit. At last he had said to her, 'Shouldn't you put down your sewing now, beauty?'

Aliénor and Christine had both raised their heads. No one had ever called Aliénor beauty before, no matter what they thought of her. I think she is beautiful, especially her hair, which is long and golden – but I would be ashamed to say so. It is hard for me to say such things. She would probably laugh at me and tell me I am a fool. She treats me as a younger, silly brother, even though I am a few years her elder.

'It's so dark over where you are,' Nicolas continued. 'You'll get a squint. You should sit closer to the window where the light is better. Besides, I've heard of all the rules you Brussels weavers work by. No work outside of daylight, no work on Sundays. Would that Paris painters had such easy lives, to save their eyes so.'

Christine and I stared at him in astonishment, but Aliénor bowed her head over her work, trying not to laugh. She did, though, and then Christine burst out laughing, and I joined them.

'What is so funny?' Nicolas demanded. That made us laugh even harder. I wondered if we should take pity on him and tell him what he had not seen.

It was Aliénor herself who decided. 'Such rules don't apply to women,' she said when we had finally stopped laughing. 'We're not weavers, we're just family.'

'I see,' Nicolas said. He looked puzzled, though, for that didn't explain our laughter. We weren't going to tell him, though. It was good to have a joke on the Paris man.

We got little done that evening, Nicolas and I. Soon

after we went to Le Vieux Chien with Georges Le Jeune and Luc, and Georges later joined us, to raise a cup to the finished tapestry, and to the new commission. Nicolas was very lively, and got us to drink more than we are used to.

He is a boaster, that Paris artist. I have not been to Paris. I don't leave the city walls except to collect firewood and mushrooms in the nearby forests, or to fish sometimes along the River Senne. But I've met enough Paris men to know I wouldn't like it there. They are too sure of their ways. Always they know best – they have the best wine, the best shoes, the best cloth, the best brushes, the best ways of making paint. Their women bear more children, their hens more eggs, their cows more milk. Their churches are taller, their ships faster, their roads smoother. They hold their beer better, they sit their horses more gracefully, they always win when they fight. Probably their shit smells sweeter too.

No, I was glad to be without him in the workshop now. I gazed down at the designs. My head was sore from the noise and smoke and drink of the tavern, for I don't go there often.

I will say this of Nicolas – his Paris ways may bother me, but he is a fine artist. He knows so too, and because of that I will never tell him how good his paintings are.

It's easy enough to find fault with them as tapestry designs. To him they are paintings – he hasn't seen that with tapestries there needs to be an even pace to the design to make them smooth, so that nothing jumps out. That is what I do when I draw a cartoon – I make the design big and paint it as I know the wool will look when woven, with less blending of colours and more bright, even patterns. Cartoons are not so beautiful as paintings, but they are essential for the weaver to follow as he works. That is how I often feel – essential but unnoticed, just as Nicolas des Innocents is a painting you cannot take your eyes from.

I was still looking at the paintings when Georges came into the workshop. His face was bleary and his hair stuck out everywhere, as if he had rolled his head about in his sleep. He stood next to me and looked down at the paintings. 'Can you make them into proper designs?'

'Yes.'

'*Bien*. Make some small sketches of the changes for Léon to see. When he's satisfied you can start on the cartoons.'

I nodded.

Georges stared at the painting of the Lady with the unicorn in her lap. He cleared his throat. 'Nicolas is to stay on and paint the cartoons.'

I stepped back. 'Why? You know I can paint as well as he. Who –'

'Léon wants it. It is part of the terms of the work. Monseigneur Le Viste is buying the cartoons, and may hang them in place of the tapestries when those travel with him. Léon wants to be sure the cartoons look exactly as Nicolas has painted the designs. We have so little time to weave them that it helps us if he stays here to work on them.'

I wanted to protest but knew I mustn't. Georges is the *lissier* – he decides what is to be done and I do it. I know my place. 'Am I still to draw the cartoons or will he do that too?'

'You will draw them, and make the changes needed.

And you'll help with the painting. You'll work together, but he will be the master.'

I was silent.

'It's only for a few weeks,' Georges added.

'Does Nicolas know?'

'Léon is telling him. In fact I'm going to see him now, to go over the contract.' Georges looked down at the paintings and shook his head. 'These are going to bring me trouble. Poor wages, little time, a difficult patron. I must be mad.'

'When do we start?'

'Now. Georges Le Jeune and Luc have gone to buy the linen and will be back soon. You and Nicolas can take it back to your house and work there if you prefer, or you can stay here.'

'Here,' I said quickly. I always prefer to work on the rue Haute when I can. It is lighter than my father's house near one of the city wall's towers, and despite the looms there's more room. My father is also a painter and not so well off as Georges. With my older brothers working with him there is little room for the youngest.

Also when I work here I am near to her. Not that she cares. She has never shown any interest in men – until now.

'If the weather holds you can paint in Aliénor's garden,' Georges said over his shoulder as he was going. 'That will keep you out of the weavers' way – it will be crowded in here with two looms.'

Even better to be in her garden – though I wasn't sure I wanted Nicolas around Aliénor so much. I didn't trust him.

Even as I thought of her, she appeared in the doorway with my morning beer. She is a little thing, small and neat. The rest of her family is much taller. 'I'm here, Aliénor,' I said. She came towards me with a little smile, her face bright, but stumbled over the bag of drawing things that I had foolishly left in the middle of the floor. I caught her before she fell, but much of the beer slopped over my sleeve.

'*Dieu me garde*,' she muttered. 'I'm sorry. Where did it spill? Not on the paintings, I hope!'

'No, just on my sleeve. It doesn't matter. It's only small beer.'

She felt my wet sleeve and shook her head, angry at herself.

'Really, it doesn't matter,' I repeated. 'I was stupid to leave my bag there. Don't trouble yourself over the beer – I wasn't so thirsty anyway.'

'No, I'll get you more.' She didn't listen to me, but hurried out again and came back a few minutes later with another full mug, stepping carefully this time.

She stood at my side, the designs at our feet, while I drank. I tried not to gulp my beer loudly. When I'm with Aliénor I'm always aware of how noisy I am – my boots creak, my teeth chatter, I scratch my hair, I cough and sneeze.

'Tell me about the story,' she said. Her voice is low and smooth – smooth like the way she walks or turns her head or picks up something or smiles. She is careful in everything she does.

'What do you mean?' I asked. My voice is not so smooth.

'The tapestries. The Lady and the unicorn. What is the story?'

'Ah, that. Well, in the first there is a Lady standing in front of a blue tent with words on it. *À mon seul désir.*' I read it slowly.

'*À mon seul désir,*' Aliénor repeated.

'The lion and the unicorn sit holding open the flaps as well as the banner and standard of the Le Viste family.'

'Are they very important, these Le Vistes down in Paris?'

'I expect so, if they are having tapestries as grand as these made. So, the Lady is taking jewels from a casket, and she wears them in the other tapestries. Then there are three tapestries where the Lady draws the unicorn nearer. Finally he sits in her lap and looks at himself in a mirror. In the last one she leads him away, holding onto his horn.'

'Which Lady is the prettiest?'

'The one feeding her parakeet. That is meant to be Taste, of the five senses. There's also a monkey eating something at her feet. This Lady is more spirited than the others. The wind blows through the scene, making her headscarf flap. And the unicorn is lively.'

Aliénor ran her tongue over her bottom lip. 'Already I don't like her. Tell me about the other senses. What stands for each?'

'The unicorn looking in the mirror is Sight, and the Lady holding his horn is Touch. That's clear enough. Then there is Sound, where the Lady plays an organ. And in this one –' I peered at the painting – 'this one is Smell, I think, for a monkey sits on a bench and sniffs a flower.'

'What kind of flower?' Aliénor always wants to know about the flowers.

'I'm not sure. A rose, I think.'

'You can see for yourself, beauty.' Nicolas was leaning in the doorway, watching us. He looked bright and fresh, as if the drink had not touched him. I suppose he lives in taverns in Paris. He stepped into the workshop. 'You keep a garden, I've heard – you must know a carnation from a rose when you see it. Surely my painting is not so bad as that, eh, beauty?'

'Don't call her that,' I said. 'She's the daughter of the *lissier*. She should be treated with respect.'

Aliénor had turned red, though whether from Nicolas' words or mine, I don't know.

'What do you think of my paintings, beau—Aliénor?' Nicolas persisted. 'They're fair, *non*?'

'Designs,' I corrected. 'These are designs for tapestries, not paintings. You seem to forget that they are merely a guide for works someone else will make – Aliénor's father and son, and other weavers. Not you. They'll look very different as tapestries.'

'As good?' Nicolas smirked.

'Better.'

'I don't see that they can be much improved on – do you?'

Aliénor pursed her lips – she prefers modesty to boasting.

'What do you know of unicorns, beauty?' he said with a sly look I did not like. 'Shall I tell you about them?'

'I know that they are strong,' she answered. 'It says so in Job and in Deuteronomy – "his horns are like the horns of unicorns: with them he shall push the people together to the ends of the earth".'

'I prefer the Psalms: "But my horn shalt thou exalt like the horn of an unicorn." Do you know about the unicorn's horn?' Nicolas winked at me as he said it.

Aliénor didn't seem to be listening to him, but was wrinkling her nose in disgust. Then I smelled it, and a moment later Nicolas did too. '*Bon Dieu*, what is that?' he cried. 'It smells like a barrow full of piss!'

'It's Jacques Le Bœuf,' I said. 'The woad dyer.'

'Is that what woad smells like? I've never been near the stuff. In Paris they have to work outside the city walls in a place no one goes near.'

'Here too, but he still comes into town. The smell clings to him but you can't ban a man from his business. Mind you, his dealings are always brief.'

'Where's the girl?' Jacques Le Bœuf's booming voice came from inside the house.

'Georges is out, Jacques,' we heard Christine say. 'Come back another day.'

'Not him. I want to see her, just for a moment. Is she in the shop?' Jacques Le Bœuf poked his shaggy head around the door. His smell always makes my eyes water. 'Hello there, Philippe, you rascal. Where's Georges' girl, then? Is she hiding from me?'

Aliénor had dropped to the floor and was crouching behind the loom.

'She's gone out,' Nicolas said, cocking his head to one side and crossing his arms over his chest. 'She's gone to get me some oysters.'

'Has she, now?' Jacques pulled his whole body into view. He is a big man, like a barrel with a scraggly beard and hands stained blue from the woad. 'And who are you to be telling her what to do?'

'Nicolas des Innocents. I've designed the new tapestries for Georges.'

'The Paris artist, are you?' Jacques crossed his arms as well and leaned against the doorway. 'We don't think much of Paris men, do we, Philippe?'

I made to answer, but Nicolas got in before me. 'I wouldn't bother waiting for her. I told her to get the best oysters, you see – only what is fit for Parisians to eat. That may take her some time to find in this city, for I do not think much of your fish market.'

I stared at Nicolas, wondering why he would dare to provoke a man so much bigger than he. Didn't he want to keep his face pretty for the women? I heard Aliénor shift beside the loom and tried not to look at her. Perhaps she was thinking of coming out, to save Nicolas from his rash words.

Jacques Le Bœuf also seemed surprised. He didn't respond with his fists, but narrowed his eyes. 'Is that your work, then?' He came to stand next to us and look down at the paintings on the floor. I tried not to gag at the smell. 'More red than blue in them. Maybe it's not worth my while for Georges to work on them.' He grinned and made to step on the painting of the Lady with the unicorn in her lap.

'Jacques, what are you doing?'

Christine's sharp words made Jacques Le Bœuf freeze,

his foot dangling over the painting. He took a step back, the sheepish look on his big face comical.

Christine hurried up to him. 'If this is your idea of a jest, it's not funny. I said Georges was out. He'll come to speak to you soon about the blue wool for these tapestries – if you don't ruin them first. Off you go, now – we're busy here.' She opened the door onto the street and stood aside.

It was like watching a dog round up a cow. Jacques hung his head and shuffled to the door. Only when he was in the street did he pop his head back through a window and say, 'Tell the girl I was asking for her.'

When we were sure he was gone, his rank smell fading, Nicolas leaned over and smiled at Aliénor by the loom. 'You can come out now, beauty – the beast is gone.' He held out a hand. After a moment she reached out and took it, then let him help her up. When she was standing she raised her face to his and said, 'Thank you, Monsieur.'

It was the first time she had looked at him in the way that Aliénor looks – her eyes trying but not able to meet anyone's – and Nicolas' smile disappeared as he gazed into her face. He looked as if he had been winded by a blow. Finally, I thought, he sees. For an artist he is not very attentive.

Aliénor knew that he finally understood – she had chosen to let him see. She does that sometimes. Now she pulled her hand from his and bowed her head.

'Come, Aliénor,' Christine said with a fierce look at Nicolas, 'or we'll be late.' She went out through the same door Jacques Le Bœuf had.

101

'Mass,' Aliénor reminded me, before running out to join her mother.

'Mass?' Nicolas repeated. He glanced up at the sun coming through the window. 'It's too early for Sext, isn't it?'

'It's a special Mass for weavers at Notre Dame du Sablon,' I said. 'A church not far from here.'

'They have their own Mass?'

'Three times a week. It is a powerful guild.'

After a moment he said, 'How long has she been like that?'

I shrugged. 'All her life. That's why it is so easy not to notice. It is natural for her.'

'How does she –' Nicolas waved at the Adoration of the Magi tapestry, which was draped over the loom it had been woven on.

'Her fingers are very skilled and sensitive. Sometimes I think her eyes must be on her fingers. She can tell the difference between blue and red wool because she says the dyes feel different. And she hears things that we don't. She told me once that each person has a different footstep. I can't hear it, but she can always tell who is coming, if she has heard them before. She will know your footstep now.'

'Is she still a girl?'

I frowned. 'Don't know what you mean.' Suddenly I did not want to talk about her.

Nicolas smiled. 'You do know what I mean. You've thought about it.'

'Leave her be,' I said sharply. 'Touch her and her father will tear you apart, Paris artist or not.'

102

'I have plenty whenever I like. It's you I was thinking of. Though I expect the girls like you well enough, with those long lashes of yours. Girls love eyes like that.'

I said nothing, but reached for my bag and pulled out paper and charcoal.

Nicolas laughed. 'I can see that I will have to tell you both about the unicorn's horn.'

'Not now. We need to start work. They can't begin the weaving until we've painted one of the cartoons.' I gritted my teeth as I said 'we'.

'Ah, yes, the painting. Luckily I have my own brushes with me. I wouldn't trust a Brussels brush – if I painted my unicorn with one it would probably look like a horse!'

I knelt by the paintings – it kept me from kicking him. 'Have you ever drawn or painted cartoons?'

Nicolas stopped smirking. He doesn't like to be reminded of what he does not know.

'Tapestries are very different from paintings,' I said. 'Artists who haven't worked on them don't understand this. They think that whatever they paint can simply be made bigger and woven just as they have made it. But looking at a tapestry is not like looking at a painting. A painting is usually smaller so that you can see everything at once. You don't stand up close, but a step or two back, as if it is a priest or a teacher. With a tapestry you stand close as you would to a friend. You see only a part of it, and not necessarily the most important part. So no thing should stand out more than the rest, but fit together into a pattern that your eye takes pleasure in no matter where it rests. These paintings don't have that pattern in them.

The *millefleur* background will help, but we will still have to change them.'

'How?' Nicolas said.

'Add things. More figures, for a start. The Lady should at least be attended by a lady-in-waiting, *n'est-ce pas*? Someone to hold carnations for her as she weaves them in Smell, or to work the bellows of her organ in Sound, or to hold out a bowl of something for her to feed to the parakeet in Taste. You have a servant holding the jewellery casket in À Mon Seul Désir. Why not in the others?'

'In a seduction a lady should be alone.'

'Ladies-in-waiting must have witnessed seductions.'

'How would you know – have you ever seduced a noble-woman?'

I turned red. I could not dream of being in a noble-woman's private chamber. I'm rarely in the same street as nobles, much less the same room. Only at Mass do we share the same air, and even then they are far away in the front pews, separate from the rest of us. They leave before we do, their horses taking them away quickly before I have reached the church porch. Aliénor says noblemen smell of the fur they wear, but I've never been close enough to smell it. Her nose is keener than most.

Clearly Nicolas had been with noblewomen. He must know all about them. 'What do noblewomen smell like?' I asked before I could stop myself.

Nicolas smiled. 'Cloves. Cloves and mint.'

Aliénor smells of lemon balm. She is always treading on it in her garden.

'Do you know what they taste like?' he added.

'Don't tell me.' I quickly picked up the charcoal and, choosing the painting of Smell to copy, began to sketch. I drew a few lines for the woman's face and head-dress, then her necklace, bodice, sleeves and dress. 'We don't want large blocks of colour. For instance, the yellow under-dress needs more pattern. Elsewhere you've used a pome-granate brocade – in Taste and À Mon Seul Désir. Let's add it here, like this, to break up the colour.'

Nicolas watched over my shoulder as I filled in the tri-angle of cloth with leaves and flowers. '*Alors*, you have the lion and the unicorn holding their banners to the left and right. Between the Lady and the unicorn a monkey sits on a bench holding a carnation. That is good. What if we add a servant between the Lady and the lion? She can hold a plate of flowers the Lady will use to make her crown.' I drew the outline of a lady-in-waiting in profile. 'Already this is much better. The *millefleurs* behind will fill out the scene. I won't draw them here, but on the cartoon. Aliénor can help us with them then.'

Nicolas shook his head. 'How can she be of use to us?' He gestured at his eyes.

I frowned. 'She always helps her father with the *mille-fleurs*. She keeps a fine kitchen garden and knows the plants well, knows their uses. We'll speak to her once we begin the cartoons. *Alors*, among the *millefleurs* we will add some animals.' I sketched as I spoke. 'A dog somewhere for fidelity, perhaps. Some hunting birds for the Lady's hunt of the unicorn. A lamb at her feet to remind us of Christ and Our Lady. And of course a rabbit or two. That is Georges' signature – a rabbit holding a paw to its face.'

I finished drawing, and we looked at the painting and the sketch side by side. 'Still not right,' I said.

'What do you suggest, then?'

'Trees,' I said after a moment.

'Where?'

'Behind the standards and banners. It will make the red coat of arms stand out better from the red background. Then two below, behind the lion and unicorn. Four trees, to mark the four directions and the four seasons.'

'A whole world in a picture,' Nicolas murmured.

'Yes. And the added blue will please Jacques Le Bœuf.' Not that I want to please him, I thought. Far from it.

I drew an oak beside the standard – oak for summer and for the north. Then a pine behind the banner, for autumn and the south. Holly behind the unicorn, for winter and the west. Orange behind the lion, for spring and the east.

'That is better,' Nicolas said when I was done. He sounded surprised. 'But can we make such a big change without the patron agreeing to it?'

'It's part of the *verdure*,' I said. 'Weavers are allowed to design the plants and animals of the background – it's only the figures we can't change. There was a law passed about it some years ago in Brussels, so that there wouldn't be problems between patrons and weavers.'

'Or between artists and cartoonists.'

'That too.'

He looked at me. 'Are there problems between us?'

I sat back on my heels. 'No.' Not about work, at least, I added to myself. I am not brave enough to say such things aloud.

'Good.' Nicolas picked up Taste and pushed Smell aside. 'Now do this one.'

I studied the Lady feeding her parakeet. 'You've painted her face with more care than the others.'

Nicolas fiddled with the charcoal, touching it and then rubbing the black smudge until it turned grey between his fingers. 'I'm used to painting portraits, and prefer to make the women here real if I can.'

'She stands out too much. The Lady in À Mon Seul Désir as well – she is too sad.'

'I won't change them.'

'You know them, though, don't you?'

He shrugged. 'They are noblewomen.'

'And you know them well.'

He shook his head. 'Not so well. I've seen them a few times, but – '

I was surprised to see him wince.

'The last time I saw them was at May Day,' Nicolas continued. 'She – ' he pointed to Taste – 'was dancing around a maypole while her mother watched. They wore matching dresses.'

'The pomegranate brocade.'

'Yes. I couldn't get near her. Her ladies made sure of that.' He frowned at the memory. 'I still think there should be no servant in these tapestries.'

'The Lady needs a chaperone, otherwise it wouldn't look right.'

'Not for the seduction itself,' he insisted.

'Why don't we put servants in all but the one in which she captures the unicorn? In Sight, when he lies in her lap.'

'And Touch,' Nicolas added, 'when she is holding his horn. You don't want a chaperone then.' He smiled. He had become himself again, his mood like a storm suddenly spent. 'Shall I tell you about the unicorn's horn, then? It may help you.'

Before I could answer, Aliénor poked her head through the window where Jacques Le Bœuf had been earlier. Nicolas and I jumped. 'Here we are, Aliénor,' I said. 'By the loom.'

'I know,' she said. 'Maman and I are back already. That Jacques Le Bœuf made us so late that Mass was over before we'd sat down. Will you take some beer?'

'In a moment,' Nicolas answered.

When she had gone into the house he turned to me. 'If you don't want to know about the unicorn's horn I will tell you something else instead.'

'No.' I didn't want him to talk like that with Aliénor so close.

He grinned at me. He would say it anyway. 'Women may smell of cloves but they taste of oysters.'

ALIÉNOR DE LA CHAPELLE

The men found me weeding among the strawberries. I have planted them so that there's a place for me to kneel easily and weed. I don't think much of them as plants – the flowers don't smell and the leaves are neither soft nor prickly nor thin nor fat. But the fruit is heavenly. Now in early summer the berries have begun to grow but are still small and hard and have little scent. Once the fruit is ripe, though, I would happily spend all day in this square of the garden, crushing the berries between my fingers to smell and taste.

I heard Philippe on the path between the squares – he scrapes one of his toes when he walks – and Nicolas des Innocents' bouncing step behind him. The first time Nicolas came into my garden he said, 'Sainte Vierge, it's a paradise! I have never seen such a kitchen garden in Paris. There are so many houses that there is no room for anything – or perhaps a row of cabbages if you're lucky.' It was the only time I've heard him praise something in Brussels as better than Paris.

People are always surprised by my garden. It has six

squares, laid out as a cross, with the fruit trees – apple and plum and cherry – at the corners. Two squares are of vegetables, where I grow cabbages, leeks, peas, lettuce, radishes, celery. One square is of strawberries and herbs – that was where I was weeding. Then there is a rose bed, which I do not much like – the thorns prick me – but it pleases Maman, and two beds for the flowers and more herbs.

I am happiest in my garden. It is the safest place in the world. I know every plant, every tree, every stone, every clod of dirt. It is surrounded by a trellis woven of willow and covered with thorny roses to keep out animals and strangers. Most often I am alone in my garden. Birds do come in and sit on the fruit trees, stealing cherries when they are ripe. Butterflies fly among the flowers, though I know little of them. Sometimes when I am sitting still I've felt the air stirred near my cheek or arm from their fluttering, but I've never touched one. Papa told me there is dust on their wings that comes off when you touch it. Then the butterfly can't fly, and birds eat it. So I leave them alone and have others describe them to me.

I smiled now when Philippe announced, 'It's only us, Aliénor – myself and Nicolas des Innocents. Here we are, by the lavender.' He has known me all my life, yet he still tells me where he is when I already know. I could smell the woody, oily scent of the lavender they were brushing against.

I sat back on my heels and raised my face to the sun. Early summer is good for sun, as it is directly overhead for longer during the day. I have always loved heat, though not from the fire. Fires scare me. I have singed my skirts too often by the fire.

'Will you pick me a strawberry, Mademoiselle?' Nicolas asked. 'I have a thirst.'

'They're not ripe yet,' I snapped. I had meant to sound pleasant but he made me feel strange. And he was talking too loudly. People often do when they discover I'm blind.

'Ah. Never mind, I expect they'll ripen before I go back to Paris.'

I leaned forward again, feeling the ground around the strawberry plants, crumbling the sun-baked earth between my fingers as I gently searched for chickweed, groundsel, shepherd's purse. There were few weeds, and none more than a seedling – I had worked among the strawberries only a few days before. I could feel both men's eyes on me, like pebbles pressed into my back. It is strange how I can feel such things when I don't know what it is like to see.

As they watched me I knew what they were thinking – how could I find the weeds and know them for weeds? But weeds are just like other plants, except unwanted – they have leaves and flowers and scents and stems and juices. By feel and smell, I know them as well as any other plant.

'Aliénor, we need your help with the *millefleurs* for the tapestries,' Philippe said. 'We've drawn some of the design large for the cartoon. But we want you to point out flowers for us to use.'

I sat back on my heels again. I am always glad to be asked for help. I have spent my life being useful so that my parents will never find me a burden and send me away.

People often praise my work. 'How even your stitches are,' they say. 'How bright your flowers, how red your cherries. Such a pity you can't see them.' Indeed, I can hear the pity in their voices, as well as the surprise that I can be so useful. They can't think of the world without eyes, just as I cannot think of the world with them. Eyes are simply two bumps on my face that can move, the way my jaw can chew or my nostrils flare. I have other ways of knowing the world.

For instance, I know the tapestries I work on. I can feel each ridge of warp thread, each bead of weft. I can trace the flowers of the *millefleur* pattern and follow my stitches around a dog's hind leg or a rabbit's ear or the sleeve of a peasant's robe. I feel colours. Red is silky smooth, yellow prickles, blue is oily. Underneath my fingers is a map made by the tapestries.

People talk about seeing with such reverence that I sometimes think if I did have eyes the first thing I would see is Our Lady. She would be wearing a robe all blue and silky in my fingers, and Her skin would be smooth and Her cheeks warm. She would smell of strawberries. She would lay Her hands on my shoulders and they would feel light but firm too, so that once She had touched me I would always feel the weight of Her hands.

I wonder sometimes if seeing would make honey taste sweeter, lavender smell richer, the sun feel warmer on my face.

'You must describe the tapestries to me,' I said to Philippe.

'I did so the other day.'

'In more detail now. Where is the Lady looking – at the unicorn or at the lion? What is she wearing? Is she happy or sad? Does she feel safe in her garden? What is the lion doing? Is the unicorn sitting or standing? Is he glad to be caught or does he want to get away? Does the Lady love the unicorn?'

Philippe began rustling paper, laying out the designs. The sound annoyed me. I turned to Nicolas. 'Monsieur, you have made the designs. Surely you know them so well that you can describe them without looking at your drawings.'

Philippe stopped rustling.

'Of course, Mademoiselle,' Nicolas replied. There was a smile in his voice. The pebbles crunched under his feet as he knelt by the edge of the square.

'You're stepping on mint,' I said sharply as its scent reached me.

'Oh. *Pardon*.' He moved a little. '*Bon*, what were all of those questions you asked?'

I couldn't think now what I wanted to know from him. I wasn't used to the attentions of such a man. 'How much blue is in the tapestries?' I said at last. I'm not happy when the tapestries my father makes have much blue in them. Then I know we will have too many visits from Jacques Le Bœuf, with his heavy tread, his lewd words, and of course his smell – the smell only a broken, desperate girl would live with.

'How much would you like there to be, Mademoiselle?'

'None, unless you are willing to stay and fight with Jacques Le Bœuf each time he comes.'

Nicolas laughed. 'The Lady stands on blue grass that makes up the bottom part of each tapestry. But if you like we can make that grassy part smaller. Perhaps an island of grass floating among red, encircling the Lady and the unicorn and lion. Yes, that could work very well. And we can make that change ourselves, can't we, Philippe? It is part of the *verdure*, *n'est-ce pas*?'

Philippe didn't answer. His angry silence hung in the air.

'Thank you, Monsieur,' I said. '*Eh bien*, what does the Lady look like? Describe her to me. Describe Taste.' I chose the Lady I did not like.

Nicolas grunted. 'Why that one?'

'I am punishing myself. Is she really very beautiful?'

'Yes.'

I was feeling among the strawberries and accidentally picked one. I threw it down. 'Is she smiling?'

'A small smile, yes. She is looking to her left and thinking of something.'

'What is she thinking of?'

'The unicorn's horn.'

'Don't, Nicolas,' Philippe said sharply.

That made me more curious. 'What about his horn?'

'The unicorn's horn is a magical thing,' Nicolas said, 'with special powers. They say that if a unicorn dips his horn into a poisoned well, the water will become pure again. He can make other things pure as well.'

'What other things?'

There was a pause. 'That's enough about it for now. Perhaps I'll tell you another time.' Nicolas added the last under his breath so that only I heard. My ears are sharper than Philippe's.

'*Bon*,' I said. 'Let me think. There should be mint among the *millefleurs*, for it guards against poison. Solomon's seal as well. And speedwell and daisies and marigolds – those are for stomach ailments. Strawberries too, for resisting poison, and for Christ Our Lord, for the Lady and the unicorn are also Our Lady and Our Lord. So you will want flowers for the Virgin Mary – lily of the valley, foxglove, columbine, violets. Yes, and dog roses – white for Our Lady's purity, red for Christ's blood. Carnations for Our Lady's tears for Her son – be sure to put those in the tapestry with the unicorn in the Lady's lap, for that is like the Pietà, *n'est-ce pas*? Which one is that?' I already knew – I remember everything. I wanted to tease them.

There was a pause. Philippe cleared his throat. 'Sight.'

'Ah.' I moved on lightly. 'Carnations too in the one where the Lady is making the bridal crown, yes?'

'Yes, in Smell.'

'There is periwinkle sometimes in bridal crowns too, for fidelity. And you will want stock for constancy, and forget-me-nots for true love.'

'*Attends*, Aliénor, you go too fast. I'll get some more paper for sketches, and stools so that we can sit.' Philippe ran to the workshop.

I was alone with Nicolas. I had never been alone with a man like him.

'Why do they call you Nicolas des Innocents?' I asked.

'I live near the Cemetery of the Innocents in Paris, off the rue St Denis.'

'Ah. I didn't think you yourself were innocent.'

Nicolas chuckled. 'Already you know me well, beauty.'

'I would like to touch your face, so that I will know you better.' It was bold of me – I've not even asked to touch Philippe's face, and I've known him since we were children.

But Nicolas is from Paris – he is used to boldness. '*Bien sûr*,' he said. He stepped into the strawberries, crushing mint and lemon balm and unripe fruit beneath his boots. He knelt in front of me and I put my hands up to his face. He had soft hair to his shoulders, and his chin and cheeks were sandy with stubble. His forehead was broad. His chin had a cleft in it. There were deep creases on either side of his wide mouth. I squeezed his long thin nose and he laughed.

I felt his face only for a moment before he jumped up and leapt to the path. When Philippe returned, dragging stools through the pebbles, we were as we had been before.

'Do you want to see the flowers you will sketch?' I stood up so quickly I felt dizzy.

'Yes,' Philippe said.

I stepped into the path and led them to the flower beds. 'Many of them are flowering now, though you have missed a few. There are no more violets, nor lily of the valley, nor periwinkle. The leaves, yes, but no flowers. And the Solomon's seal are beginning to shrivel. But the foxglove and speedwell are blooming already, and one or two of the marigolds. Do you see them, near the plum trees?'

'Yes,' Nicolas said. 'You grow everything here, then? Why do you take such care when you can't see them?'

'I grow them for others to see, but especially for Papa, so that he may know the flowers he weaves and can copy their true shapes and colours. It works best that way. That is the workshop's secret – that's why our *millefleurs* are so fine.

'*Bon*, here is the stock. I plant it in the corners of the squares for the smell, so that I know where I am. Here is the columbine, everything in three – three leaves in three clusters on three stems, for the Holy Trinity. Here are the carnations and daisies and marguerites. What else do you want?'

Philippe asked me about other plants he saw there and I knelt and felt them – blue gromwell, saxifrage, soapwort. Then he sat and began to sketch, his charcoal scraping along the rough paper.

'You may want some of the early spring flowers too,' I reminded him. 'Snowdrops and hyacinths. Of course they're not blooming now but you can look at some of Papa's designs if you don't remember them. And narcissus too, for the unicorn in Sight – gazing at himself in the mirror as Narcissus did.'

'You must have talked to Léon Le Vieux when he was here – you both think the unicorn is a vain, cocky fellow,' Nicolas said.

I smiled. 'Léon is a wise man.' Indeed, Léon Le Vieux has always been kind to me, treating me almost like a daughter. He once told me that his own family had been Jews, though he attends Mass with us when he is here. So he too knows of what it is like to be different, and of the need always to fit in and be useful.

'Nicolas, bring out the linen where I've begun drawing

Sound, and I'll add the *millefleurs*,' Philippe said sharply.

I thought Nicolas might say something sharp back, but instead he went without a word to the workshop. I didn't know why, but suddenly I didn't want to be alone with Philippe, in case he wanted to say something to me. Before he could do so I slipped away to join Maman inside.

I could smell what she was cooking for dinner – trout, new carrots from the garden, dried beans and peas boiled into a mush. 'Will Nicolas and Philippe be eating too?' I asked, setting out mugs on the table.

'I should think so.' Maman clunked something heavy onto the table – the pot with the pea mush. Then she moved back to the fire, and after a moment I heard the sizzle of more fish frying. I began to pour the beer – I can hear when it reaches the top of the mug.

I am not so confident by the fire as I am in the garden. I prefer things that do not change quickly. That is why I like tapestries – they take a long time to make, growing over months like the plants in my garden. Maman always moves things as she cooks – I can never be sure a knife will be where I left it, or a sack of peas put away so that I don't trip over it, or a bowl of eggs placed against a wall so that I don't knock it over. I am not so useful to her at the hearth. I can't tend the fire – many times it has gone out on me. Once I built it too high and the chimney caught fire, almost burning us down but for my brother beating it out with a bit of wool doused in water. After that Papa forbade me to touch it. I can't roast meat or fowl. I can't move pots on or off the fire. I can't stir pots either – soup has slopped onto my hands.

But I can chop vegetables – Maman says I slice carrots more evenly than they need be, but I can't do otherwise or I might take off a finger. I can scrub pots. I can get things out and put them away. I can season food, though slowly, as I must feel the mace or cinnamon or pepper in my hand first and taste the food often. I try hard to help.

'What do you think of this Nicolas des Innocents?' Maman said.

I smiled. 'A vain, cocky fellow.'

'That he is. Handsome, though. I expect he's got many girls into trouble back in Paris. I hope he won't be trouble here. You be careful around him, *ma fille*.'

'What would he want with a blind girl like me?'

'Eyes are not what he's after.'

My face went hot. I turned from her and opened the wooden bread box. The sound inside told me there was nothing in it but crumbs. I felt around the small table by the hearth, then the big trestle table. 'Is there any bread? Even for trenchers?' I asked at last. I hate to admit when I can't find something.

'Madeleine has gone for some.'

I used to feel it was my fault that we had a servant. Madeleine was with us to be my eyes, doing all of the things a daughter is meant to do to help her mother. But as Papa's workshop became known for its *millefleurs* and he took on more and more work, he needed Maman and me to help him, and it was just as well that Madeleine was here. Now we couldn't do without her, though Maman still prefers to cook when she can – she says Madeleine's stews are too dull, and give her bellyache. But when we are busy in the workshop we are glad enough to eat Madeleine's meals, to wash with the water she fetches, to sit by the fire she has made with the wood she has collected.

Madeleine came in now with the bread. She is a big girl, as tall as Maman and broader. I have felt her arms and they are like legs of lamb. The men like her. I've heard her in the garden of an evening with Georges Le Jeune. They must think I won't hear their grunts or notice that my narcissi by the willow trellis have been trampled. I say nothing, of course. What would I say?

Just after Madeleine came in, Papa and the boys returned from meeting with the wool merchant. 'I've ordered the wool and silk,' Papa said to Maman. 'There is enough at Ostend for the warp and a bit to start the weaving – they'll bring it in a few days so that we can dress the loom. The rest depends on the sea and the passage between England and here.'

Maman nodded. 'The meal is ready. Where are Philippe and Nicolas?'

'In the garden,' I said. I could feel her eyes on my back as I went to fetch them.

As we ate, Papa asked Nicolas about Paris. We are always keen to hear about other places. Papa has been to Ostend, and to other weaving towns like Lille and Tournai, but never as far as Paris. Maman and Georges Le Jeune went with him once to Antwerp, but I've never been outside our city walls – I would be too frightened. It is enough for me to know the places I do in Brussels – Notre Dame de la Chapelle close by, with the *place* in front for the market, Notre Dame du Sablon, the gate to pass through the inner walls to get to the Grand-Place, the Church of St. Michel and St. Gudule. That is the world I know. I like to hear about other places, though, and imagine what it must be like. The sea, for example – I would love to smell salt and fish all around me, to hear the boom and suck of the waves, and to feel the spray of water on my face. Papa has described it to me, but I would like to be there to feel for myself how big and powerful water can be.

'What is Notre Dame de Paris like?' Papa asked. 'I've heard it's even bigger than St. Michel and St. Gudule here.'

Nicolas laughed. 'Your church is a shepherd's hut compared to Notre Dame. Notre Dame is heaven brought straight down to earth. It has the most beautiful towers, the loudest bells, the most stunning stained glass. What I would give to design such glass.'

I was about to ask more about the bells when Philippe said quietly, '*En fait*, we Brusselois are proud of St. Michel and St. Gudule. The western façade will be complete later this year. And our other churches – Notre Dame de la Chapelle is also impressive, and the little Church of Notre Dame du Sablon is very beautiful, what has been built of it. The stained glass there is as fine as any Paris glass.'

'It may be beautiful but it's not grand the way that the Paris Notre Dame is,' Nicolas insisted. 'I like to stand outside and watch people look up at it with their mouths hanging open. There are more pickpockets at Notre Dame than anywhere else in Paris because people are staring so much they don't notice the thieving.'

'People steal from each other?' Maman asked. 'Don't they fear the noose?'

'There are plenty of hangings in Paris, and plenty of thieves too. There are so many riches that thieves can't resist. At Notre Dame you will see noblemen and women going in and out all day long, wearing the finest clothes in the world. Women in Paris are better dressed than anywhere else.'

'Have you been to other cities?' Georges Le Jeune asked.

'Oh, many.'

'Where?'

'Lyons. Lovely women.'

'And?'

'Tournai.'

'Papa has been to Tournai. He said it was a lively place.'

'Dreadful city, Tournai,' Nicolas said. 'I vowed never to go back.'

'There is fine weaving comes out of Tournai,' Papa said. 'Some of it rivals any we produce in Brussels.'

'The women were flat-chested and always frowned.' Nicolas spoke with his mouth full.

I frowned.

'Have you been to Norwich?' Papa said. 'That's a place I should like to visit one day, to see the wool market.'

'Venice, that is where I would go,' Nicolas said.

'Why, Monsieur?' I asked. 'Do you prefer silk to wool?'

'It's not just the silk. Everything passes through Venice – spices, paintings, jewels, furs. Whatever you could wish for. And then all the different people – Moors, Jews, Turks. It's a feast for the eyes.' He paused. 'Ah. *Pardon*, Mademoiselle.'

I shrugged. Everyone talks of seeing to me – I am used to it.

122

'The Venetian women would please you as well, I suppose?' Philippe asked.

Madeleine and I giggled. I knew Philippe said that to make things easy again. He is like that.

'What is the house of Jean Le Viste like?' Maman interrupted. 'Is it very grand?'

'Grand enough. It is just beyond the city walls, by the Abbey of Saint-Germain-des-Prés – a very fine church, the oldest in Paris. His wife goes there often.'

'Monseigneur Le Viste as well?'

'He's a busy man – always doing something for the King. I don't expect he has time for Mass.'

'No time for Mass!' Maman was indignant.

'Has he any children, Monsieur?' I asked, picking at my trencher. I had left some pea mush there – I was too excited to eat.

'Three daughters, Mademoiselle.'

'No sons? He should have prayed more,' Maman said. 'That must be a trial for him, not to have an heir. What would happen to this workshop, after all, if not for Georges Le Jeune?'

Papa grunted. He doesn't like to be reminded that the workshop will be Georges Le Jeune's one day.

'How long does it take to walk across Paris?' Luc asked.

'At least as long as two masses said together,' Nicolas said. 'And that is if you don't stop at any of the stalls or taverns, or to say hello to those you know. The streets are jammed with people, day and night. You can see whatever you fancy and buy whatever you like.'

123

'It doesn't sound so different from Brussels – only bigger, and with more strangers,' Georges Le Jeune said.

Nicolas snorted. 'It is very different from here.'

'How? Apart from the women, I suppose?'

'Actually, Brussels women are better-looking than I'd first thought. You just have to look more closely.'

I flushed. Madeleine giggled again and shifted on the bench so that I was pushed against Maman.

'That's enough, Monsieur,' Maman said sharply. 'Show some respect in this house or – Paris artist or no – you'll be out on your arse!'

'Christine!' Papa said, while Georges Le Jeune and Luc laughed.

'I speak as I feel. Apart from myself there's Aliénor and Madeleine to think of. I don't want some honey-tongued charmer worming his way among them.'

Papa began to say something, but Nicolas interrupted. 'I assure you, Madame, that I meant no disrespect to you or your daughter, nor to the fair Madeleine.'

Madeleine squirmed again and I had to nudge her with my toe.

'We'll see,' Maman said. 'And you'd best show your respect by attending Mass. You haven't been once since you arrived.'

'You're right, Madame – I've lapsed unforgivably. I shall make up for it by going to Nones this afternoon. Perhaps I'll go along to your Sablon so I can have a look at this famed stained glass as well.'

'No,' Papa said. 'Mass can wait. I need that first design painted as soon as possible so that we can start. You and

Philippe work until you finish it – then you can go to Mass.'

Maman's anger made her quiver, but she said nothing. She would never put work before Mass, but Papa is the *lissier* – it is for him to decide such things. She didn't stay angry at him for long, though. She never does. After dinner she and Papa went into the workshop. Although she's not meant to weave – the Guild would fine Papa if she did – she often helps him with other work. Her father was a weaver, and she knows how to dress a loom, thread heddles, wind and sort wool, and work out how much wool and silk are needed for each tapestry, and how much time they will take to make.

I can't help her with these things, but I can sew. At night when the weavers are done I sit for hours and feel my way around the tapestry on the loom, finding the slits that form when one colour stops and another begins. That way I get to know the tapestries as well as the weavers who work on them.

Of course, if the patron is willing to pay enough and the design allows for it, Papa will dovetail colours, weaving different coloured threads into each other, interlocking them so that there are no slits to sew. It is fiddly work that takes longer and costs dear, so many patrons don't ask for it, as Monseigneur Le Viste did not. It seems he is too mean and too rushed – just as I expected of a Paris nobleman. There will be much sewing for me these next months.

While they were in the workshop I worked out in the garden again, weeding and showing the men the flowers they needed as they drew and painted the cartoon on a piece of large linen cloth. We were peaceful together, and I was glad – I prefer that we are not always battling.

Later Georges Le Jeune and Luc came out to the garden and watched Nicolas and Philippe paint. The sun had dropped from above. I picked up two buckets to get water for the plants, and was passing through the kitchen on my way to the well down the street when I heard the name Jacques Le Bœuf spoken. I stopped just beside the doorway leading into the workshop.

'I saw him today, to tell him I would order the blue soon,' Papa was saying. 'He asked about her again.'

'There's no rush, is there?' Maman said. 'She's only nineteen. Plenty of girls wait longer than that, to make the right match or for their husbands to get themselves sorted out, or to sew for their trousseau. And it's not as if women are waiting outside his door to marry him.'

'The smell would kill them, for a start,' Papa said.

They chuckled.

I held my buckets very still and did not breathe for fear my parents would hear me. Then I felt someone from the garden stop in the doorway behind me.

'It is an offer, though,' Papa said. 'The only offer she has had. We shouldn't dismiss it out of hand.'

'There are other things she can do besides marry a woad dyer. Is that what you want for your daughter?'

'It's not so easy, finding a husband for a blind girl.'

'She doesn't have to marry.'

'What, and be a burden to the workshop all her life?'

I flinched. Clearly I had not been useful enough.

Whoever was behind me moved a little, and after a moment stepped quietly back into the garden, leaving me to my silent tears. That is one use my eyes share with others – they do make tears.

CHRISTINE DU SABLON

I couldn't take my eyes from the clothes. The Lady playing the organ wears a lavish outer dress in a yellow and red pomegranate pattern. All around the edges are pearls and dark jewels to match those she wears around her neck. The underdress is blue, with pointed sleeves that fall gracefully from her arm. Georges will be able to show off his hachure on those sleeves, dark blue into light.

Even the servant pumping the organ's bellows wears beautiful clothes – finer than anything Aliénor or I own. I suppose that is how Parisian ladies-in-waiting dress. Of course her dress is simpler than her mistress's, but it is still a deep blue moiré with red trim – more hachure for Georges – and long yellow sleeves, round rather than pointed. If I wore such a dress those sleeves would dangle in the soup and get tangled in the warp threads.

The lady-in-waiting also wears two neck chains with flower pendants. They are not so rich as her mistress's necklace, but the chains are of gold. And she wears jewels on her head-dress. I should like to have such jewels. I do have a necklace of rubies set in enamel that Georges gave me when the workshop became his. I wear it to Guild banquets, walking through the Grand Place like a queen.

Sometimes I think about how well off we are, even if we don't look it, and wonder what Georges would say if I decided to be a lady like those in these tapestries. What if I wore fine clothes and ate sugared almonds and had ladies to wait on me – dress my hair, carry my prayer book and baskets and handkerchiefs, set my things straight and warm a room for me. Madeleine is meant to build up the fire first thing, but often as not she is still asleep when I get up and I have to do it myself.

I am nothing like the ladies in these designs. I don't know how to play an organ, and I don't have the time to feed birds or plait carnations or gaze into mirrors. The only Lady I understand a little is she who has grasped the unicorn by the horn. That is what I would do – make sure I've got a firm hold on him.

We have money but Georges does not spend it on fine things. Our house is larger than most, that is true – we have put two houses together so that there's a large room for the workshop, and there are beds for the apprentice and others helping us. I have my necklace and we have a good bed made of chestnut. The cloth for our dresses, though plain, is of good quality and well cut. And Aliénor and I have three dresses each, where others have only two, or one. But we wear clothes for working in, not for show. Our sleeves don't get in the way of our work.

Georges does not flaunt our wealth, but uses it to buy tapestry designs – he has more than most other *lissiers* in this city. And we have two good horizontal looms where another workshop like ours would have but one. He pays handsomely for Masses to be said for our family, and for part of the building of the Church of Notre Dame du Sablon.

It is only now and then that I wish my dress were blue instead of brown, and had a bit of silk in it rather than just wool. I would like a fur to keep me warm, and the time to dress my hair, and a lady to do it properly. Madeleine tried once but it looked like a bird's nest. I would like my hands to be soft as the rose petals these Ladies in the tapestries must soak theirs in. Aliénor has made an ointment from petals for me but I handle too much rough wool for it to be of use.

I would like always to have a fire to sit by, and more food than I need.

Only sometimes do I think of these things.

I had been so busy stringing heddles in the workshop with the others that it was good to stand in the garden and just look for a moment at what Nicolas des Innocents and Philippe have painted. This cartoon – Sound – was the only one painted large so far, and was pinned up on the wall in the garden, where the men were working. Philippe did all the drawing, as Nicolas did not understand that we weave back to front and so need cartoons that are mirror images of the final tapestries. There is a special talent in taking a small design and drawing it large and left to right rather than right to left. We all laughed at the look on Nicolas' face when he first saw Sound drawn backwards. But he got used to it, and has managed the painting well. Cocky as he is, he is a fine artist and learns fast.

Aliénor and Nicolas were in the garden when I came out – he painting, she on a ladder pruning the cherry trees. Philippe had gone to his father for more paints. Though they were at far ends of the garden from each other and were busy with their work, I did not like them being alone together. There was little I could do about it, though – I have too much to do to chaperone my daughter. She is a sensible girl, though I have seen her change when he walks into the room.

Nicolas was working now on the next cartoon, painting onto a large piece of linen where a sketch had been made in charcoal. This one was of Smell, with the Lady making a bridal crown out of carnations, the flower of betrothals. This Lady must think she was sure to catch her unicorn if she was already making her crown. Nicolas was painting her face but had not yet started on her dress. I was impatient to see it.

He stopped painting and came to stand with me in front of Sound. 'What do you think of the painting, Madame? You've said nothing about it. Very pretty, *n'est-ce pas*?'

'You're never one to wait for a compliment, are you? You're happy to make one to yourself.'

'Do you like her dress?'

I shrugged. 'The dress is fine, but even better are the *millefleurs*. Philippe has done a fine job, and with the animals in the grass too.'

'I've done the unicorn and the lion. What do you think of them?'

'The unicorn is too fat, and is not as vigorous as I expected him to be.'

Nicolas frowned.

'There's no time to change it now,' I added. 'It will do. The lion at least is full of character. You know, with his round eyes and wide mouth he looks a bit like Philippe.'

Aliénor chuckled from up the cherry tree.

I moved over to Smell. 'What is the Lady's dress like in this one? And the servant's?'

Nicolas smiled. 'She wears the red pomegranate brocade under a blue dress, with the overdress hitched up and fastened at her waist so that you can see the red underside. The servant's dress mirrors her mistress's – blue overdress, red underdress – but the cloth is a plainer moiré.'

He sounded so smug as he described them that I had to say something. 'A servant should not wear two necklaces,' I said. 'One would do, and a plain chain at that.'

Nicolas bowed. 'Anything else, Madame?'

'Don't be cheeky.' I lowered my voice. 'And stay away from my daughter.'

Aliénor's steady rustling in the tree stopped. 'Maman!' she shouted. I am always surprised by what she can hear.

Before either could say more Georges called us all into the workshop to warp the loom. We had already begun preparing the loom for weaving – setting the warp threads into a raddle and attaching them to the beam at one end of the loom. Now it was time to wind the warp onto the back beam before attaching it to the front beam to make the surface to weave on.

Warp threads are thicker than the weft, and made of a

coarser wool as well. I think of them as like wives. Their work is not obvious – all you can see are the ridges they make under the colourful weft threads. But if they weren't there, there would be no tapestry. Georges would unravel without me.

To warp a loom for a tapestry of this size you need at least four people to hold bundles of warp threads and pull on them while two men turn the roller to wind the warp around the back beam. Someone else checks the tension of the threads as they go. That must be just right at the start, otherwise there are problems with the weaving later on. Aliénor always does this – her hands are so sensitive they are well suited to the task.

Georges and Georges Le Jeune were already standing at each end of the roller when we came in. Aliénor went to join her father while I showed Nicolas the bundles of warp threads laid out for us. Luc stood holding some at one end.

We were one person short. 'Where's Philippe?' Georges asked.

'Still at his father's,' Nicolas said.

'Madeleine, put the lentils at the back of the fire and come out here!' I called.

Madeleine appeared from the fire, sooty and hot. I had her stand between me and Luc so that she wasn't next to Nicolas – I didn't want them making eyes at each other when they should be working. We took up a bundle in each hand and stood at a distance from the loom. I showed Nicolas and Madeleine how to hold the threads tightly and evenly around their hands and pull firmly. It's not easy to do this so that each thread is as taut as the next. We held our bundles and were pulled slowly towards the loom as Georges and Georges Le Jeune turned the cranks at each end of the roller. When they stopped for a moment, Aliénor stepped up to the warp as it lay across the roller and walked along, brushing her hand over the threads. Everyone was quiet. Her face was bright and attentive, a look I see on Georges' face when he is weaving. For a moment I almost thought she could see. When she reached the end she turned and walked back, stopping with her hand across threads Nicolas held. 'Too loose,' she said. 'Here, and here.' She reached along and touched threads of Madeleine's. 'Pull harder with your left,' I ordered both. 'Those are your weak hands – always pull harder with them.'

When the threads were even, Georges and Georges Le Jeune turned the crank again, slowly winding the warp around the beam as we four strained against it. When we were pulled all the way up to the loom we let go of the warp and then began again, taking up the threads further along. Aliénor checked the tension again. This time Nicolas' right hand was too loose, then part of Luc's left hand. Then Madeleine, and then Nicolas again. Aliénor and I told them how much to pull.

Nicolas groaned. 'This could take hours. My arms ache.'

'Pay attention and it will go faster,' I snapped.

As Georges and Georges Le Jeune turned the crank I smelled something burning. 'The lentils!'

Madeleine jumped. 'Don't let go!' I cried. 'Aliénor, go and take the lentils off the fire.'

134

A fearful look crossed Aliénor's face, chasing away her brightness. I knew she does not like fire, but there was nothing for it – she had the only free hands.

'Madeleine, did you move those lentils to the back as I asked you?' I said as Aliénor ran from the workshop.

The girl scowled at the threads in her hands. Her fingers were red and white from the threads wound around them so tight.

'Stupid girl.'

Nicolas chuckled. 'She's like Marie-Céleste.'

Madeleine raised her head. 'Who's that?'

'A girl who works at the Le Viste house. Just as saucy.'

Madeleine made a face at Nicolas. Georges Le Jeune frowned at them both.

Aliénor came back. 'I've put the pot on the floor,' she said.

We went back to the warping, with us pulling, the Georges cranking, Aliénor testing. It was not so much fun now. My arms ached too, though I would never have admitted it. I fretted too about dinner and what I would serve. I would have to run to the baker's wife for a pie – she sells them from her house while her husband is at the Bread Hall. Madeleine huffed and sighed and sulked next to me, and Nicolas began rolling his eyes from boredom. 'What do you do after you finish this tedious task?' he asked.

'We thread the heddles, to make the shed,' I said.

Nicolas looked blank. 'Heddles are strings that pull every other thread apart so that you can run the weft through them,' I explained. 'You push a pedal and the warp separates into two. The space between those sets of threads is the shed.'

'Where do you put the tapestry as you're weaving it?'

'It gets wound onto this beam here in front of us.'

Nicolas thought for a moment. 'But then you don't see it.'

'No. Only the strip you're working on, then it gets wound on. You don't see the whole tapestry at once until you've finished.'

'That's impossible. It would be like painting blind!' Even as he said it he winced and looked at Aliénor, who continued feeling the threads as if she had not heard him.

Still he kept asking questions. 'Where will the cartoon go?'

'On a table we put underneath the warp, so we can look at it as we weave. Philippe will trace the design onto the warp threads as well.'

'What's that for?' He pointed at the wool mill in the corner.

'Lord, will he never stop talking?' Georges Le Jeune said what we were all thinking. Ours is a quiet workshop, where others are louder and more boisterous. When Georges brings in other weavers to help out – as he will for these tapestries – he always chooses quiet ones. Once we had in a weaver who talked all day, and Georges had to let him go. Nicolas talks all the time too – Paris gossip, mostly, all of it nonsense. He asks so many questions I want to slap him. It is just as well he is mostly working in the garden, otherwise Georges would shout. He's a mild man but he cannot abide silly talk.

Nicolas opened his mouth to ask another question, but Aliénor plucked at some threads then and he pulled his left hand tight.

'Less talk, more thought to your work,' Georges said. 'Or we'll be at this till nightfall.'

It was not as long as that, though. We were finished at last, and I could go and sort out dinner.

'*Viens*, Aliénor,' I said. 'You can help me choose the pie that smells best.' Aliénor loves going to the baker's house.

'Please, Madame, I'll fetch one for you if only you'll let me have some as well,' Madeleine said.

'It's scorched lentils for your dinner, girl. You just fetch the men some drink when you're done here and then get to scrubbing that pot.'

Madeleine sighed, even though Nicolas winked at her. Georges Le Jeune frowned again. When Nicolas took a step back and put his hands up as if to show that he hadn't touched her, I suddenly wondered at my son and Madeleine. Perhaps Nicolas had seen something I hadn't.

I looked over Aliénor as we left. She keeps herself well but sometimes she gets soot on her cheek and doesn't know it, or, as I found now, cherry twigs in her hair. She is fair enough, with long gold hair like mine, a straight nose and a round face. It is just her big empty eyes and her crooked smile that make people sorry to look at her.

Aliénor held my sleeve just above my elbow as we stepped along the rue Haute. She is spry on her feet and those who don't know her don't guess, just as Nicolas did not. She knows her way so well that she doesn't really need me to guide her, except for the dung or slops from chamberpots that she would tread through or have flung on her, or the horses that bolt. Apart from that she walks through the streets as if angels were leading her. As long as she has been there before, she can find a place. Though she has tried to explain how she does it – the echoes of her footfalls, the counting of the number of steps, the feel of the walls around her, the smells to tell her where she is – her surefootedness is still a miracle to me. She prefers not to walk alone, though – she would rather hold my arm.

Once when she was a girl I did leave her alone. It was a market day in autumn, and the Place de la Chapelle was heaving with people and wares – apples and pears, carrots and pumpkins, bread and pies and honey, chickens, rabbits, geese, leather, scythes, cloth, baskets. I saw an old friend who'd been abed many weeks with a fever, and she and I got to wandering and gossiping to catch up. I didn't even notice Aliénor was gone until my friend asked after her and I felt then that her fingers weren't on my sleeve. We looked everywhere and finally found her standing in the middle of the bustle, dead eyes teary, moaning and wringing her hands. She'd stopped to fondle a lamb skin and let go of my sleeve. It is rare to see her blindness get the better of her like that.

Ahead of us I could smell the baker's wife's beef pies. She puts juniper berries in them, and stamps the crust with a jester's laughing face. That always makes me smile.

Aliénor was not smiling. Instead she was wrinkling her nose, her face screwed up with misery and disgust.

'What's the matter?' I cried.

'Please, Maman, can we go to the Sablon, just for a moment?' Without waiting for my answer, she pulled me into the rue des Chandeliers. Even upset, she had still counted her steps and knew where she was.

I stopped. 'The baker's wife will stop selling soon – we don't want to miss her.'

'Please, Maman.' Aliénor kept pulling my arm.

Then I smelled what she already had underneath the beef and juniper. Jacques Le Bœuf. Suddenly that foul stench was everywhere. 'Come.' Now I was pulling her along. We reached the rue des Samaritaines and were ducking into it when I heard Jacques call, 'Christine!'

'Run,' I whispered, and put my arm around her shoulders. We stumbled over the uneven stones, bumping into walls and passers-by. 'This way.' I pulled her to the left. 'The Sablon's too far – let's go to the Chapelle instead. He's not likely to look there.' I led her quickly through the *place*, where the stall keepers were packing up to go home to their dinners.

We reached the church and ducked inside. I pulled Aliénor into the Chapel of Our Lady of Solitude not far from the door and pushed her to her knees where a pillar would block Jacques Le Bœuf's view if he came in. I knelt and whispered a prayer, then sat back on my heels. We didn't say anything for a time but let our breaths go quiet. If it hadn't been Jacques we were running from, I might have laughed then, as we must have looked comical. But I did not – Aliénor's face was full of woe.

I looked around. The church was empty – Sext had ended and people were at home eating. I like the Chapelle well enough – it is big and light with all its windows, and it is very close to us – but I prefer the Sablon. I grew up a stone's throw from its walls, and it has served the weavers in this area well. It is smaller and made with more care, with better stained glass and stone animals and people peering down from the outside walls. These things are lost on Aliénor, of course – the best parts of a church mean nothing to her.

'Maman,' she whispered, 'please don't make me go to him. I would rather join a convent than live with that smell.'

That smell – of the fermented sheep's piss they soak the woad in to fix the colour – is what has kept woad dyers marrying their cousins for many generations. In Aliénor Jacques Le Bœuf must see fresh blood as much as a dowry and a tie to the workshop of a fine *lissier*.

'How can I live with that stink just to produce a colour I can't even see?' she added.

'You work on tapestries you can't see either.'

'Yes, but they don't smell bad. And I can feel them. I can feel the whole story of them with my fingers.'

I sighed. 'All men have faults, but that is nothing compared with all that you get from them – food and clothing, a house, a livelihood, a bed. Jacques Le Bœuf will give you all of those things and you should thank God that you have them.' I sounded more forceful than I felt.

'I do, but – why shouldn't I have a man more to my liking, as other women do? No one else wants him, the smelly brute. Why should I?' Aliénor shuddered, her body rippling with disgust. Hers would not be a happy bed with

Jacques Le Bœuf, I could see that. It was hard to think of his blue hands on my daughter's body without shuddering myself.

'It's a good business match,' I said. 'If you marry Jacques you will help his woad business and your father's workshop. He'll get steady orders from Georges, and Georges will get cheaper blue from him. *Tu sais*, your father and I married so that our fathers' workshops would be combined. My father had no son, and chose Georges as his own by having him marry me. That hasn't stopped us from making a good marriage.'

'Mine is not a business match,' Aliénor said. 'You know it's not, Maman. You could have married me to any other business – one of the wool merchants, or a silk merchant, or another weaver, or even an artist. Yet you would have me be with the one man with so many faults of his own that he will overlook mine.'

'That's not true,' I said – though it was. 'Anyone can see how useful you are to us, that your blindness doesn't stop you from keeping a house and helping in the workshop and growing your garden.'

'I've tried so hard,' Aliénor muttered. 'I've worked so hard to please you, but in the end it's made no difference. What man would choose a blind girl over someone with eyes that aren't broken? There are many girls in Brussels who will be chosen before I am, just as most men will be accepted before Jacques Le Bœuf will. He and I are what is left when the barrel is empty. That is why we are meant to have each other.'

I said nothing – she had done my arguing for me,

141

though she did not look persuaded. Her brow was crumpled and she was wringing out a bit of her skirt. I placed a hand over hers to stop them. 'Nothing's decided,' I said, pushing her hands away and smoothing the crushed cloth. 'I will talk to your father. Anyway, we need you for these new tapestries – we can't spare you just yet. *Tiens*, Jacques must be gone by now. Let's get to the baker's house before they eat our pie.'

The baker was home already, and the family sitting down to eat. I only got his wife to sell us a pie by promising her a basket of peas from Aliénor's garden. There were no beef pies left, only capon. Georges does not like those so much.

When we were close to our house, Aliénor shied like a horse and clutched my arm. The sheep's piss stench was there – Jacques Le Bœuf must have been coming to see Georges when he first spied us on the rue Haute. Of course he chose the hour when we eat for his visit so that we would have to feed him.

'Go and stay with the neighbours,' I said. 'I'll come and get you when he's gone.' I led her to the door of the cloth weaver two houses from us and she slipped inside.

Jacques was drinking beer with Georges in the garden. Unless it is very cold we always take him there when he visits. I suppose he must be used to such treatment. Nicolas' paintings of Sound and Smell were still tacked up on the wall, but the painter was gone. Jacques Le Bœuf has that effect wherever he goes. 'Hello, Jacques,' I said, stepping into the garden to greet him and trying not to gag.

'You ran away from me just now,' he rumbled. 'Why did you and the girl run away?'

'I don't know what you mean. Aliénor and I were just going to the Chapelle to pray before we stopped at the baker's house. We had to hurry before the baker shut, so we were running, but not from you. You will stay to dinner, *bien sûr* – there's pie.' Unbearable or not, asking him to stay was the decent thing to do, especially if he was to be our son-in-law.

'You ran away from me,' Jacques repeated. 'You shouldn't have done that. Now, where's the girl?'

'She's out – visiting.'

'*Bien.*'

'Jacques wants to talk to us about Aliénor,' Georges interrupted.

'No, I want to talk to you about your pitiful order for blue in these tapestries.' Jacques Le Bœuf gestured at Sound. 'Look at that – hardly any blue there, especially with all those flowers. This taste for *millefleurs* will be the death of me, all red and yellow. And even less blue in this one, it looks like.' He peered at Smell, sketched out but only the Lady's face and shoulders painted. 'You told me there would be much more blue in these tapestries – half of the ground would be blue for grass. Now it's just islands of blue, and all this red instead.'

'We added trees to the designs,' Georges replied. 'The blue in them will make up for most of the missing grass.'

'Not enough – half of the leaves are yellow.' Jacques Le Bœuf glowered at Georges.

It was true that we had changed the amount of blue we

were ordering from him. Now that we had one of the designs to scale, Georges and I had sat down the night before and worked out how much we would need for all of the tapestries. Georges had sent Georges Le Jeune around this morning to tell Jacques Le Bœuf.

'The designs have changed since we first spoke,' Georges said calmly. 'That often happens. I never promised you a certain amount of blue.'

'You misled me, and you'll have to make up for it,' Jacques insisted.

'Will you take your pie out here?' I cut in. 'It is nice to eat outside sometimes. Madeleine, bring out the pie,' I called inside.

'Jacques, you know I can't guarantee quantities,' Georges said. 'That's not how the business works. Things change as we go.'

'I'm not supplying you with any blue until you agree to what I ask for.'

'You will deliver that wool tomorrow, as promised.' Georges spoke slowly, as if explaining something to a child.

'Not until you make a promise too.'

'Promise what?'

'Your daughter.'

Georges glanced at me. 'We haven't discussed this with Aliénor yet.'

'What's to discuss? You give me her dowry and she'll be my wife. That's all there is to say to her.'

'We need Aliénor yet,' I interrupted. 'These tapestries are the biggest commission we've taken on, and we need everyone working. Taking away even Aliénor may mean we can't complete them in time, and then that will mean no orders of blue to you at all for them.'

Jacques Le Bœuf ignored me. 'Make your daughter my wife and I'll supply you with blue wool,' he said as Madeleine brought out the pie and a knife. She was holding her breath so that she wouldn't breathe in his smell, but she let it out in a surprised huff when she heard what he said. I frowned and shook my head at her as she dropped the pie on the table and hurried back inside.

'Christine and I need to discuss it,' Georges said. 'I'll give you my answer tomorrow.'

'Good,' Jacques said. He picked up the knife and cut himself a large wedge. 'You give me the girl and you'll get your blue. And don't try to go to other woad dyers – they know me better than they know you.' Of course they did – they were all cousins.

Georges had been about to cut himself some pie, but paused with the knife held over the crust. I closed my eyes so as not to see the anger in his face. When I opened them again he had plunged the knife tip into the pie and left it sticking straight up. 'I have work to do,' he said, getting up. 'I'll see you tomorrow.'

Jacques Le Bœuf took a great gulp of pie – he didn't seem insulted by Georges walking away from him as he ate.

I backed away as well, and went to find Madeleine. She was bent over the lentil pot, her face red from the heat. 'Don't you say a word to Aliénor,' I hissed. 'She doesn't need to know about this just now. Besides, nothing has been decided.'

Madeleine glanced up at me, tucked a stray clump of hair behind her ear, and began scrubbing again.

Jacques ate half of our pie before he left. I didn't touch it – I had no stomach for it now.

Aliénor didn't say anything when I fetched her from the neighbour's – she went straight to her garden and began picking the basket of peas for the baker. I was glad, for I don't know what I would have said.

Later she offered to take the peas to the baker's wife on her own. When she was gone I pulled Georges to the far end of the garden by the rose-covered trellis so that no one could hear us. Nicolas and Philippe were working side by side on Smell, Nicolas painting the Lady's arms while Philippe began the lion.

'What are we going to do about Jacques Le Bœuf, then?' I demanded.

Georges gazed at some pink dog roses as if he were listening to them rather than me.

'*Alors?*'

Georges sighed. 'We will have to let him have her.'

'The other day you were joking that the smell would kill her.'

'The other day I didn't know we would cut back on the blue in the tapestries. If I don't get that blue soon we'll run late already and be fined by Léon. Jacques knows that. He has me by the balls.'

I thought of Aliénor's shudders in the Chapelle. 'She detests him.'

'Christine, you know this is the best offer Aliénor will get. She's lucky to have it. Jacques will look after her. He's not a bad man, apart from the smell, and she'll get used to that. Some people complain of the smell of the wool here, but we don't notice it, do we?'

'Her nose is more sensitive than ours.'

Georges shrugged.

'Jacques will beat her,' I said.

'Not if she obeys him.'

I snorted.

'Come, Christine, you're a practical woman. More so than me most of the time.'

I thought of Jacques Le Bœuf chomping his way through half of our pie, and of his threat to ruin Georges' business. How could Georges agree to such a man for his daughter? Even as I thought it, though, I knew there was little I could say. I knew my husband, and he had already decided. 'We can't spare her now,' I said. 'We need her to sew on these tapestries. Besides, I've made nothing for her trousseau.'

'She won't go yet, but she could when the tapestries are almost done. You could finish the sewing on the last two. By the end of next year, let us say. She could certainly be at Jacques' by that Christmas.'

We stood silent and looked at the dog roses growing along the trellis. A bee was worrying one, making its head bob up and down.

'She must know nothing about this for the moment,' I said at last. 'You make it clear to Jacques that he can't go about bragging of his wife-to-be. If he says a word the betrothal is broken.'

Georges nodded.

Perhaps that was cruel of me. Perhaps Aliénor should

be told now. But I couldn't bear to live with her sad face for the next year and a half while she waited for what she dreaded. Best for everyone if she knew only when it was time.

We walked back through Aliénor's garden, which was bright with flowers, tangles of peas, neat rows of lettuce, clipped bushes of thyme and rosemary and lavender, of mint and lemon balm. Who will look after this when she's gone? I thought.

'Philippe, stop your painting now – I need you to draw on the warp once we've put the cartoon underneath,' Georges said, stepping ahead of me. He went up to Sound. '*Tiens*, help me take this inside, if it's dry. Georges, Luc!' he called. He sounded stern and brisk – Georges' way of leaving behind our talk.

Philippe dropped his brush into a pot of water. The boys hurried out from the workshop. Georges Le Jeune climbed up a ladder to detach the cartoon from the wall. Then, one man at each corner, they carried it inside to the loom.

With the cartoon gone the garden suddenly felt empty. Nicolas and I were alone. He was painting the Lady's hands now as she held a carnation. In his own hand he too held one. He did not turn around but kept his back to me. That's unlike Nicolas – he doesn't usually give up the chance to talk to a woman alone, even if she is older and married.

He was holding his back and head very stiff and straight – from anger, I realized after a moment. I gazed at the white carnation between his fingers. Aliénor grew them near the roses. He must have come over to pick one while Georges and I were back there talking.

'Don't think badly of us,' I said softly to his back. 'It will be best for her.'

Nicolas didn't answer immediately, but held his brush up to the cloth. He did not paint but remained with his hand suspended in the air. 'Brussels is beginning to bore me,' he said. 'Its ways are too boorish for me. I'll be glad to leave. The sooner the better.' He glanced at the carnation he held, then threw it down and crushed it under his heel.

That evening he painted until very late. These summer nights it is light almost to Compline.

III

PARIS
AND CHELLES

Eastertide 1491

NICOLAS DES INNOCENTS

I didn't expect ever to see the tapestries or their designs
again. When I paint a miniature or a shield, or design
stained glass, I see it only as I work on it. What happens
after doesn't concern me. Nor do I think of it after, but
go on instead to paint another miniature, or a carriage
door, or a Madonna and Child for a chapel, or a coat of
arms on a shield. It's like that with women – I will plough
one and enjoy it, then find another and enjoy that. I don't
look back.

No, that is not wholly true. There is one I do look back
to, one I think of all the time, though I've not had her.

Those Brussels tapestries stayed with me for a long time.
I would think of them at odd moments – when I saw a
posy of violets on a market stall along the rue St Denis,
or smelled a plum tart through an open window, or heard
monks singing during Vespers in Notre Dame, or chewed
a clove seasoning a stew. Once when I was with a woman,
I suddenly wondered if the lion in Touch looked too much
like a dog, and my staff wilted under the girl's fingers like
a limp lettuce.

Most work I quickly forget, but I could recall many details in the cartoons – the long orange sleeves of the servant in Sound, the monkey pulling at the chain around its neck in Touch, the flip of the Lady's scarf as the wind caught it in Taste, the darkness in the mirror behind the unicorn's reflection in Sight.

I had proven something with those designs. Léon Le Vieux now treated me with more respect, almost as if we were equals rather than a wealthy merchant tolerating a lowly painter. Though I still painted miniatures, he began to get me commissions from other noble families for tapestries. He shrewdly held onto the paintings I'd made of the six Ladies, making excuses to Jean Le Viste about returning them, though they were Monseigneur's to keep. He showed them to other noblemen, who told others, and from the talk came demands for more tapestries. I designed other unicorn tapestries – sometimes sitting alone in the woods, sometimes being hunted, sometimes with a Lady, though I was always careful to make them different from the Le Viste Ladies. Léon was gleeful. 'See how excited people are now, just with the small designs,' he would say. 'Wait till they see the real tapestries hanging in Jean Le Viste's Grande Salle – you'll have work for the rest of your days.' And money for his pocket, he might have added. I was happy, though – if things continued this well I would never have to paint another shield or coach door.

One day I went to Léon's house to discuss a new tapestry commission – not of unicorns, but of falconers out hunting. Léon has done well by his commissions. He has a large house off the rue des Rosiers, with his own chamber for business. Dotted about the room are beautiful objects from far away – silver plates with strange letters scratched onto them, filigree spice boxes from the East, thick Persian carpets, teak chests inlaid with mother-of-pearl. As I looked around I pictured my plain room above Le Coq d'Or and frowned. He has probably been to Venice, I thought. He has probably been everywhere. One day soon, though, I too will have earned enough for such fine things.

As we talked about the commission I sketched a falcon's wings and tail. Then I threw down my charcoal and sat back. 'With the weather better I may go away when I've finished this design. I'm bored of Paris.'

Léon Le Vieux also sat back. 'Where?'

'I don't know. A pilgrimage, perhaps.'

Léon rolled his eyes. He knew my church-going was not regular.

'Truly,' I insisted. 'South, to Toulouse. Maybe all the way to Santiago de Compostela.'

'What do you expect to find when you get there?'

I shrugged. 'What one always finds on a pilgrimage.' I didn't tell him I'd not been on one before. 'But that's not something your kind know much about,' I added, to tease him.

Léon didn't bother with such a gibe. 'A pilgrimage is a long journey for possibly little reward. Have you thought of that? Think of all the work you will give up to go and see – well, very little. A tiny part of the whole.'

'I don't understand you.'

'These relics you go to look at. Doesn't Toulouse hold

a splinter of our Saviour's cross? How much of a cross can you see in a sliver of wood? You may see it and be disappointed.'

'I wouldn't be disappointed,' I insisted. 'I'm surprised you haven't been on a pilgrimage, good Christian that you are.' I reached over and picked up one of the silver spice boxes. The filigree was cleverly wound to make a door with hinges and a lock. 'Where did this come from?'

'Jerusalem.'

I raised my eyebrows. 'Perhaps I should go there.'

Léon laughed loudly. 'I would like to see that, Nicolas des Innocents. Now, you speak of travel. The roads between Paris and Brussels are clear now and I've had word of your tapestries from a merchant I know. He stopped in at Georges' workshop for me.'

Léon and I had not spoken of the tapestries in months. By the beginning of Advent the roads were too poor for most to make the journey easily between Paris and Brussels. Léon had no more word of their progress and I had stopped asking. I set down the spice box. 'What did he say?'

'They finished the first two after Christmas and began the next two at the Epiphany – the two long ones. They've fallen behind on them, though. Some in the house were ill.'

'Who?'

'Georges Le Jeune and one of the outside weavers brought in for the work. They're better now, but time was lost.'

I was relieved to hear it was not Aliénor. That surprised

me. I picked up the charcoal and drew the falcon's head and beak. 'How do the tapestries look?'

'Georges showed him the first two – Sound and Smell. The merchant said they are very fine.'

I added an eye to the falcon's head. 'What about the two they're making now? Where have they got to?'

'They were weaving the dog that sits on the train of the Lady's dress in Taste. In À Mon Seul Désir they have reached the servant. Of course you can only see a little strip of what they're working on.' He smiled. 'A tiny part of the whole.'

I tried to remember the details of the designs. For a long time I knew them so well I could draw them with my eyes shut. I was surprised to have forgotten that a dog sat on the Lady's dress. 'Léon, get out the paintings. I want to look at them.'

Léon chuckled. 'You haven't asked to see them in some time,' he said as he took his keys from his belt and unlocked the teak chest. He pulled them out and laid them on the table.

I looked at the dog in Taste and began to estimate how long it would take the weavers to reach the Lady's face. Claude's face.

It was months since I'd seen Claude Le Viste. I hadn't been inside the house on the rue du Four after returning from Brussels in the summer. There were no other commissions for me there, and the family was at their château near Lyons. At Michaelmas I heard they'd returned, and sometimes stood near Saint-Germain-des-Prés, waiting for a glimpse of Claude. One day I saw her on the rue du

Four with her mother and her ladies. As she passed I began to walk alongside on the other side of the road, hoping she would look over and see me.

She did. She stopped then as if she'd stubbed her toe. The ladies poured around either side of her until there was just her and Béatrice left standing in the road. Claude waved on her lady and knelt as if to adjust her shoe. I let a coin drop near her and stepped over to pick it up. As I knelt next to her we grinned at each other. I did not dare to touch her, though – a man like me does not touch a girl like her in the street.

'I've wanted to see you,' Claude whispered.

'And me you. Will you come to me?'

'I'll try, but –'

Before she could finish or I could tell her where I lodged, Béatrice and the groom escorting them rushed up to us. 'Go away,' Béatrice hissed, 'before Dame Geneviève sees you!' The groom grabbed me and hustled me away from Claude, who remained kneeling in the street, her light eyes gazing after me.

After that I saw her once or twice from a distance, but there was little I could do. She was a noblewoman, after all – I couldn't be seen with her out in the street. Though I was keen to have her in my bed, I doubted I could ever get through the guard of ladies around her. I went with other women, but none satisfied me. Each time I finished feeling I was not completely emptied, like a mug with a mouthful of beer still left at the bottom. Looking at the Lady in Taste now made me feel the same way. It was not enough.

Léon reached over to gather up the paintings. '*Un moment*,' I said, laying my hand on À Mon Seul Désir, where the Lady stood frozen with her jewels in her hands. Was she putting them on or taking them off? I was not always sure.

Léon clicked his tongue and folded his arms across his chest.

'Don't you want to look at them?' I said.

Léon shrugged. 'I've seen them.'

'They don't please you, do they, even though you speak so highly of them in front of others.'

Léon picked up the spice box I'd been playing with and set it back on the shelf with the others. 'They're good for business. And they will make Jean Le Viste's Grande Salle a room worth feasting in. But no, I am not seduced by your Ladies. I prefer useful things – plates, chests, candlesticks.'

'Tapestries are useful too – they cover rough walls and make rooms warmer and brighter.'

'So they do. But for myself I prefer their designs to be purely decorative – like this.' He pointed at a small tapestry hanging on one wall that was just of *millefleurs*, with no figures or animals. 'I don't want ladies in a dream world – though perhaps for you they are real.'

I wish they were, I thought. 'You're too down-to-earth.'

Léon tilted his head to one side. 'That is how I survive. That is how we have always survived.' He began to collect the paintings. 'Are you going to draw something now or not?'

I drew quickly – falcons attacking a heron as men and ladies looked on, with dogs running along the bottom, all to be filled in with *millefleurs*. I had designed enough tapestries now that it all came easily to me. Thanks to Aliénor's garden, I could even draw the *millefleurs* accurately.

Léon watched as I drew. People often do – drawing for them is magical, a show at a fair. For me it has always been easy, but most people who take up the charcoal draw as if they're holding a candle stub.

'You've learned much over these months,' he said.

I shrugged. 'I too can be down-to-earth.'

That night I dreamt of a strip of tapestry with Claude's face on it, and woke sticky. That had not happened in some time. The next day I found a reason to go to Saint-Germain-des-Prés – a friend there could tell me more about hunting with falcons. Of course I could have asked someone on the rue St Denis, but this way I could walk down the rue du Four and look up at the Le Viste house. I had not done that in some time either. The windows were shuttered, though it was only just after Easter and I didn't think the family would have already gone to Lyons. Though I waited, no one came in or out.

My friend was not in either, and I wandered back towards the city. As I passed through the city walls at the Porte St Germain and pushed through the market stalls surrounding it, I saw a familiar woman, frowning at some early heads of lettuce. She was not so fat now.

'Marie-Céleste.' I called her name without knowing I'd remembered it.

She turned and looked at me without surprise as I stepped up to her. 'What do you want?' she demanded.

'To see you smile.'

Marie-Céleste grunted and turned back to the lettuces. 'This one's got spots all over it,' she said to the man selling them.

'Find another, then,' he shrugged.

'Are you buying those for the Le Vistes?'

Marie-Céleste sorted through the lettuce heads, her mouth a grim line. 'Don't work there now. You should know that.'

'Why not?'

'I had to go away to have the baby, didn't I. Claude was to put in a word for me, but when I came back there was another girl in my place and mistress didn't want to know.'

Hearing Claude's name made me shiver with desire. Marie-Céleste glared at me and I tried to think of something else. 'So, how is the baby?'

Marie-Céleste's hands stopped moving for a moment. Then she began shifting the heads again. 'Gave her to the nuns.' She picked up a lettuce and shook it.

'What? Why?'

'I had to go back to my job, to keep my mother. She's too old and sick to look after a baby. It's just what I had to do. Then I didn't even have a job to come back to.'

I was quiet, thinking about a daughter off somewhere with nuns. It wasn't what I expected of any children I might have.

'What did you name her?'

'Claude.'

I slapped Marie-Céleste so hard the head of lettuce flew from her hand.

'*Holà!*' cried the lettuce seller. 'You drop it, you pay for it.'

Marie-Céleste began to cry. She grabbed her basket and ran.

'Pick that up!' the lettuce man shouted.

I scooped up the lettuce – leaves falling from it – and tossed it on top of the others before running after her. When I caught up, Marie-Céleste was red in the face from running and crying at the same time. 'Why did you name her that?' I shouted, grabbing her arm.

Marie-Céleste shook her head and tried to pull away from me. A crowd was gathering – in a market anything is entertainment. 'You going to hit her again?' a woman jeered. 'If you are, wait till my daughter comes back so she can get a look.'

I pulled Marie-Céleste away from the crowd and into an alley. Sellers had thrown their rubbish there – rotting cabbage heads, old fish, horse dung. A rat ran off as I pushed her past the festering pile.

'Why did you call my daughter that?' I said in a lower voice. It was strange using the word daughter.

Marie-Céleste looked at me wearily. She had stopped crying. Her doughy face looked like a bun with two currants pressed into it, and her dark hair dangled loose from her cap. I wondered why I had ever wanted to bed her.

'I told Claude I would,' she said. 'I was so grateful to her offering to set me straight with the mistress. But then she didn't – when I spoke to Dame Geneviève she swore

Mademoiselle hadn't said a thing. Mistress thought I'd run off and that was that. So the baby has Mademoiselle's name for nothing, after all I done for her when she was a girl. Lucky for me I got another place, with a family on the rue des Cordeliers. The Bellevilles. Not so rich as the Le Vistes, but they'll do. They even entertain the Le Viste ladies sometimes.'

'The Le Viste ladies come to you?'

'I stay well out of sight when they do.' Marie-Céleste had recovered herself now. She looked around the alley and smiled a little. 'I never thought I'd end up in an alley again with you.'

'Which Le Vistes visit? Only Dame Geneviève, or does she bring her daughters?'

'Usually Claude comes with her,' Marie-Céleste said. 'There's a daughter her age she likes to see.'

'Do they come often?'

Marie-Céleste furrowed her brow like the old woman she would become one day. 'What do you care?'

I shrugged. 'Just curious. I've worked for Monseigneur Le Viste, as you know, and wondered what his women are like.'

A cunning look came over Marie-Céleste's face. 'I suppose you want to come and see me there, don't you?'

I gaped at her, amazed that she was flirting with me after all that had happened. But then, she could be useful to me. I smiled and brushed a feather from her shoulder. 'Might do.'

When she reached over and pressed her hand against me, my groin grew hard very fast, and her face suddenly looked less doughy and more rosy. She took her hand away just as quickly, though. 'I've to get back. Come and see me one day.' She described the house on the rue des Cordeliers.

'Maybe I'll come when the Le Vistes are visiting,' I added. 'Then I can have a look to satisfy my curiosity.'

'If you like. *En fait*, they're visiting the day after to-morrow – I heard my mistress say.'

It was too easy. Once Marie-Céleste had left, swinging her basket as she went, I wondered for a moment what she meant to get from this, apart from a moment's pleasure between her legs. But I didn't think for long. I would see Claude Le Viste and that was enough.

Of course it was too easy. Marie-Céleste was not as for-giving as that.

The Belleville house was indeed not as grand as the Le Vistes'. There were two levels and glass in some of the windows, but it was squeezed in among other houses, and some of the timber was rotting. I studied it while I waited across the road for Marie-Céleste, wondering if I would see Claude go in. I didn't know how I could get her on her own. There would be her mother and Béatrice about, as well as the ladies of the house. And there was Marie-Céleste – I might have to plough her just to be rid of her. I had no plan but to keep my wits and look about. At the least I would try to see Claude for a moment to arrange another meeting. I'd even paid a man to write a note for me – Claude would be able to read it even if I couldn't.

The man had smirked at my words, but he'd written it. Men will do most things if a coin or two is the reward.

Marie-Céleste opened the front door and peeked out, then beckoned to me. I ran across and slipped inside. She led me through one room, then another where tapestries were hanging – though it was too dark to see them properly – then back through the kitchen where the cook glared at me as he squatted by a pot on the fire. 'Don't make noise or there'll be trouble,' he growled.

I couldn't remember if Marie-Céleste had been noisy when she opened her legs, but I played along, leering at him as we went out the back door. 'Idiot,' the cook muttered.

I didn't have time to understand the warning behind that word. As I stepped into the back garden, I heard a sound behind me and took such a blow to my head that I saw stars. I staggered, and couldn't even turn around to see my assailant before I was kicked in the back and fell to the ground. Then he began kicking me in the side and head. I managed to look up through the blood trickling into my eyes and saw Marie-Céleste standing with her arms crossed. 'Mind the laundry,' she said to the man I couldn't see. It was too late – the sheet behind her was spattered with blood.

I got enough breath back to groan before the man kicked it out of me again.

It was strangely quiet, with only the sound of thumps and Marie-Céleste's shoe crunching the ground as she shifted from one foot to the other. I was curled up in a ball, trying to protect my innards and take the blows on my back. After one or two kicks to the head everything went black for a time. When I woke I heard a high-pitched whine, like a rabbit caught in a trap. Why is Marie-Céleste making that noise? I thought. 'Be quiet,' Marie-Céleste hissed, and I realized the sound came from me.

'Kick him in the balls,' Marie-Céleste said to my attacker. 'Kick him so he'll not get anyone else with child.'

The man aimed a kick in my knees to uncurl me and flatten me on my back. As he readied himself for the *coup de grâce*, I closed my eyes. Then I heard the creak of a window shutter swinging out. I opened my eyes and looked up into Claude's face peeking over a window sill high above me. Her eyes were wide and clear. She looked like a strip of tapestry.

'*Arrêtez!*' Marie-Céleste yelled. The man paused, looked up, then in a flash was gone. I had not thought someone could disappear so fast. I did see enough of his face, though, to recognize the Le Viste steward. Watch my back, indeed. He had always hated me – enough, apparently, to risk his position. Either that or he fancied Marie-Céleste himself.

'What's happened? Is that you, Marie-Céleste?' Claude called. 'And –' she started – 'Nicolas?'

Other faces appeared by Claude's – Geneviève de Nanterre, Béatrice, Madame and Mademoiselle de Belleville. It was so peculiar seeing their heads huddled together peering down at me – like birds in a tree looking at a worm – that I closed my eyes again.

'Oh, Mademoiselle, a man has attacked Monsieur!' Marie-Céleste cried. 'I don't know where he came from – he just jumped on him!'

The pain of my blows suddenly struck me everywhere. Despite myself I groaned. I could taste blood.

'I'll come down,' Claude said.

'No, you won't,' her mother said. 'Béatrice, go and help Marie-Céleste tend to him.'

When I opened my eyes the heads were gone save Claude's. She gazed down at me. It was very quiet. We smiled at each other. Looking at her face was like seeing blue sky through the leaves of a tree. Then she disappeared suddenly, as if she had been pulled away from the window.

'Don't you say a thing,' Marie-Céleste hissed. 'You was visiting me and he tried to rob you.'

I lay still. I would gain nothing from telling Béatrice what had really happened – if I did Marie-Céleste might tell Béatrice we had a daughter, and she would tell Claude. I didn't want Claude to know.

Béatrice appeared with a bowl of water and a cloth. She knelt by me, took my head in her lap, and began mopping the blood from my face. Just the moving of my head made me feel queasy and I had to close my eyes.

When Marie-Céleste repeated her story about a man setting on me and trying to rob me, Béatrice said nothing. That made Marie-Céleste frantic – she began to spin a more and more complicated web, with grudges and purses of money and friends of brothers and angry words. She got herself into a terrible tangle.

At last Béatrice cut her off. 'How did the man get in the house? He must have known someone here.'

Marie-Céleste started to speak, but finally understood

that words were her enemy and went silent as if someone had just stuffed a rag in her mouth.

Béatrice opened my tunic and pressed her cloth on my shoulders and chest, making me wince and moan. My cries loosened Marie-Céleste's tongue again. 'Don't know what that man was doing – '

'Go and get some clean water,' Béatrice interrupted. 'Some warm water.'

As Marie-Céleste ran inside someone must have appeared in the doorway behind me, for Béatrice turned her head. 'Ask if they have any leopard's bane. If not that, then a handful of dried daisies or marigolds in the warm water will help.'

Whoever it was made a movement and was gone.

'Was that Claude?' I asked. I could barely move my lips.

When Béatrice did not answer I opened my eyes and looked up into her brown eyes that filled so much of her plain face.

'No,' she said. 'It was the daughter of the house.'

I could not guess if she was lying. Turning my head, I spat from my mouth two teeth. They missed Béatrice's blue moiré skirt and bounced on the ground.

'What have you done to get such a beating?' Béatrice asked softly. 'Whatever it was, you probably deserved it.'

'Béatrice, put your hand in my pocket.'

Her arched, painted eyebrows made even higher arcs into her forehead.

'Please. There's something there I want you to deliver.'

She hesitated, then reached in and pulled out the note from my doublet. There was blood on it.

'Give it to Claude.'

Béatrice glanced behind her. 'You know I can't do that,' she whispered.

'Yes, you can. Please. She would want you to. You are her woman, *non*? You must do what's best for her.' I gazed deep into her eyes. Women have often said my eyes are what they like best about me. Just as well it wasn't my teeth.

Béatrice's face softened, her chin tucking into her neck and her nose flaring. She said nothing, but stuffed the note up her sleeve.

Marie-Céleste came back then with a bowl that smelled of flowers. I closed my eyes and let her and Béatrice wash me. Another time I would have enjoyed the attentions of two pairs of women's hands on me, but now I was so sore that I just wanted to sleep to escape the pain. Madame de Belleville appeared briefly to order that men be called to cart me home. I was drifting to sleep when she turned her harsh voice on Marie-Céleste.

I was abed three days before I could move properly again. My joints were stiff, my eyes black, my nose swollen, and a rib was cracked so that a sharp pain flashed through me when I tried to move. I stayed in bed and drank beer but ate nothing, and slept much of the day, though at night I lay awake cursing at the pain.

I was waiting for Claude to come. On the fourth day I heard steps on the stairs, but it was not she who opened the door. Instead Léon Le Vieux stood in the doorway and surveyed the cold, dirty room – the girl from Le Coq d'Or had not yet come up to light the fire and clear away the food she'd brought me the day before. Léon does not usually visit me, but sends a messenger to fetch me to his house. I struggled to sit up.

'You've been a naughty lad, haven't you?'

I started to protest, then stopped. Léon seemed to know everything – there was no point in lying to him. I lay back. 'I did take quite a beating.'

Léon chuckled. 'Get some rest now. You need to be well soon – for your pains I'm sending you on a pilgrimage.'

I stared at him. 'What? Where?'

Léon smiled. 'Not south, but north. To see a Brussels relic.'

GENEVIÈVE DE NANTERRE

Claude would not look at me as we walked back to the rue du Four. She strode so fast that she almost trod on a sweeper boy who was clearing the street of dung and rubbish. Béatrice hurried after her. She is smaller than Claude, who takes after her father in size. Another day I would laugh to see Béatrice trotting after her mistress like a little dog. Today I did not laugh.

I stopped trying to keep up with my daughter and walked at a more sedate pace with my ladies. Soon they were far ahead, giving much trouble to the groom sent along to escort us to and from the rue des Cordeliers. He ran back and forth between the two parties, but didn't dare ask Claude to slow down, nor me to speed up. He did speak to Béatrice, but it had no effect – by the time we reached the Porte St Germain Claude and Béatrice were out of sight.

'Leave them,' I said to the groom when he came back to us. 'They're not far from the house anyway.'

The ladies clucked their tongues. Indeed it must have seemed strange. For the past year I've kept Claude under close guard, yet now I was letting her out of my sight just as the man I was guarding her from came to the very house we were visiting. How could Claude have arranged such a meeting under our noses? I couldn't quite believe it, even though I had recognized Nicolas des Innocents the moment I saw him flat on the ground, his face bruised and bloodied. I was shocked at the sight, and had to stand very still so that Claude wouldn't see me flinch. She too had not moved, as if to hide what she felt. And so we two had stood side by side and still as stones, looking down on him. Only Béatrice had buzzed about like a bee worrying flowers. It was a relief to send her down to him.

I was tired of thinking about Claude. I was tired of caring what happened to her, when she clearly didn't care herself. For a moment I was even tempted to push her into the painter's arms and shut the door on them for good. Of course I couldn't do so, but I let her and Béatrice disappear ahead of us and half-hoped she would do it for me.

When we got back the steward told me that Claude had gone to her room. I went up to my own chamber and sent for Béatrice, one of my ladies sitting in her place with Claude.

When Béatrice came in she dropped to her knees by my chair and began to speak before I could say a word. 'Madame, she says she knew nothing of Nicolas des Innocents being at the rue des Cordeliers. She was as surprised as we when she saw him out there, and in such a state. Claude swears by Our Lady that she's had no contact with him.'

172

'And you believe her?'

'She can't have, or I would know. I've been with her all these months.'

'At night as well? You must sleep.'

'I never fall asleep before her. I pinch myself to stay awake.' Béatrice's eyes were as wide as I've ever seen them. 'And when she falls asleep I tie a silk cord around her ankle so that she can't get up without my knowing.'

'Claude knows how to untie knots.' I was rather enjoying Béatrice's anxiety. Clearly she feared for her position.

'Madame, she has not seen Nicolas. I swear to you.' Béatrice reached into her sleeve and pulled out a piece of paper. There was blood on it, as well as on her sleeve and her bodice. 'Here, perhaps this will tell us how it came about. He gave this to me to give to her.'

I took the paper and carefully unfolded it. The blood was dry now.

Mon Amour –
Come to me – the room above Le Coq d'Or, off the rue St Denis. Any night, as soon as you can.
Ça c'est mon seul désir.
        Nicolas

The scream tore my throat out. Béatrice fell backwards in fright, scrambling away from me as if I were a boar about to charge. The ladies all stumbled to their feet.

I couldn't help it. Seeing my own words – for I knew at once that he was echoing me – written on a bit of bloody paper in a crude hand, by some drunkard sneering in a tavern, was too much to bear.

Claude would pay for it. If I couldn't have *mon seul désir*, I would be sure that she didn't either.

'Go and wash your dress,' I said to Béatrice, crumpling the paper. 'It looks slovenly.'

She stared at me, then pulled her dress around her with shaking hands and got to her feet.

When she was gone I said to my ladies, 'Come change my dress and do my hair. I am going to see my lord.'

I had not said a word to Jean about the troubles with our unruly daughter over the past year. I knew what he would do – throw my words back in my face and blame me for not looking after Claude well enough. He is not close to Claude or his other daughters – though perhaps he is softer with Jeanne – but she is his heir, for better or worse. Certain things are expected of her, and it is up to me to make her ready. If Jean knew the truth – that Claude would prefer to lose her maidenhead to a Paris artist than preserve it for her husband – he would beat me, not her, for not having taught her obedience.

Now I had to break my silence. What I proposed to do with her would require his consent – the very consent Père Hugo had counselled me against the year before.

Jean was in his chamber with the steward, going over the household accounts. It was a task I was meant to do, but Jean preferred to be in charge, as he does in all things. I curtsied low beside the table where they sat. 'Monseigneur, I would like to speak with you. Alone.'

Jean and the steward both jerked their heads and

frowned, as if they were puppets being worked by the same man. I kept my eyes fixed on the fur collar of Jean's gown.

'Can't it wait? Steward's been out and we've only just sat down.'

'I'm sorry, Monseigneur, but it is urgent.'

After a moment Jean said to the steward, 'Wait outside.'

The steward nodded as if he had slept badly and his neck was stiff. I rose as he did. He bowed briefly to me and left us.

'What is it, Geneviève? I'm very busy.'

I would have to tread carefully. 'It's about Claude. She is to be betrothed next year, as is proper, and you will decide soon – or perhaps you have done so already – who will be her lord and husband. I've begun preparing her for her new life – teaching her how to keep herself and wear her clothes, to handle servants and household matters, to entertain and dance. She is doing well in all of these things.'

Jean did not speak but tapped a finger on the table. His silence often has the effect of making me use more words to try to fill it. Then he just looks at me, and all that I have said feels like the words of a jester in the market.

I began to walk up and down. 'There is one area, however, where she needs more guidance than I can give her. She has not yet truly absorbed the ways of the Church, of Our Lady and Our Lord Jesus Christ.'

Jean flicked his hand. I know that impatient gesture, have seen it when men speak to him of things that matter little to him. Claude's indifference to the Church may well stem from her father's – he has always dismissed its

175

importance to his soul, and has been concerned only for its power over his King. To him priests are simply men to make deals with, Mass a meeting place for Court business.

'It's important for a noblewoman to have strong faith in the Church,' I said firmly. 'She must be spiritually as well as physically pure. Any true nobleman will expect that of her.'

Jean scowled, and I wondered if I had gone too far. He does not like to be reminded that some don't think him truly noble. I remembered then the shock I had felt when my father told me I would be betrothed to Jean Le Viste. My mother had locked herself in her chamber and cried, but I was careful not to show how I felt at being linked to a man whose family bought its way into the nobility. My friends were kind to me but I knew that they laughed behind my back and pitied me – poor Geneviève, a pawn in her father's games with the Court. I never knew what Father won by giving me to Jean Le Viste. Certainly Jean won – the support of my father's family was the making of him. It was I who lost. I had been a happy girl, not so different from Claude at her age. But years with a cold man ground away my smiles.

'Make your point,' Jean said.

'Claude is restless and can be difficult at times,' I said. 'I think it would do her good to stay in a convent until her betrothal.'

'A convent? My daughter is no nun.'

'Of course not. But a stay there will help her to know the value of Mass, of prayers, confession, communion. Now she mumbles her prayers, the priest says she makes up her confession, and I'm not sure she always swallows her communion – one of my ladies thought she saw Claude spitting it out in the cloisters after Mass.'

Jean looked scornful, and I resorted to something closer to the truth. 'There is a wildness in her that no husband will like to see. I fear it will bring her harm. The convent will settle her. There is one outside of Paris at Chelles where I'm sure the nuns can help her.'

Jean shuddered. 'I've never liked nuns. My sister became one.'

'She won't become a nun. She'll be safe there and can get up to no mischief. The walls are very high.'

I should not have added that last part. Jean sat up straight and knocked a piece of paper to the floor. 'Has Claude been going out alone?'

'Of course not,' I said, reaching for the paper. He got to it before me, his knees cracking. 'But I think she would like to. The sooner she's married the better.'

'Why don't you keep a closer eye on her rather than imprison her with nuns?'

'I do watch over her carefully. But there are distractions in a city like Paris. And this would be a way of completing her religious education as well.'

Jean picked up a quill and made a mark on the paper. 'People will think you can't control your daughter, or that there is something wrong with her if you have to hide her away.'

He meant that she might be with child. 'It is not wrong for a lady to stay in a convent before her betrothal. My grandmother did, and my mother too. And Claude may visit us occasionally, for some of the Holy Days – the Assumption of Our Lady, All Souls' Day, the Advent – so that people may see there's nothing wrong with her.' I could not keep the scorn from my voice.

Jean just looked at me.

'Or we could bring the betrothal forward if you prefer,' I said quickly, 'if you have finished your talks with the man's family. Do it now rather than next spring. The feast may not be so grand with less time to prepare, but that doesn't matter.'

'No. It won't look right to rush her marriage so. And the tapestries won't be done until next Easter.'

Those tapestries again. I had to bite my lips to keep from spitting. 'Is it really necessary for the tapestries to hang for the betrothal?' I tried to sound offhand. 'We could have it at Michaelmas when we've returned from d'Arcy, and give Claude the tapestries as a wedding gift later when they're ready.'

'No.' Jean threw down the quill and stood. 'The tapestries are not a wedding gift – if they were they would have the husband's coat of arms in them as well. No, they are celebrating my position at Court. I want my new son-in-law to see the Le Viste coats of arms in them and be reminded of what family he is marrying. So he will never forget.' He went over to the window and looked out. It had been sunny earlier but it was starting to rain now.

I was silent. Jean glanced at my stony face. 'We could bring the betrothal back a month or two,' he said to placate me. 'Isn't there a betrothal day in February?'

'The Feast of St Valentine.'

'Yes. We could have it then. Léon Le Vieux told me the other day that the Brussels workshop is a little behind in making the tapestries. I'll send him to chivvy them along by cutting off two months – that will get them working harder. I've never understood why tapestries take so long to make. It is just weaving, after all. Bits of thread wound in and out – even women can do that.' He turned from the window. 'Send Claude to me before you take her to the convent.'

I curtsied. 'Yes, my lord.' When I straightened I looked him in the eye. 'Thank you, Jean.'

He nodded, and though he didn't smile at me, his face softened. He is a hard man, but he does listen to me sometimes.

'Who will she marry, Monseigneur?' I asked.

He shook his head. 'That is my business and not for you to be concerned with. Worry about the bride instead.'

'But –'

'Since you did not give me a son, I must choose one.' He turned away then, and the tender moment was lost. He was punishing me for having only daughters. I could weep but I'd already used up my tears over that.

When I got back to my chamber I sent for Béatrice again. She appeared in a yellow brocade, which I thought too bright, but at least the artist's blood was not staining it.

'Pack Claude's things,' I said. 'Only her simplest clothes, and no jewels. I am taking you both on a journey.'

'Where to, Madame?' Béatrice sounded fearful, as well she might. Nine months in the convent would be punishment for her too. Yet I was still fond of her. 'Don't worry,' I said.

'Look after Claude well and you will yet have your reward.'

I sent for a groom and told him to make ready my carriage, as well as to send a messenger ahead with news of our visit. Then I sent Claude to her father. I sorely wanted to creep outside his door and listen, but it would not be dignified, and I busied myself instead with my own preparations – changing out of the brocade I had worn for Jean and into the simple dark wool I had worn on Good Friday, removing the jewels from my hair, changing my jewelled cross for a wood one.

There was a knock on the door and Claude entered. Her eyes were red and I wondered what Jean had said to her. I'd asked him not to tell her where she was going, so she couldn't be crying over that. She came straight to me and knelt. 'I'm sorry, Maman. I will do whatever you ask of me.' I heard fear in her voice, and some obedience, yet underneath it there was still defiance. Instead of keeping her eyes lowered in respect, she looked at me sideways the way I have seen birds do when under a cat's paw, searching for a way of escaping.

The nuns would have their hands full with her.

I accompanied them in the carriage. They were both surprised to see it – they had been expecting to ride, prob-ably thinking we were going to my mother's in Nanterre. We did not go that way, though – once we crossed the Seine over the Pont de Notre Dame we turned east and drove out of Paris past the Bastille. Claude sat far from me, with Béatrice squeezed between us. We spoke little. My carriage is not made for long journeys, but for simple jaunts across the city. We were jolted often, and at times

I wondered if the wheels would fall off. I could not sleep, though Claude and Béatrice managed a little once it was dark and they couldn't watch the passing fields.

When we arrived at the town walls it was almost daybreak. Lauds would soon be said. Claude had never been to Chelles, and didn't react when we stopped outside the small door set in the high wall. Béatrice recognized it at once, though, and sat up, her face wrinkled with concern as I climbed out and rang the bell next to the door. 'Madame –' she began, but I waved her to silence.

Only when a woman opened the door and Claude saw the white cloth framing her face in the torchlight did she suddenly understand. 'No!' she cried, pushing herself into the corner of the carriage. I ignored her and spoke in a low voice to the nun.

Then I heard a noise, and Béatrice cried, 'Madame, she has run off!'

'Go and get her,' I said in a low voice to the grooms, who were wiping down the horses. One of them dropped his cloth and ran down the road into the darkness beyond the torch. This was why I had brought Claude in a carriage – if we had gone on horses she could have ridden away. In a few minutes he was back, carrying Claude in his arms. She had gone limp like a sack of rye and would not stand when he tried to put her down by me. 'Carry her inside,' I said. With the nun holding high her torch, we made our sorry entrance into the convent.

They took Claude away, Béatrice trailing behind like a chick that has lost its mother. I joined the nuns in the chapel for Lauds, sinking to my knees with a lightness

I had not felt for some time. Afterwards I joined the Abbess for a glass of wine before having a short sleep. I slept better on the narrow straw pallet than I ever do at the rue du Four in my big bed with my ladies close by.

I did not see Claude again before I left. I did send for Béatrice, though, who looked worn and subdued. Her curtsy was less brisk than usual, and she'd had trouble dressing her hair – normally my ladies take turns fixing each other's hair, and there are no mirrors at Chelles. I was glad to see that she'd changed from the yellow brocade to something more sober. We walked around the cloisters and then into the central garden, where nuns were at work planting and weeding, digging and tying. I am no gardener but I can appreciate the simple pleasure of a flower's colours and scent. There were still some daffodils in flower, and hyacinth, some violets beginning to bloom, and periwinkle. Sprigs of lavender, rosemary and thyme were poking out from their bushes, and new mint was growing in clumps. Standing in that peaceful garden in the morning sun, with nuns quietly busy around me and the bell soon to ring for Terce, I felt a stab of envy that Claude would stay here when I couldn't. I'd thought of this place as a punishment for her as well as a protection and an education. But it was a punishment for me too, to know that she would have what I could not.

'Look at this garden, Béatrice,' I said, pushing away my thoughts. 'It's like Paradise. Like Heaven on Earth.'

Béatrice did not respond.

'Where were you at Lauds? I know it was early, but you will get used to that.'

'I was attending Mademoiselle.'

'How is she?'

Béatrice shrugged. She wouldn't normally use such a rude gesture. She was angry at me, though of course she couldn't say so. 'She hasn't spoken since she arrived. Nor has she eaten – not that she missed much.'

It is true that the gruel here is thin, the bread hard. 'She will get used to it in time,' I said gently. 'This is the best place for her, you know. She'll be the better for it.'

'I hope you're right, Madame.'

I drew myself up. 'Are you questioning my decision to bring her here?'

Béatrice bowed her head. 'No, Madame.'

'She'll be much happier by Candlemas.'

Béatrice jerked her head. 'Candlemas? Candlemas is long past.'

'I mean next Candlemas.'

'We're to stay here until then?' Béatrice's voice rose.

I smiled. 'It will go by faster than you think. And if you are both good and behave yourselves – both of you,' I repeated so that she would understand, 'I will arrange a marriage for you at the end of it, if you wish.'

Poor Béatrice had a split face – a sad mouth but hopeful eyes.

'You know that you will be well looked after here,' I said. 'Be cheerful with Claude, obey the Abbess, and all will be well.'

With that I left her in the lovely garden, tearing myself away to get in my carriage for the long journey back to the rue du Four. I confess I cried a little as I watched the fields pass, and again when we reached the Paris gates. I did not want to go back to the rue du Four. But I must.

At the house I stopped the grooms before they took the horses away, and paid them handsomely to keep their mouths shut about where we had been. No one but they and Jean knew where Claude was – I had not told even my ladies where we were going. I didn't want Nicolas finding out and pestering the nuns there. I had been careful but I was still uneasy, and wished that Nicolas were far away. I didn't trust him. I saw the way he looked at my daughter as he lay bloodied on the ground – a look I never had from Jean. It made my gut turn from jealousy.

As I stepped across the courtyard I had an idea, and hurried back to the stables. 'I'm going back out,' I said to the surprised grooms. 'Take me to the rue des Rosiers.'

Léon Le Vieux was also surprised – it is rare for a noble-woman to visit him, and alone. However, he was very gracious, making me comfortable by the fire. He has done well for himself – it is a fine house, filled with rugs and carved chests and silver plates. I counted two servants, though his wife herself brought us sweet wine and made me a deep curtsy. She looked happy enough, and there was silk woven into the wool of her dress.

'How do you fare, Dame Geneviève?' he asked as we sat. 'And Claude? And Jeanne and Petite Geneviève?' Léon never forgets to ask after each of my daughters. I have always liked him, though I fear for his soul. His family has been converted to the Church, yet still he is not like us. I looked around for signs of this, but saw only a crucifix on the wall.

'I need your help, Léon,' I said, sipping my wine. 'Have you heard from my husband?'

'About the tapestries? Yes, this morning. I was just arranging how I might go to Brussels when you arrived.'

'I would ask something of you. It may be in your favour as well. Send that Nicolas des Innocents to Brussels instead.'

Léon paused, his glass half-raised to his lips. 'That is an unexpected request. May I ask why, Dame Geneviève?'

I wanted to tell someone. Léon is a discreet man – I could talk to him without it becoming the next day's gossip. So I told him everything I had kept from Jean – how Claude and Nicolas met the first time in Jean's chamber, all I had done to keep them apart since, and the meeting at the rue des Cordeliers. 'I've taken her to Chelles,' I finished, 'where she'll stay until her betrothal. No one knows she's there but you and me and Jean. That's why we've moved the betrothal back to just before Lent rather than after Easter. But I don't trust Nicolas. I want him out of Paris for a time until it's certain he won't find her. You have dealings with him – tell him to go to Brussels in your stead.'

Léon Le Vieux listened impassively. When I was done he shook his head. 'I should not have left them together,' he muttered.

'Who?'

'Nothing, Dame Geneviève. I will do as you ask. It suits me as well – a trip to Brussels now is not so convenient for me.' He grunted. 'These tapestries seem to be causing trouble, *non*?'

I sighed and looked at the fire. 'Indeed – more than any tapestry is worth!'

CLAUDE LE VISTE

At first I would not leave my room, nor eat, nor speak to anyone except Béatrice – and very little to her either, once I'd looked in my bags. She had packed my plainest dresses – no silk, no brocade, no velvet. There were no jewels for my hair or throat, no head-dresses but simple scarves, nothing to paint my lips with, and only a wood comb. When I accused her of knowing where we were going and not telling me, she denied it. I do not believe her.

It was easy enough not to eat – the food they gave me wasn't fit for pigs. The room, though, was so small and plain that after only a day I longed to be free of it. There was room only for a straw pallet and a chamberpot, and the stone walls were bare except for a small wooden crucifix. Béatrice couldn't fit her pallet in there – she slept outside my door. I've never slept on straw before. It is prickly and noisy and I miss my soft feathers at home. Papa would be so angry if he could see his daughter sleeping on straw.

Béatrice had brought paper and a quill and ink, and I thought of sending word to Papa to come and get me.

He'd said nothing about convents when he spoke to me in his chamber, but only reminded me that I carried his name and that I was to obey Maman in everything. That may be true but I don't think he meant I was to be shut up in a convent, sleeping on straw and breaking my teeth on bread as hard as stone.

I've never been able to talk freely with Papa. I wanted to tell him that his steward is not to be trusted – that I had seen him beating Nicolas at the rue des Cordeliers. But of course I could not mention Nicolas, so I had to say nothing, but listen to him go on about the husband I am to marry one day, and how important it is for me to remain chaste and pious in honour of the family name. Afterwards I cried from frustration. I have not cried since, but I am still angry with everyone – Papa, Maman, Béatrice, even Nicolas for playing a part in trapping me here, even if he doesn't know it.

By the fourth morning I was so bored with my room that I broke my silence with Béatrice and begged her to find a messenger. She came back later and told me the Abbess said I am neither to send nor receive messages. So I truly am imprisoned.

I sent Béatrice away, then came out of my room with a note I had written my father. I tied it to a stone and tried to throw it over the wall, hoping some nobleman on the other side would find it, take pity on me and somehow get it to Papa. I tried again and again but the note kept fluttering off the stone, and besides I was too weak to get it over that high wall.

I did cry then, very bitter tears. I didn't go back inside,

though. It was sunny out, and there was a garden in the middle of the cloisters to sit in that was much preferable to my tiny room. I sat on one of the stone benches set around the sides of the cloisters, not caring if the sun burned me. A few nuns were working in the garden, and gave me curious looks. I ignored them. In front of me a bed of roses was just beginning to bloom and the bush nearest me was dotted with tight white buds. I looked at them, then reached over and squeezed a thorn into the flesh of my thumb. A drop of blood appeared, and I held it up and let it drip down my hand.

Then I heard a noise I had not expected ever to hear in a convent. From somewhere inside a child laughed. After a moment little pattering steps came from the door nearest me, and a tiny girl appeared in the archway. She was wearing a grey dress and a white cap, and reminded me of Petite Geneviève when she was much younger. She was really still a baby, and lurched along with uneven steps, any moment about to fall and break open her head. She had a funny little face, very determined and serious, as if walking were a game of chess she must win. I couldn't say if she would be fair when she grew older – her face was like an old woman's, and that is not always pleasant in a baby. She had fat cheeks and a low brow that jutted over pinched brown eyes – eyes that could do with being lighter than they were. But her hair was lovely, a dark red like chestnuts, in big tangled ringlets.

'Come here, *ma petite*,' I called, wiping my bloody hand on my dress. 'Come here and sit with me.'

Behind the girl a nun appeared in her long white habit.

They wear white here at Chelles. At least I'm not surrounded by black – black does not suit a woman's face.
'There you are, you naughty thing,' the nun scolded.
'Come here.' She might as well have been talking to a goat,
for the girl paid no attention. She tottered out the door
and tripped down the step, sprawling into the cloisters,
her arms before her. 'Oh!' I cried, and jumped up to run
over to her. I needn't have bothered, though – the girl
hopped up as if nothing had happened and ran along one
side of the cloisters square.

The nun did not follow but stood looking me up and
down. 'So you've come out now,' she said sourly.

'I won't be here for long,' I said quickly. 'I'll be going
home soon.'

The nun did not respond but kept looking at me. She
seemed very taken with my dull dress. But then, mine was
not so dull when compared to hers – coarse white wool
that hung like a sack. Mine may have been brown, but
the wool was fine, and there was tiny yellow and white
embroidery on the bodice. She was staring at this, so I
said, 'One of our servants did that. She is – was – very
good with her needle.'

The nun gave me a funny look, then gazed after the girl,
who had tottered along two lengths of the square and was
rounding the third corner. '*Attention, mon petit chou!*' the
nun called. 'Watch where you run!'

Her words seemed to do just what they were meant to
prevent. The girl fell again, and this time lay still and began
to cry. The nun ran around the square, her dress dragging
behind her. When she got to the girl she stood over her

and began to scold. Clearly she was not used to children. I strode over to them, then knelt and put my arms around the girl, lifting her onto my lap as I had done with Petite Geneviève many times. 'There now,' I said, patting her arms and knees, and brushing off her little dress. 'There now, that must have hurt. Where does it hurt? Your hands? Your knees?'

The girl kept crying, and I wrapped my arms tight around her and rocked her back and forth until she was quiet. The nun went on scolding, though of course the baby could scarcely understand a word. 'Really you have been very silly, running so fast when you shouldn't. This wouldn't have happened if you had obeyed me the first time. You'll be on your knees doing penance during Sext.'

I snorted at the thought of trying to get such a small girl to pray for forgiveness. She could scarcely say 'Maman', much less 'Notre père, qui est aux cieux . . .' We didn't take Petite Geneviève to Mass until she was three and even then she was a noisy thing who would not sit still for more than a moment. This girl didn't look much older than a year. She was like a little doll folded into my lap.

'Are you sorry now, Claude? Are you sorry?'

I glared up at the nun. 'You're to call me Mademoiselle. And I have nothing to be sorry for – I've done nothing wrong, whatever Maman has said! It's an insult for you to say such a thing to me. I shall tell the Abbess.'

The baby began to cry again when she heard my angry voice. 'Shush-shush,' I whispered, turning my back on the nun. 'Shush-shush.' I began to sing a song Marie-Céleste had taught me.

I am so gay
so sweet, so pleasing,
such a young little maid
of not yet fifteen years.
My little breasts
are budding as they should.
I should be learning
about love
and amorous ways,
but I am
in prison.
May God curse the one
who put me there!

The nun tried to say something but I sang louder, rocking back and forth.

It was evil, villainy, and sin
to put this little maid
in a convent.
It was indeed,
by my faith.
In the convent
I live in great chagrin,
God, for I am such a young thing.
I feel the first sweet pangs beneath my little belt.
Cursed be the one who made me a nun!

The girl had stopped crying and made little noises in between her sniffles, as if she too were trying to sing but didn't know the words. It was very pleasant, rocking and singing taunting words that the nun could hear. The song might as well have been written for me.

I heard steps behind us and knew it was Béatrice, my gaoler. She was as bad as the nuns.

'Don't sing that song!' she hissed.

I ignored her. 'Do you want to run again?' I said to the girl. 'Shall we run together? Come, let's run all around the cloisters as fast as we can.' I set her on her feet, took her hand and began to pull her along, so that she was half running, half dangling from my hand. Her squeals and my shouts echoed in the arches of the cloisters. The convent had not heard so much noise since a pig escaped or a nun got ants running up her legs while she gardened. Nuns appeared in doorways and windows to stare at us. Even Abbess Catherine de Lignières came out and stood watching us with her arms crossed over her bosom. I caught the girl up in my arms and ran and ran, once – twice – five times around the cloisters, shouting all the way, and no one stopped us. Each time we passed Béatrice she looked more ashamed.

In the end it was not a person who stopped us but a bell. When it rang the nuns immediately disappeared. 'Sext,' the nun next to Béatrice announced as I ran by, before going off herself. Béatrice looked after the nun, then at me. I ran still faster, the girl jiggling in my arms. When I got all the way around the cloisters a sixth time Béatrice had gone too, and we were alone. I ran a few more steps and then stopped, as there was no longer any reason to run. I dropped onto a bench and set the girl down next to me. She immediately laid her head in my lap. Her ruddy face was flushed, and after a moment she was asleep. It's funny how fast a baby can fall asleep when she is tired.

'That's why you were crying, *chérie*,' I whispered, stroking her ringlets. 'You need sleep, not prayers. Those silly nuns don't know anything about little girls and what they need.'

At first I was glad to sit on the bench with her on my lap in the sun, left alone with a garden to look at. But soon my back began to ache with having to sit still and straight when there was nothing to lean against. It grew hot and as I wore no hat I worried the sun would bring out freckles on my face. I didn't want to look like a common woman out sowing in the fields. I began to wish someone would come along that I could hand the girl to, but there was no one – they were still at their prayers. There is nothing wrong with prayers but I don't see why they should say them eight times in a day.

I didn't know what else to do with the little thing, so I gathered her up and carried her to my room. She didn't wake when I laid her on my pallet. I searched in my bag for a bit of embroidery, then went back out and sat on another bench in the shade. I don't much like embroidery, but there was nothing else to do. There is no riding or dancing or singing here, no playing backgammon with Jeanne, or having my writing lessons, or flying falcons with Maman in the fields beyond Saint-Germain-des-Prés, or visiting my grandmother at Nanterre. There are no fairs or markets to go to, no jesters or *jongleurs* for entertainments. There are no feasts – *en fait*, there is no food at all that I can bear to eat. I will be nothing but bones by the time I leave – whenever that is. Béatrice won't tell me.

There are no men to look at, not even a stooped old gardener pushing a barrow. Not even a suspicious steward. I never thought I would welcome the sight of my father's mean-faced steward, but if he were to walk through the convent gate now I would smile at him and give him my hand to kiss, even if he did beat Nicolas.

Now there are only women to look at, and dull ones at that, their faces staring at me from oval frames of white, with no hair or jewels to soften them. They look rough and red, their cheeks and chins and noses sticking out like a jumble of parsnips, their eyes small as currants. But then, nuns are not meant to be fair.

Béatrice once told me that Maman has long wanted to join Chelles. I had never thought much of that until I was here. Now I can't picture Maman's delicate face made coarse by a habit, nor see her hoeing among the leeks and cabbages, nor scurrying to prayers eight times a day, nor living in a plain cell on straw. Maman thinks convent life is much like her visits here, when the Abbess pampers her, preparing lavish dishes from food the convent would normally sell at market. I expect there is a lovely room for her to stay in too, full of cushions and tapestries and gilded crosses. If Maman were to join and become a bride of Christ, the convent would receive a large dowry. And so the Abbess is very kind to Maman and other rich women who visit.

There are no cushions on my seats, no tapestries to warm the walls. Wooden crosses will have to satisfy me, rough wool and plain shoes, pottage without spices and bread made from coarse brown flour.

All this I had worked out for myself after only four days at the convent.

I frowned at my embroidery. I was meant to be making a falcon for a cushion cover, but it looked like a snake with wings. And I had just stitched the wrong colour, red where it should be brown, and the threads had become all tangled. I sighed.

Then I heard footsteps, and someone said, 'Oh!' I looked up. Marie-Céleste stood across the cloisters from me, looking very confused. 'Ah, Marie-Céleste, I am glad you're here,' I called out. 'You can help untangle my threads.' It was as if she and I were at home on the rue du Four, working our needles in the courtyard while Jeanne and Petite Geneviève played around us.

But we were not there. I sat up straight. 'What are you doing here?'

Marie-Céleste curtsied, and then she began to cry.

'Come here, Marie-Céleste.'

She was so used to me commanding her that even now she didn't hesitate, except in choosing which way around the cloisters to walk. She reached me and curtsied again, wiping her eyes on her sleeve.

'Have you come to get me out?' I asked eagerly, for I could not see why else she would be here.

Marie-Céleste looked even more confused. 'You, Mademoiselle? I didn't know you was here. I've come to see my daughter.'

'Hasn't my father sent you? Or Maman?'

Marie-Céleste shook her head. 'I don't work at your house now, Mademoiselle. You know that, and you know

195

why too.' She frowned in a way that was strangely familiar, like suddenly getting a taste in your mouth of an almond cake you'd eaten earlier.

'Why else would you come here, if not for me?' I could not let go of the idea that Marie-Céleste would be my means of escape.

Marie-Céleste looked around. 'My daughter – they said she was out here. I know I'm not meant to come, and she don't even think of me as Maman, but I can't help it.'

I gazed at her in surprise. 'The girl is your daughter?'

Marie-Céleste looked equally surprised. 'Didn't you know? They didn't tell you? Her name is Claude, you know – like yours.'

'They tell me nothing here. *Alors*, she's asleep in there.' I pointed down a passageway towards my room. 'Four doors along.'

Marie-Céleste nodded. 'I'll just have a look at her, then, Mademoiselle. *Pardon*.' She stepped across the cloisters and down the corridor.

As I waited for her I thought back to the day Marie-Céleste had said she would name her baby after me. Then I remembered something – I had been meant to tell Maman that Marie-Céleste had gone to tend to her mother, and would be back. I had forgotten. Maman had been so awful to me then and every day since that I spoke to her as little as I could. And so Marie-Céleste did not work for us any more. I am not used to feeling guilty, but now I felt sick with it.

When she came back out I moved over on the bench. 'Come and sit with me,' I said, patting the space beside me.

Marie-Céleste looked uneasy. 'I should be getting back, Mademoiselle. My mother didn't know I was coming here, and she'll be expecting me.'

'Just for a moment. You can help me with my sewing. *Regarde*, I'm wearing some of your work.' I smoothed my bodice.

Marie-Céleste sat down warily. She must be angry with me. I would have to make things right if I wanted to get her to help me.

'How do you know this place?' I asked, as if we were good friends chatting. We had been, once.

'Been coming since I was a girl. We live close by, and Maman used to work here. Not as a nun, of course, but she helped in the fields and with the cooking. Them nuns are so busy praying that they need the help.'

Now I understood. 'And Maman got you from here.'

Marie-Céleste nodded. 'She wanted a new maid and asked the nuns to find one. She came here three or four times in a year, your mother. She wanted to join, but of course she couldn't.'

'And you named your baby after me.'

'Yes.' Marie-Céleste looked as if she regretted that, as well she might.

'Has the father seen her?'

'No!' Marie-Céleste shook her head as if she were shooing away a fly. 'He don't care nothing for me or the baby. He had me once and didn't care what happened after. Then two years later he has the cheek to come around and see me. Wants it again, and won't care again if there's another babe. Well, I showed him, didn't I?' She clenched

197

her hand into a fist. 'Deserved all he got. If you hadn't poked your head out the window – ' She stopped, her eyes suddenly fearful.

My sister Jeanne has a toy she likes to play with – a wooden cup on the end of a stick, with a ball tied to the stick with a string. She tosses the ball up and tries to catch it in the cup. I felt as if I had been tossing and tossing the ball, and suddenly I caught it with the click of wood against wood.

Perhaps the convent was already having an effect on me. If I had been anywhere else and discovered such a thing I would have shrieked. Now, though, sitting in that quiet garden, I did not scream, or scratch out Marie-Céleste's eyes, or cry. I would cry later. I simply said very quietly, 'Nicolas des Innocents is Petite Claude's father?'

Marie-Céleste nodded. 'It was only the once, when he came to see your father about some painting. That was all.'

'Then why were you with him in the courtyard the other day? Having him beaten, it looked to me.'

Marie-Céleste gazed at me fearfully and began to cry again.

I gritted my teeth. 'Stop it. Stop that crying!'

She gulped and swallowed, then wiped her eyes and blew her nose on her sleeve. Marie-Céleste really is very stupid. If we were in Paris she would go straight into the stocks – or worse – for having a man attacked like that. But I was trapped in the convent – there was nothing I could do to have her punished.

That thought must have come to her too, for when she

had stopped her crying she looked at me sideways. 'What are you doing here, Mademoiselle? You never said.'

Of course I could say nothing of Nicolas. Marie-Céleste didn't know what I felt for him or what I'd done with him – or tried to do, and that she had already done. I hated her now, but I could not let her see that. I would have to sound as if I wanted to be here. I picked up my embroidery so that I could keep my eyes on it. 'Maman and Papa decided it would be best for me to spend the last months before my betrothal here, better to learn the ways of the Church. When a woman marries, she's no longer pure in body as she was when she was a maiden. It is important that her spirit remain pure, that she not be seduced by lust into forgetting Our Lady and the sacrifice made by Our Lord Jesus Christ.'

I sounded just like Maman, except not so convincing. I didn't convince Marie-Céleste, I could see that – she rolled her eyes. But then, she had lost her maidenhead long ago, I was sure, and didn't place such value on it as my family did on mine.

'He was asking about you,' Marie-Céleste announced suddenly.

'He? Who?' My heart beat faster. I stabbed at the embroidery with my needle. Marie-Céleste frowned at the mess I was making of the threads. She held out her hand and I surrendered it to her.

'That bastard artist,' she said, plucking at the strings to untangle them. 'Wanted to know what you looked like and when you would visit the Bellevilles.'

So Nicolas had indeed come to see me at the rue des

Cordeliers. I knew it couldn't have been for Marie-Céleste. I gazed at her head bowed over my embroidery, deftly unpicking all my faults. How could I get word to him through her without her becoming suspicious? She was stupid but she could often guess when I was lying.

From my room we heard a cough and a yelp. Marie-Céleste looked at me anxiously. 'You go to her, Mademoiselle,' she begged.

'But you are her mother!'

'She don't know that. I come to have a look at her but I don't talk to her or hold her. It hurts too much after.' There was another cough and Marie-Céleste winced as if someone had stepped on her toe. For just a moment I felt sorry for her.

I went to the doorway of my room and looked in. Petite Claude was shaking her head, rolling it along the pillow in her sleep. She frowned, then suddenly let go of the dream, and her face relaxed into a smile. Now that I knew, I was amazed I had not seen Nicolas in the girl – her pinched eyes, her chestnut hair, her strong jaw. When she smiled she looked like him, and like her mother when she frowned.

'She's fine,' I said when I came back. 'Demons were visiting her in her sleep but they have gone now.' I didn't sit down, but scraped my toe in the pebbles.

Marie-Céleste nodded. She had been rapidly sewing, and already my falcon looked less like a snake and more like itself.

Watching Petite Claude had given me an idea. 'Has Nicolas helped you with the child?'

Marie-Céleste snorted. 'He threw some coins at me. Weren't nothing, though.'

I didn't care what Nicolas did or didn't do for his daughter – as far as I could see, Marie-Céleste had got into her own trouble. I didn't say so, though. 'He should be giving you more than just a few coins,' I said, strolling up and down in front of the bench. 'He has designed tapestries for my father, you know, that will bring him money and are sure to bring him fame. He should be paying something for Petite Claude.' I let her think on that while I took a little turn around the square of roses. My thumb ached pleasantly from where I'd pierced it on the thorn. When I came back to the bench I said, 'Perhaps I could help you get money from him – get him to pay for Petite Claude so that she may leave here and stay with you and your mother.'

'How?' Marie-Céleste asked quickly.

I brushed a fly from my sleeve. 'I could tell him my father won't pay him for the tapestries until he does.'

'Could you really do that, Mademoiselle?'

'I will write a note now, and you can take it to him.'

'Me?' Marie-Céleste looked put out. 'Why don't you, Mademoiselle? Or one of your ladies?' She looked around. 'You must have one with you. Probably Béatrice – your mother always meant her for you, didn't she? She'll be surprised to be living here again.'

'Again? Has she before?'

Marie-Céleste shrugged. '*Bien sûr*. She grew up here, same as me.'

I'd not thought of it before, but Béatrice did seem

familiar with the convent and its ways – she knew where things were and even some of the nuns.

'She can take the note for you, Mademoiselle,' Marie-Céleste added.

I had forgotten that Marie-Céleste didn't know I was imprisoned here – she thought Béatrice and I could come and go as we pleased. And she mustn't know. If she did she might not help me to reach Nicolas.

'I'm not meant to leave,' I said. 'Nor Béatrice. It's part of the purification of the soul before the betrothal. I don't see other people, especially not men.'

'But I can't go to him – not after what happened. He might beat me, or worse.'

It's no more than you deserve, I thought. 'Leave it in his room, when he's not there,' I suggested. When she continued to look dubious I added, 'Do you want me to tell Papa that you had his steward beat the very artist my father admires?'

Marie-Céleste knew she was trapped. She looked as if she might cry again. 'Give me the note, then,' she mumbled.

'Wait there.' I hurried to my room before she could change her mind. I rummaged through my bag for more paper, then knelt on the floor and quickly wrote a note, telling Nicolas where I was and begging him to rescue me. I had no sealing wax but that did not much matter – Marie-Céleste certainly couldn't read it, and I doubted she knew anyone else who could.

I wasn't quiet enough. As I was finishing Petite Claude sat up on the pallet and began to cry and rub her eyes. Her dark red curls swirled around her face. She looked so like Marie-Céleste that I wanted to laugh. 'Come, *chérie*,' I whispered, picking her up. 'Come and see your silly mother.'

When we came out, the nuns were coming back from Sext and Marie-Céleste was standing with Béatrice. They looked peculiar together, a giant with a doll. It was hard to picture them here as girls. They jumped apart when I got to them, and Marie-Céleste would not look at Petite Claude. 'Take her for a moment,' I said, handing the baby to a surprised Béatrice. 'I'm going to walk Marie-Céleste to the gate.'

Béatrice gave me a look with her doggish eyes. 'They won't let you out, you know.'

I made a face at her and tucked my hand through the crook of Marie-Céleste's arm. When I was sure Béatrice couldn't see I stuffed the note into her hand. 'Do you know where he lives?' I whispered.

Marie-Céleste shook her head.

'Steward will – he sent messengers there for Papa. Find out from him – I'll have him punished if he doesn't tell you.'

Marie-Céleste nodded and pulled her arm from my grasp. She looked weary. The thought of sharing the same man with her disgusted me. How Nicolas could have wanted her – especially if he could see her now, with her red nose and her small eyes and her scowl – I did not understand.

At the gate a nun handed Marie-Céleste a basket filled with eggs, bread and beans – a charity basket handed out to the poor. She didn't look back at me or her daughter as she left.

When I got back to Béatrice – still holding a squirming Petite Claude – I said, 'You and Marie-Céleste grew up here together.'

Béatrice looked startled, then nodded. 'My mother was widowed when I was young, and joined the convent.'

Petite Claude reached over and pulled a loose strand of Béatrice's hair. Béatrice yelped, and Petite Claude and I chortled.

'Are you pleased to be back, then?' I asked.

To my surprise Béatrice looked at me sadly. 'The happiest day of my life was when your mother chose me to come and be her lady. It is a horror for me to have to live here again.'

I set Petite Claude down so that she could totter through the garden. 'Then help me to escape.'

Béatrice shook her head. 'It's better for you to be here, Mademoiselle. You know that. Why do you want to wreck the path of your life? You will marry a nobleman and live grandly. Why would you want anything other than that? There is no greater joy for a woman than to be married, *n'est-ce pas*? Every woman.'

I picked up the embroidery Marie-Céleste had left folded on the bench, the needle threaded through it. I took the needle and jammed it into my finger, just to feel the jolt of pain.

'Oh dear,' I said. 'Look what I have done.' Then, to torment Béatrice for acting as my gaoler rather than my lady, I began to sing the song that had upset her. She had probably sung it when she was a girl here:

I should be learning
About love
And amorous ways,
But I am
in prison.
May God curse the one
Who put me there!

IV

BRUSSELS

May Day 1491–
Septuagesima 1492

GEORGES DE LA CHAPELLE

By the time he arrived we had already been working for hours. Silence had settled on the workshop. No one had spoken even to ask for wool or a bobbin or needle in at least an hour. Even the shifting of the loom pedals was quiet, as if they were muffled with cloth. The women too were quiet, or out – Christine was winding a bobbin with wool thread, Aliénor was working in her garden, and Madeleine was at the market.

I work best when it's quiet. Then I can weave for hours without noticing time pass, thinking of nothing but the coloured threads under my fingers as I pull them back and forth between the warp. But one restless weaver or a chattering woman can make the whole shop unable to settle. We need this silence now to do proper work, if we're ever to finish the tapestries in time. Even when it's quiet these days, often all I can think of is time – of what has gone and what is left, of how we shall manage and what we can do to catch up.

I was sitting between Georges Le Jeune and Luc, finishing the jewels the Lady held in À Mon Seul Désir, while also keeping an eye on my son as he began the hachure on the Lady's shoulder, yellow into red. He was making a good job of it – really I no longer needed to watch as he did it. It is a habit that's hard to break.

The two hired weavers, a father and son called Joseph and Thomas were working on *millefleurs* in Taste. They have done *millefleurs* for me before, and are good and quick at them. And they're quiet, though Thomas uses the pedals on his loom more than he needs to. Sometimes I think he does it on purpose to make noise, as the young often do. I had to teach Georges Le Jeune to shift his pedals quietly and only when he was making a large enough shed. Of course I cannot tell another weaver what to do, but I grit my teeth when Thomas makes such a racket.

It's not easy being the *lissier*. Apart from watching over the others, I weave the hardest parts – the faces and hands, the lion's mane, the unicorn's face and horn, the intricate cloth. I jump between the two tapestries, trying to keep up as the other weavers press on with *millefleurs* and animals, waiting for me to fill the hole in the centre.

I've told the weavers they must be sitting at the looms, ready to start, when the bells of the Chapelle ring – earlier now May has begun. We began at seven this morning. Other workshops may use the bells as a signal to begin preparing for the day, but there's nothing in the Guild rules to say that weavers can't arrive early and study the cartoon to see what they will be weaving that day and make their bobbins ready. Then they can begin the moment the bells sound.

I don't worry about Georges Le Jeune or Luc – they

know we have no time to dawdle in the mornings. The other two weavers have managed so far, but it's not their workshop or commission, and though I trust their work – their *millefleurs* are as fine as mine – I wonder sometimes if there will come a day when they find other work that's not so demanding and don't turn up when they should. Joseph hasn't complained, but I've seen Thomas sit down to the loom and stare at it after the bells ring until at last he lifts his hands to the threads as if he had stones tied to his wrists. Yet I need ten months' more work from him, noisy pedals or not. It could be he hasn't properly recovered from his illness this winter. Though Aliénor dosed him and Georges Le Jeune through their fevers, it took them a long time to get well. We have not yet recovered the time lost.

Pray, Christine is always saying. But it takes too much time to pray, and I tell her to go to the Sablon and say our prayers for all of us so that we may remain here and weave instead.

Now I heard voices in the kitchen. Madeleine had come back from market, and brought a man with her. I thought little of it – Madeleine often has swains buzzing around her. One day she'll be stung by one of them.

Then Aliénor came in from the garden, a strange look on her face.

'What is it?' Christine asked, breaking the workshop's precious silence.

Aliénor was listening to the sounds in the house. 'He's come back.'

Georges Le Jeune looked up. 'Who?'

211

He needn't have asked. I knew who. Our peace was about to be wrecked – that man can never keep quiet.

Madeleine appeared in the workshop with a silly smile on her face. 'The Paris man's here,' she announced.

Nicolas des Innocents appeared behind her, still splattered with mud from the journey, and grinned at us. 'You're all sitting just as I left you last summer,' he scoffed. 'The world goes on, but Brussels never moves.'

I stood. 'Welcome,' I said. 'Christine, drink for our guest. Small beer.' Although he was a nuisance, I would not have it said of me that I don't welcome visitors, especially those who've travelled far.

Georges Le Jeune began to stand as well, and Luc, until I shook my head at them. Nicolas needn't disrupt everyone's work.

Christine nodded at him as she passed. 'So you've come for another look, have you?' She made a gesture with her head that took in both the looms and Aliénor still idling in the doorway.

'I have indeed, Madame. I had hoped to see Aliénor dancing around a maypole, but I've arrived too late.'

Christine disappeared inside without telling him we'd worked through May Day – though I had let Luc and Thomas go early to see the fair.

As Nicolas stepped down into the workshop, he winced as if he'd stepped on a nail. 'Are you all right?' I asked.

Nicolas shrugged but held his elbow against his side. 'A little battered from the journey, that's all.' He turned to Aliénor. 'And you, Aliénor – how do you keep?' When he smiled at her I saw that two side teeth were missing, and there was a trace of bruising around his eye. Either he had fallen off a horse or been in a fight. Perhaps there had been thieves along the road.

'Very well, Monsieur,' Aliénor said, 'but the garden is even better. Come and smell the flowers.'

'In a moment, beauty. I want to have a look at the tapestries first.'

Aliénor smiled wryly. 'You want to see her, don't you? Well, you've come too early.'

I didn't know what she meant until Nicolas looked at the strip of Taste on the loom. 'Ah,' he said, crestfallen. What he could see was a Lady's arm with the hand holding a parakeet, a fold of an overdress, the beginnings of a monkey and the tip of a magpie's wing. And *millefleurs*, of course. To a weaver there was much to admire, but I could see that for a man like Nicolas the strip must be a disappointment. He glanced at À Mon Seul Désir, perhaps hoping for a face there. But there was only another Lady's arm reaching out with her jewels, more overdress, a monkey, and a blue tent flap with golden flames dotted on it.

'It could be worse,' Aliénor said. 'We might already have woven her face and wound her around the roller so that you couldn't see her until the tapestry was done.'

'Unless you unwound her for me, Mademoiselle.'

'Papa unwinds tapestries for no one,' Aliénor replied sharply. 'It ruins the tension in the warp.' That was the answer of a *lissier's* daughter.

Nicolas smiled again. 'Well, then, I shall have to stay until you've woven her.'

213

'Is that why you've come all this way – just to see a strip of tapestry?' I said. 'That is a long trip for a woman's face.'

Nicolas shook his head. 'I have business with you, on behalf of Léon Le Vieux.'

I frowned. What could Léon want now? He knew I was too busy for other commissions. And why send this artist rather than come himself? The weavers were all looking at me. Whatever it was, I wanted them working, not listening. 'Come into the garden, then,' I said, 'so you can see Aliénor's flowers. We can talk there.'

I led the way. As Nicolas followed me through the doorway to the garden, Aliénor stepped aside to let us pass. 'Go and help your mother,' I said as she began to follow us. Now it was her turn to look crestfallen, but of course she did as I ordered.

Aliénor's garden is at its best in May. The flowers are fresh and new, not yet faded by the sun. Solomon's seal, periwinkle, violets, columbine, daisies, carnations, forget-me-nots – they were all blooming. Best of all, Aliénor's lily of the valley had its brief flowers, and its strange seductive smell was everywhere. I sat on a bench while Nicolas wandered for a few minutes, sniffing and admiring.

'I had forgotten how beautiful this garden is,' he said as he came back to me. 'It's like a healing balm, especially after many days on the road.'

'What's brought you here, then?'

Nicolas laughed. 'As abrupt as ever.'

I shrugged. My hands were twitching – they needed to be weaving. 'I am a busy man. We've much to do yet.'

Nicolas reached out and plucked a daisy. Aliénor hates people picking her flowers – they're trouble enough to grow without killing them. He began to twirl the bud between his fingers. 'That's why I'm here,' he said finally. 'Jean Le Viste is concerned about getting his tapestries on time.'

That damned merchant, poking around the workshop back during Lent. I knew he was spying for Léon Le Vieux, though he said he was keen to commission me. I hadn't heard from him since.

There was a rustle behind me – Aliénor was crouching in the herb bed with a pair of kitchen shears. She was trying not to be seen, but a blind girl is never good at hiding. 'What are you doing there, girl?' I growled. 'I told you to help your mother.'

'I am,' Aliénor faltered. 'She wanted chervil for the soup.'

Her mother had sent her to listen. I know my wife – she doesn't like to be excluded. I didn't send Aliénor back – she and Christine would know soon enough anyway. 'Don't repeat what you hear,' I said to her. 'Not to weavers, nor the neighbours, nor anyone.'

She nodded and began to cut herbs into her apron.

'It's nothing to be worried about,' I said to Nicolas. 'We did fall behind during the winter because of illness, but we're catching up now. We'll have them done for next Easter as Monseigneur Le Viste has asked.'

Nicolas cleared his throat and squatted to sniff at some carnations and finger their petals. There was something more he wanted to say, I knew, but he was taking his time about it. When Christine appeared with mugs of beer he looked relieved. 'Ah, thank you, Madame,' he cried, jumping up and stepping forward to meet her.

Normally Christine would send Madeleine or Aliénor to serve the beer, but this time she had come herself, hoping to hear the news from Nicolas rather than later, second hand, from me. I took pity on her. 'Sit,' I said, making room on the bench next to me. Christine might as well hear it too. Whatever it was, it would not be good. We faced Nicolas on the bench, with Aliénor clipping quietly behind us, and waited.

When Nicolas finally got to it – after drinking from his beer and admiring more flowers – he said it bluntly. 'Jean Le Viste wants his tapestries by Candlemas.'

Aliénor stopped rustling behind us.

'That's impossible!' Christine cried. 'We're working flat out as it is – every moment God gives us.'

'Can you hire more people?' Nicolas suggested. 'Put three weavers on each loom?'

'No,' I answered. 'We can't afford to pay another weaver – if we did that we'd be losing money. I'd be paying Jean Le Viste for the privilege of making the tapestries.'

'If you finish them sooner you can begin other work sooner, and that will bring you money.'

I shook my head. 'I have nothing spare to pay anyone – I wouldn't be able to hire a weaver without paying him something first.'

Nicolas made a futile gesture with his hands. 'Jean Le Viste wants them by Candlemas and is sending soldiers to collect them then. If they aren't done he'll have them seized and not pay what's owed.'

I snorted. 'Whose soldiers?'

After a pause Nicolas said quietly, 'The King's.'

'But the contract says Easter,' Christine said. 'He can't break that.'

I waved away her words. Nobles can do what they like. Besides, Léon still held over me the threat of the Magi's green hose. If I had to pay a fine for them, I would certainly be ruined. 'Why didn't Léon come himself?' I said with a scowl. 'I would prefer to discuss this with him.'

Nicolas shrugged. 'He was too busy.'

Aliénor's rustling stopped again. My daughter is like me in judging people. She has an ear for lies, as I have an eye for them. She heard something in his voice, just as I saw the lie in his eye as it cast about but did not meet mine. He was leaving out part of the story. I didn't ask him, though, for I suspected I wouldn't get it out of him here – perhaps later, in a place where he felt more at home.

'We'll talk more later,' I said. 'At Le Vieux Chien.' I turned to Christine. 'Is dinner ready?'

She jumped to her feet. 'Soon.'

I left him in the garden to finish his beer and went back to the workshop. I did not start weaving again, but stood in the doorway and watched the weavers. They were leaning over their work and sitting very still, like four birds lined up along a tree branch. Occasionally one would push the pedals to shift the threads and change the shed, but apart from that clunk of wood, it was quiet.

Christine came to stand next to me. 'You know what we have to do,' she said in a low voice.

'We can't,' I answered as quietly. 'Apart from breaking

Guild rules, it's hard on the eyes, and the candles drip onto the tapestries. The wax is hard to get out, and leaves an easy clue for any Guild member who wants to make a fuss.'

'I didn't mean that. No one weaves well at night – not even you.'

'You want us to weave on Sundays? I'm surprised you would suggest such a thing. Though perhaps you could bribe the priest – you've got his ear.'

'That's not what I meant either. Of course we don't weave Sundays – they're sacred.'

'What do you mean, then?'

Christine's eyes were bright. 'Let me weave *millefleurs* and Georges Le Fils can do the harder parts along with you.'

I was silent.

'As you said, we can't afford to pay another weaver,' she continued. 'But you have me. Use me, and let your son do what he is able to do.' She looked hard at me. 'You've taught him well. Now it's time to let him be his own weaver.'

She was trying to make that be what mattered, but I knew what was really behind her words – she wanted to weave.

'*Écoute*, I'm hungry,' was all I said. 'Isn't the meal ready yet?'

Directly after the bells rang to end the day's work I took Nicolas to Le Vieux Chien. I didn't much fancy being among loud men, but it might be a better place to haggle with him over Jean Le Viste's demands. Georges Le Jeune came with us, and I sent Luc to fetch Philippe as well. We had not made a night of it in some time.

'Ah,' Nicolas sighed, looking around and smacking his lips as he drank. 'Brussels beer and Brussels company. How could I forget this? Taverns like graves where they serve water and call it beer. For this I've travelled ten days on bad roads?'

Myself I was glad it was quiet. 'It will be livelier later. You'll have your fun.'

Georges Le Jeune wanted to know about Nicolas' journey – how his horse was to ride, who rode with him, where he stayed. He's much taken by the thought of other places, though when he has come with me to Antwerp or Bruges he's slept poorly, eaten little and been fearful of strangers. Always he's happy to return home. He says he wants to see Paris one day, but I know he will never go.

'Did you meet thieves on the road?' Georges Le Jeune asked now.

'No, nothing more than mud got in our way – mud and a lame horse.'

'Then how did you get that?' Georges Le Jeune pointed at the yellowish bruises around Nicolas' eye. 'And you've hurt your side.'

Nicolas shrugged. 'There was a brawl in one of the taverns where I drink in Paris. I got caught up in it, though it was naught to do with me.' He turned to me. 'How is Aliénor?' he asked. 'Is her trousseau coming on?'

I frowned. What could he know about Aliénor's trousseau? Only Christine and Georges Le Jeune knew of the agreement I'd made with Jacques Le Bœuf. Christine had insisted that we tell our son so that he would know what to expect when he took over the workshop. He had told no one else, though – he can keep secrets.

Before I could think what to answer, Philippe arrived with Luc. 'We didn't expect you back,' he said to Nicolas as he sat down. 'You painted so fast last summer I was sure you were glad to go. I thought you vowed never to leave Paris again.'

Nicolas smiled. 'I have business with Georges, and I wanted to see how the tapestries are coming on. Of course it's always a pleasure to see Christine and Aliénor. I was just asking Georges about her.' He turned to me again. 'How does she fare?'

'Aliénor is very busy now,' I said curtly. 'She sews the tapestries long into the night so that she won't be in our way during the day.'

'Then you have an advantage over the other workshops,' Nicolas said. 'If she could see she would never be able to sew in the dark. But being blind, she can work all night and not just between the bells. You may be grateful that Aliénor is such a help.'

I had not thought of it that way.

'Of course she has no time to work on her trousseau, then,' Nicolas added. Philippe started. I suppose anyone would – no one expects Aliénor to marry.

'My daughter isn't worrying about a trousseau, but about these tapestries, like all of us,' I muttered. 'And now that we're to lose two months it'll be even worse.' I had not meant to blurt it out, but Nicolas annoyed me so that I couldn't help it.

220

Georges Le Jeune stared at me. 'Why are we to lose yet more time? As it is we're behind.'

'Ask Nicolas.'

Everyone – my son, Luc, Philippe and I – looked at Nicolas, who squirmed and gazed into his beer. 'I don't know,' he said at last. 'Léon said only that Jean Le Viste wants the tapestries earlier, not why he wants them.'

If he didn't know even that, there was little we could haggle over.

'Léon must know,' I said, my voice full of scorn. 'He knows everything. Why didn't he come himself? Don't tell me he's too busy – that's never stopped him before, not when it's Jean Le Viste's business.'

Nicolas looked at me defiantly – clearly he does not like to be held in contempt. He raised his mug and drained it of beer. We all watched as he picked up the jug and filled his mug again, then drank it down in one long pull. I dug my fingernails into my palms but kept quiet, though he was drinking me dry of beer.

Nicolas belched. 'Jean Le Viste's wife told Léon to send me. She wanted me gone from Paris.'

'What did you do to her?' Philippe asked. He has a quiet voice but we heard it well enough.

'I tried to see her daughter.'

'You fool,' I muttered.

'You wouldn't think so if you could see her.'

'He has seen her,' Philippe said. 'We all have, in Taste.'

'Now we're paying for your folly,' I said. 'If Léon were here I'd be able to talk over the terms properly. He could make Jean Le Viste see reason. But you, you're just the messenger. There's no business to be done with you.'

'I'm sorry, Georges,' Nicolas said, 'but I doubt Léon Le Vieux could have helped. Jean Le Viste is a difficult man – once he's decided on something it's not so easy to get him to change. I did once, when these tapestries were meant to be a battle. But I don't think I or even Léon could manage it again.'

'You had them changed to unicorns? I should have guessed, given how much you favour your ladies.'

'It was his wife, really. *En fait*, you should blame her. Blame the women.' He raised his mug to a whore in yellow across the room. She smiled at him. Brussels whores like strangers – they think a Paris man will pay better and be gentler. Perhaps they're right. Now they were beginning to circle Nicolas like gulls around fish guts. Myself, I was with a whore just once, before Christine, and then I'd had so much beer I couldn't remember what she did. Whores sit on my knee now and then, when there are no seats left or the night is slow. But they know there is nothing to be had from me.

'*Écoute*, Georges,' Nicolas said, 'I'm sorry about all this. I'll give you a hand in the workshop for a bit if that will help.'

I snorted. 'You –' Then I stopped. I could almost hear Christine hissing in my ear, 'Take what help we can get.' I nodded. 'A new batch of wool has arrived that needs sorting. You can help with that.'

'You've not asked about the first two tapestries,' Philippe said. 'Smell and Sound. Your Taste is not the only woman in the world, after all.'

Smell and Sound were rolled up, with rosemary tucked into them to keep out moths, and locked in a long wooden box in the corner of the workshop. I never sleep so well when there are finished tapestries in the workshop. Even with Georges Le Jeune and Luc sleeping near them, to me every footstep outside is a thief come to take them, every cooking fire a blaze that will destroy them.

'You didn't change them, did you?' Nicolas said.

'No, no, they are as we painted them. And they look very fine when hung. They are like little worlds unto themselves.'

'Is that what noblewomen do all day?' Georges Le Jeune asked. 'Play music and feed birds and wear fine jewels out in the woods?'

Nicolas snorted. 'Some of them, perhaps.' He reached for the jug and shook it. There was no sound of sloshing.

'Luc, go and get more beer,' I said. I had given up being angry at Nicolas. Perhaps he was right – Jean Le Viste wanted what he wanted, and there was naught we could do about it.

Luc grabbed the jug and went to the keeper of the barrel in the corner. As he waited for the jug to fill the whore in yellow began to talk to him, gesturing at Nicolas. Luc's eyes widened – he's not yet used to the attentions of women – and he shook his head.

'Have you ever seen a unicorn, then?' Georges Le Jeune asked.

'No,' Nicolas said. 'But I have a friend who's seen one, in woods a two days' ride from Paris.'

'Really?' I'd always thought unicorns lived far away to

the East, with the elephants. But I am ignorant in such matters, so I held my tongue.

'He said it ran very fast, like a bright white light through the trees, and that he could hardly make out its features beyond its horn – though he did say it seemed to smile at him. That's why I've made it look so content in the paintings.'

'And are the women all content as well?' Philippe said.

Nicolas shrugged.

The jug was full, but the keeper handed it to the whore rather than to Luc, who trailed behind as she hugged the jug to her chest and sauntered over to us. 'Your beer, gentlemen,' she said, planting herself in front of Nicolas and bending over to show off her bosom as she set the jug on the table. 'Any space for me here?'

'Of course,' Nicolas said, pulling her down onto the bench next to him. 'A table isn't complete without a whore or two.'

I would never say such a thing to a woman, not even a whore herself, but she in yellow just laughed. 'I'll call my friends over, then,' she said. In a moment two others had joined us and our corner became the noisiest in the tavern.

I didn't stay long after that. Whores are a young man's game. As I left the yellow whore was sitting in Nicolas' lap, one in green had her arm around a red-faced Georges Le Jeune, and a third in red was teasing Luc and Philippe.

I pissed away most of the beer on the way back. When I got in Christine was sitting up waiting for me. She didn't say anything – I knew what she wanted to hear.

'Then you will weave,' I said. 'It's the only way we can finish them. Not a word to anyone, though.'

Christine nodded. Then she smiled. Then she kissed me and pulled me towards our bed. Yes, whores are best left to the young.

ALIÉNOR DE LA CHAPELLE

I never thought I would be alone with Nicolas des Innocents again in the garden. My parents left us there, so concerned with the news Nicolas brought from Paris that Maman didn't even tell me to come away. I sat back on my heels, careful not to squash the lily of the valley growing nearby. It dangled near my legs, and whenever it brushed against them a sweet scent filled the air.

When he'd left last summer I thought Nicolas would never come back. He had been comfortable with us at first, but had suddenly stopped flirting with me and become short with Maman and Papa. At the same time he began to paint more quickly. Then one day he didn't come to the workshop, and Philippe told us that Nicolas had gone and left him to finish painting the last cartoon. Perhaps we had offended him with our plain Brussels ways. Perhaps we didn't hand out enough fair words about his work. Friends of Papa's sometimes came and stood behind him as he painted and pointed out mistakes – the unicorn looked too much like a horse, or too much like a goat, or the lion looked like a dog, or the genet like a fox, or the orange tree like a walnut tree. Nicolas hated that.

He was standing over me now. I got to my feet. I did not move away but stood very close to him – so close that I could feel the heat of his tunic, smell the leather of his horse's reins on his hands and the sweat in his hair and the sun-warmed skin of his neck.

'You look tired, beauty.'

'I'm up half the night with the sewing. Now with your news I'll be up all night.'

'I'm sorry for that. I don't like bringing bad news to anyone.'

I stepped back. 'Why did you leave without saying good-bye last summer?'

Nicolas snorted. 'You are like your father – blunt to a fault.'

I said nothing.

'I had work that took me back to Paris.'

'I can hear in his voice when a man is lying.'

Nicolas scraped his feet on the path. 'What do you care, beauty? I was just a bothersome Paris artist to you and your family.'

I smiled. 'That may be, but we expect the good grace of a farewell.'

Though I would never tell him, after he'd left I did not speak for three days. No one noticed – I am a quiet girl – except Maman, who said nothing but kissed my forehead when I finally opened my mouth again. She rarely kisses anyone.

Nicolas sighed. 'I found out things then I would rather not know. Maybe I'll tell you one day. Not now.'

Before we could say more, Maman called us in for our meal. Afterwards Nicolas went off and didn't come back till evening bells had rung the end of our work. Papa and the boys took him off to the tavern while Maman sewed Taste and I sewed À Mon Seul Désir. We were very quiet – Maman was worrying about the tapestries, and didn't even ask what I thought of Nicolas returning to us.

Later Papa came back and he and Maman went into the house while I stayed up sewing. Much later, Georges Le Jeune and Luc returned. Luc was very sick with the beer and kept going out into the street.

I didn't want to ask but couldn't help myself. 'Didn't Nicolas come with you?' I said to Georges Le Jeune, who had thrown himself down onto his pallet near my feet. He smelled of beer and smoke from the tavern fire and – I wrinkled my nose – a cheap flower water the whores buy from the market.

My brother laughed – loudly, as he'd drunk too much to know he was being loud. I shushed him so that he wouldn't wake our parents or Madeleine. 'He's not likely to be back tonight. He's found his own pallet, and it's yellow.' Georges Le Jeune began to laugh again.

I got up and stepped over him towards the house. I would rather go to my bed than stay in the workshop with his stink and silliness, no matter how much sewing there was yet to do. I would get up early and work while the men were still asleep.

Nicolas didn't return till late the next morning, when we'd already been working many hours, except for Luc, who'd been so sick that he was still no use to us, and was asleep in the house. The weavers were at the looms. Maman and I were working with the batch of new wool that had just arrived – some of it for the tapestries we were weaving now, the rest to be prepared for the last two tapestries. Maman was sorting it, using a waist-high wooden mill to wind the wool thread into hanks, then hanging those by colour on rollers. I was preparing bobbins by pulling strands of thread together from the rollers and winding them onto the little wooden sticks, ready for the weavers to use.

'Where is he?' Maman kept saying as she pulled at the wool.

Papa didn't seem bothered. 'He'll come when he's ready.'

'We need him now.'

I didn't know why she was so angry. Nicolas owed us nothing, nor did we need him. If he wanted to sleep the morning away with his whore, that was his choice. We did not have to care where he was.

Then he arrived, stinking almost as much as Jacques Le Bœuf. He was still merry after a night at Le Vieux Chien, where others were silent with their sore heads. He thumped Papa and Georges Le Jeune on their backs and called out to Maman and me.

'Did you know,' he said, 'that Philippe is now a man of the flesh? He found his way with a whore last night, or rather, she showed him the way, He'll know what he's doing now.' Those last words seemed to be aimed like an arrow that flew straight across the room at me. I bowed my head over the bobbin and wound faster.

Maman put her hand over mine to slow me down. I could feel her fury in her touch. 'Don't talk of such sinning in front of Aliénor,' she muttered. 'You can take your whoring straight back to Paris.'

'Christine –' Papa said.

'I won't have such muck in my house, I don't care how much we need his help.'

'Stop now,' Papa said.

Maman stopped. When Papa uses a certain voice she always does stop. He cleared his throat and I stopped winding the bobbin – he usually makes that noise when he is going to say something worth hearing.

'So, Nicolas,' Papa began, 'you said last night that you would help us for a bit. Perhaps the beer has washed away those words, so I'm repeating them for you to remember. You can help with this new batch of wool – you and Aliénor will sort it so that Christine doesn't have to. Aliénor will show you what needs doing, and you can be her eyes.'

I sat back in surprise. I didn't want him sitting next to me, smelling of other women.

Then Papa surprised us even more. 'Christine, you weave at Luc's place for the moment. When he's well again you'll take your son's place. Georges Le Jeune, you're to do the figures in À Mon Seul Désir.'

'The figures?' my brother said. 'Which parts?'

'All of them. You can start on her face once the wool is prepared. You're ready for such work without me standing over you.'

Georges Le Jeune pushed the pedals under his feet with a crash. 'Thank you, Papa.'

'Go on, Christine,' Papa said.

The bench creaked as Maman and Georges Le Jeune sat down side by side. Otherwise the room was silent.

'We have to make this change,' Papa said. 'Otherwise we'll never finish the tapestries in time. Not a word of this outside the workshop. If the Guild hears of her weaving it could fine us, or even shut down our looms. Christine will always work at the back loom by the garden door so that anyone looking in the front window won't see her. Joseph and Thomas, there'll be extra pay at the end for you to keep your mouths shut.'

Joseph and Thomas said nothing. What could they say? Their jobs depended on Maman working as well. As Papa had explained, we had no choice.

Nicolas came over to me. 'Well, beauty, what am I to do? Show me. Here are my hands.' He put his on mine. He smelled of a used bed.

I pulled my hands back. 'Don't touch me.'

Nicolas laughed. 'You're not jealous of a whore, are you? I thought you didn't even like me.'

'Maman!'

But Maman was chuckling about something with Georges Le Jeune. She had already forgotten her anger at Nicolas, she was that pleased to be weaving. I would have to fend him off alone.

I turned from him and placed my hands on the wool mill Maman had left, plucking the taut lines of thread with my fingers. 'We're winding this wool into hanks,' I said briskly. 'Then we prepare bobbins from them. *Tiens*, we'll have to unwind what Maman has done and start again. Hold here and wrap the thread around your hands while I unwind. Don't let it drop to the floor, or it will get dirty.'

Nicolas took up the thread and I began to turn the mill, faster and faster so that he couldn't keep up. 'Steady!' he cried. 'Remember, I've never handled wool. You'll have to be patient with me.'

'We've no time for you to be slow. You and Jean Le Viste have made sure of that. Keep up with me.'

'All right, beauty. As you wish.'

At first I was careful to stay as far from Nicolas as I could, and did not let our hands touch – not easy when working with wool. I didn't chatter to him, and answered his questions with few words. I was quick to find fault, and never praised him.

Instead of making him angry or aloof, my distance seemed to please him all the more. He began to call me Mistress of the Wool, and asked more questions the shorter my answers became. Even after he had learned to make a smooth hank on the wool mill he often got his threads tangled just so that I would have to help him unpick the knots and touch his fingers. He was a good pupil. Within a few days he could make hanks and prepare bobbins almost as well as Maman and me. Sometimes I could even leave him to work alone while I tended my plants – May is no time to neglect a garden.

Nicolas had a keen eye for colour and separated the wool into more hanks of different shades than Maman would have. He even noticed that a red wool lot was two lots dyed separately and mixed together so that they didn't quite match. Papa sent the whole lot back and demanded a fee of the dyer not to complain to the dyers' guild. That night he took Nicolas to the tavern again to celebrate. Nicolas didn't come back till late the next morning. This time no one scolded him. I simply handed him the bobbin I had been winding and escaped to the garden so that I wouldn't have to smell the whore on him.

Maman was less worried about Nicolas being with me now that he was staying to help us and she was able to weave. I've never known her so happy as when she was working at the loom. She paid little attention to Madeleine, nor me either unless Nicolas and I asked for her help with the wool. During the day she sat quietly at the loom, working as hard as any of the other weavers, and at night when I sewed her weaving I could feel that it was good, taut and even. In the evenings she would sit with Papa and talk about what she had done, and what more she might do. Papa never spoke much when she talked thus, except to say No when she asked to learn hachure.

Nicolas went most nights to Le Vieux Chien, though he didn't always stay out all night. Sometimes Georges Le Jeune went with him, but not Luc, who'd been put off beer that first night. Most often Nicolas went alone, though. Later I would hear him coming down the street, singing or talking to men he'd met at the tavern. I was surprised that he found his place among people here so readily. When he'd been with us last summer he was not so friendly and easy with others, but had acted the arrogant

Paris artist. Now he had men – and women too – calling for him and asking after him in the market.

I was often still sewing when he came back. I had even more work, for Maman was no longer helping – she was tired after the day's weaving and needed to save her eyes for the next day. Nicolas was staying with us this time, to save on the cost of an inn, and when he returned from the tavern he would lie on his pallet near the loom where Taste was being woven. Whenever I worked on that tapestry he was lying almost at my feet. Night after night we were together in the dark like that. We did not talk much, for I didn't want to wake Georges Le Jeune and Luc. But sometimes I could feel that he had turned towards me. If seeing is like a warp thread tied between two beams of a loom, I could feel his thread, taut.

One night Nicolas came back very late. Everyone was long abed but me. I was sewing the Lady's face in Taste, making careful stitches around one eye. The face was half done – soon enough Nicolas would get his wish to see her.

When he lay down on his pallet at my feet I felt the thread between us tighten. He wanted to say something, but didn't. The silence was very heavy. I waited until I couldn't any longer. 'What is it?' I whispered into the still room, feeling as if I were finally scratching a flea bite.

'Something I have long wanted to tell you, beauty. Since last summer.'

'The thing that made you leave?'

'Yes.'

I held my breath.

234

'Jacques Le Bœuf came to the tavern tonight.'

My mouth tightened. '*Alors?*'

'That man is a boor.'

'That is not news.'

'I can't bear to think –'

'To think what?'

Nicolas paused. I felt along the slit of the Lady's eye and jabbed my needle through.

'I heard your parents last summer, speaking of Jacques Le Bœuf. Your father has come to an agreement with him. About you.'

He was struggling but I didn't help him by speaking.

'You're to marry him. By Christmas, was the agreement – though that may change now the tapestries are needed sooner. But when they're done. By Lent, I should think.'

'I already knew that.'

'You know?'

'Madeleine told me. She heard it from my brother. They –' I waved my hand and did not finish what Georges Le Jeune and Madeleine were doing. Nicolas could guess. 'Though she said she wouldn't tell anyone, probably all of Brussels knows. But what do you care about what happens to me? I'm nothing to you – just a blind girl who can't admire your handsome face.'

'I don't like seeing a pretty girl married off to a brute, *c'est tout.*' His voice didn't sound as if that were all. I waited.

'It is strange,' he continued. 'These tapestries – it's as if they make me see women differently. Some women.'

'But they are not real women doing real things.'

Nicolas chuckled. 'They have real faces, though, some

235

of them. That's what I'm known for, after all – painting ladies' faces. And now, tapestries.'

'You've done well from these designs, *alors*?'

'Better than your father, it seems.'

'Poor Papa is being ground down by your Jean Le Viste.'

'I am sorry about that.'

We were silent for a bit. I could hear his steady breath.

'What will you do about Jacques Le Bœuf?' Nicolas said then.

Luc turned over and muttered something in his sleep.

I laughed softly. 'What can I do? I am a blind girl who's lucky to have an offer at all.'

'From a man who smells of sheep's piss.'

I shrugged, though I didn't feel so carefree.

'*Tu sais*, Aliénor, there is something you can do.'

His voice changed when he said that. I froze. I knew what he was thinking. I had thought of it myself. But it could leave me worse off than marrying Jacques Le Bœuf.

Nicolas seemed to have no doubts, though. 'Come, beauty,' he said, 'and I'll tell you the whole story of the unicorn's horn.'

I ran my fingers lightly over the tapestry's warp ridges, the rough, even beads of wool and silk tickling my fingertips, and let my hands rest there for a moment. Maman and the priest said it was a sin unless you were married but I had not heard that stop many – not even Maman. For all her saying that she and Papa married for the sake of their fathers' workshops, my brother was born only a month after they began to share a bed as man and wife. Madeleine and Georges Le Jeune didn't seem to fear their sin, nor Nicolas, nor the couples I heard in the alleys, nor the women laughing about it by the fountain or in the market.

I threaded my needle through the Lady's mouth so that I would know where to start again, then held out my hands to Nicolas. He took them, then pulled me up and lifted me from my seat, carrying me over the sleeping weavers and out to the garden. I clung to his neck and buried my nose in his warm skin. It smelled wonderful.

He laid me on a bed of flowers – daisies and carnations, forget-me-nots and columbine. I didn't care what got crushed but for the lily of the valley swinging over my face. It is hard to grow and lasts for such a short time, and its scent is so sweet. I shifted sideways away from it. Now my head was in a clump of lemon balm. It brushed my forehead and cheeks with its cool, fuzzy leaves. Luckily lemon balm springs back easily even when it's crushed.

I had never thought that I would at last be with a man and yet be fretting over my plants.

'What are you laughing at, beauty?' Nicolas said, his face hovering just above mine.

'Nothing,' I said, and put my hand up to touch him.

He pressed down on me, his legs over my hips, his chest on my breasts, his groin pushing hard into mine. I have never felt such weight on me, but I wasn't scared. I wanted him to press harder. He put his mouth on mine, his lips moving, his tongue filling my mouth so that I wanted to laugh again. It was soft and yet hard, and wet and moving. He sucked my tongue into his mouth and it was warm there, and tasted of the beer he'd been drinking, and of

237

something else that I didn't know – the taste of himself. He yanked at my dress, pulling the skirt up and the bodice down. I shivered as my skin met the cool air and his skin.

Every sense was working, all but one. I wondered what it would be like to see while doing this. From the little I knew about what went on between men and women – when I had heard Papa with Maman at night, or Georges Le Jeune with Madeleine in the garden, or when women joked in the market, or sang songs about it – I had always thought you needed eyes to enjoy it, that it was not something I could do, or only with a man like Jacques Le Bœuf and then it would hurt, and I would always dread it. But now it hurt only for a moment, when Nicolas first entered me, and then my body felt him everywhere, tasting and touching and smelling and hearing him.

'What are you looking at?' I said to Nicolas when he was pushing in and out, and we were wet between us and making sucking noises like a foot pulling out of mud.

'Nothing – my eyes are closed. It's better that way, for I feel more. It's too dark to see, anyway – there's no moon.'

So I was missing nothing. I was truly there with him, as much as anybody could be. This was a pleasure I could enjoy too, then. Something began rising in me, higher and higher with the rhythm of his pushing until I couldn't keep up with it, and I cried out as my body tensed and then released itself, a hand making a fist and then letting it go.

Nicolas clamped his hand over my mouth. 'Shhh!' he hissed, but he was laughing too. 'Do you want everyone to hear?'

238

I let out a deep breath. I was not frightened so much as surprised.

Nicolas was moving faster and making his own noises, his breathing was fast like mine, and then something hot spread out inside me. He stopped moving and slumped over me, his weight now so heavy I couldn't breathe. After a moment he rolled to the side. I heard the crunch of plants, smelled the sweetness of the lily of the valley, and knew it was crushed. But then, it was too sweet, like honey on its own without the bread to spread it on. Under the cloying scent I could smell something else, more real and like the earth. It was the bed smell I had sniffed on others, but it was fresh, like new shoots and dirt when they've been rained on.

We breathed in and out, in and out at the same time, slower and slower until we grew quiet.

'Is that what you do with your whores, then?' I said.

Nicolas snorted. 'More or less. Sometimes it's better than others. It's usually better when the woman is happy.'

I was happy.

'What's that smell?' he asked.

'Which one?'

'The sweet one. I know the other.'

'Lily of the valley. You're lying on it.'

He chuckled.

'Nicolas, I want to do it again.'

'Now?' Nicolas laughed harder. 'You'll have to give me a minute, beauty. Let me have a little rest, then I'll see what I can do.'

'Tomorrow,' I said. 'And the night after, and the night after.'

Nicolas turned his face to me. 'Are you sure, Aliénor? You know what may happen?'

I nodded. 'I know.' All of the talk, the songs, the jokes, had taught me that too. I knew what I wanted. So much had been kept from me because my eyes were broken. I would have this, and its outcome as well.

For two weeks we worked together in the workshop each day and lay together in the garden at night, crushing all of my flowers. By the end of that time the wool had been sorted, the Ladies in Taste and À Mon Seul Désir were woven, and we were done. Papa slid a mirror under Taste so that Nicolas could see the whole face of his Lady. That night he said goodbye to me in the garden. As he laid his head in my lap afterwards he said, 'Don't be sad, beauty.'

'I'm not sad,' I said, 'and I am no beauty.'

He left for Paris the next day.

CHRISTINE DU SABLON

He was a clever one, that Nicolas des Innocents. I'll give him that. He got up to mischief right under our noses and I never even guessed till long after he'd gone. The weaving must have blinded me. I was so busy keeping my eyes on my work that I didn't notice what was going on around me. I blame myself, for my sin of pride in my weaving, pride that became arrogance – that and not going to Mass at the Sablon during the week, as I'd always done before. I was neglecting Our Lady and Our Lord, and we were punished for it.

One Sunday after Mass Georges and Georges Le Jeune unrolled and hung Sound and Smell, the first two completed tapestries, for Nicolas to see. When they were ready I stood in the doorway admiring them. I did notice, however, that the Lady's hands as she plays her organ might have been better made. If only Georges had decided earlier to let me weave he would have had more time to do the hands properly. I kept this thought to myself.

'Something has made you smug, Madame,' Nicolas said just then.

I shook my head at him. 'I was just admiring my husband's skill,' I said. He continued to grin at me until I clapped my hands and stepped down from the doorway. 'That's enough gaping, now,' I said. 'Roll them up again or the moths will get them. Aliénor, cut some fresh rosemary.'

Now that Nicolas had seen the first two tapestries, and the third and fourth as they were being made, he said he wanted to look at the designs for the last two – Sight and Touch – to be sure everything was still all of a piece. So he said.

I confess I did not think much about this. Luc got out the cartoons for Nicolas and he looked at them alone in the garden while the rest of us worked. Soon after he came back in and said, 'I would like to make a change.'

'Why?' Georges said. 'They've already been agreed.'

'I want to repaint the lily of the valley, now that I've been able to see it in the flesh in Aliénor's garden.'

Behind the wool mill Aliénor giggled in a way I'd not heard from her before. That didn't tell me anything at the time, though it should have.

'We can change it when we come to weave it,' Georges said. 'Remember, weavers can change the *verdure* as they wish.'

'I'd like to anyway,' Nicolas insisted. 'I could do with a change – handling wool has made my fingers so rough I worry what women will say when they feel them.' He winked at Georges Le Jeune. Aliénor giggled again.

I frowned, but Georges just shrugged. 'As you like – the wool's almost sorted anyway. We won't be needing you much longer.'

Now that I think back on it, no one looked to see what

Nicolas did. He had proven his skill the previous summer when he painted the cartoons, and we had no time to be peeking over his shoulder. He worked on the cartoons in the garden, and when they were dry he rolled them up and stored them with the others.

His parting would have been solemn but we were too busy to think much of it. We were weaving fourteen hours a day then, with hardly a moment for meals, and I was dizzy with the pattern of the tapestry in front of me even when I wasn't weaving. I fell into bed each night and slept without moving until Madeleine woke me in the morning. There was little time left to think about a man's departure. The night before Nicolas went the men did go to the tavern, but they fell asleep over their beer. Even Nicolas came back, rather than have a last go with his yellow whore. He seemed to have gone off her those last days. Now of course I know why.

After that there was a string of unbroken summer days, one after the other, when we wove, hardly speaking. Summer days are long, with fewer feast days than other times of the year, and we were starting earlier and finishing later. Fifteen hours, sixteen hours we sat at the looms, hot and still and silent. We had stopped talking – even Joseph and Thomas no longer said much. My back ached all the time, my fingers were rubbed hard by the wool, and my eyes went red, yet I had never been happier. I was weaving.

Madeleine left us alone, bringing in beer without being asked, serving meals quickly and without fuss. Her cooking had improved since I left her to it – rather like Georges Le Jeune's weaving, which I now couldn't tell apart from his father's. Aliénor too was quiet – but then she always has been. She sewed for us and worked in her garden and helped Madeleine in the house. Sometimes she slept during the day so she could sew all night when the tapestries were free from weavers.

At the end of the summer, just after the Feast of the Birth of the Virgin, we finished. I'd known for weeks that soon we would – my fingers were slowly creeping up to the edge with different colours I was ending – green, then yellow, then red. I had thought I would celebrate, yet when I'd finished the last red edge, tied off the last bobbin, helped Aliénor to sew shut the last slit, I felt flat, like a stew with no pepper in it. The day was no different from any other.

Of course I was proud when Georges let me use the scissors for some of the cutting-off. I had never before been allowed to cut the warp threads. And when we unrolled the tapestries to see them whole for the first time, they were a joy to see. My own weaving on À Mon Seul Désir did not stand out from the others', but fitted in as if I had always been a weaver.

We had no time to rest. There were still two tapestries to weave in five months. Georges said nothing but I knew I would be weaving them too. The days were getting shorter and everyone was needed. If Aliénor had been able to see Georges would probably have had her weave too.

One Sunday after Mass we were going for a walk in the Grand Place – the only time I got out to see people now – when Aliénor grabbed my arm. 'Jacques Le Bœuf!' she hissed. Her nose was right – he was across the square, making his way to us. I confess I hadn't given the woad

244

dyer a thought all summer. We hadn't told Aliénor, nor had I stitched even a cap for her trousseau.

I moved her hand to Georges Le Jeune's arm. 'Take her to L'Arbre d'Or,' I whispered – only weavers and their families are allowed inside the weavers' guild. As my children hurried away I tucked my hand into the crook of Georges' arm and we stood close together, as if waiting for a storm to come and knock us over. We both looked up at the Hôtel de Ville, so solid and impressive with its arches and sculpture and tower. Would that we two could be so solid.

Jacques stumped up to us. 'Where's the girl gone?' he shouted. 'Always she runs from me – not much good to have a wife who runs away every time her husband comes near.'

'Shhh!' Georges hissed.

'Don't you shush me. I'm bored of keeping quiet. Haven't I kept my mouth shut all this past year? Haven't I said nothing to the market gossips who ask if I'm to marry her? Why should I keep quiet? And why shouldn't I see her? She's got to get used to me some time. It may as well be now.' He turned towards L'Arbre d'Or.

Georges grabbed his arm. 'Not there, Jacques – you know you can't go in there. And I'm only asking you to keep quiet for a little longer.'

'Why?'

Georges dropped his hand and looked at the ground. 'I haven't told her yet.'

'She doesn't know?' Jacques bellowed even louder than before. A crowd was beginning to gather, though at a spitting distance because of the smell.

I coughed. 'You must be patient with us, Jacques. As you know, we've been very busy with the tapestries, where your blue wool plays an important part. So important,' I continued, taking his arm and slowly walking him along, though my eyes filled with tears from the stench, 'that I have no doubt you will be swamped with orders for more blue once people have seen them.'

Jacques Le Bœuf's eyes gleamed for a moment – but only for a moment. 'But the girl, the girl. She'll come to me at Christmas, yes? Have you bought her bed yet?'

'I'm just going to order it tomorrow,' Georges said. 'Chestnut, I thought. We have one and it has served us well.'

Jacques chuckled in a way that made my belly turn. 'Georges will come very soon to see you about the arrangements,' I said, 'for of course we shouldn't be discussing business on the Sabbath.' I glared at him and he ducked his head. With a little more scolding I was able to get him to go, and the crowd drifted away without finding out the cause of his shouts – though from what he'd said about market gossips they already knew anyway.

Georges and I looked at each other. 'The bed,' he said.

'The trousseau,' I said at the same time.

'Where will I ever find the money for it?'

'When will I ever find the time to sew?'

Georges shook his head. 'What will he say when I tell him it won't be Christmas, but Candlemas?'

Not long after, I had answers to these questions, though not the answers I'd expected.

*   *   *

At first no one noticed. The looms were dressed for Sight and Touch, then we spent most of a day warping the looms, with Philippe and Madeleine helping. Then Georges unrolled the cartoons, ready to slide them underneath the warp. I studied the edges of the designs, checking to be sure we had the right colours ready. As I did so I glanced at the Lady in the cartoon of Sight. It took a moment for me to see it, but when I did I stepped back as if someone had thumped me in the chest. Nicolas had changed something, that was certain, and it was not just the lily of the valley.

At the same time Georges Le Jeune began to laugh. '*Regards*, Maman!' he cried. 'So that's what Nicolas was doing in the garden. You should be pleased.'

His laugh made me so angry I slapped him. Georges Le Jeune stared at me, astonished. He didn't even rub his cheek, though I'd hit him hard enough to turn it red.

'Christine!' Georges said sharply. 'What is this?'

I turned my glare to Aliénor. She was sitting on a stool, untangling thread. Of course she couldn't see what Nicolas had done to Sight.

'I was only saying to Maman that Nicolas has made her likeness in Touch,' Georges Le Jeune said. 'Then she goes and slaps me for it!'

I stared at him, then looked over at Touch. I looked for a long time. He was right – the Lady did look like me, with my long hair and long face, my pointed chin and strong jaw, and my eyebrows in high curves. I was the proud weaver's wife, smugly holding a banner in one hand, the unicorn's horn in the other. I remembered the moment he had captured, when I'd been standing in the door thinking of my weaving. Nicolas des Innocents knew me too well.

'I'm sorry,' I said to my son. 'I thought you were talking about Sight, where he has made the Lady look like Aliénor.'

Everyone looked down at Sight, and Aliénor raised her head. 'I was angry,' I lied quickly, 'because I think it cruel to have a blind girl stand for Sight.' I said nothing about the unicorn being in my daughter's lap and what that might mean. I watched Georges and the other men as they looked, but they didn't seem to notice. Men can be thick sometimes.

'It does look like you, Aliénor,' Georges Le Jeune said, 'with your crooked eyes and your crooked smile.'

Aliénor turned bright red and fumbled with the wool in her lap.

'Will we keep them like this, Papa?' Georges Le Jeune continued. 'We're not meant to change figures that have already been agreed with the patron.'

Georges was rubbing his cheek and frowning. 'We may have to use them as they are – I don't remember what the faces were like before. Do you, Philippe?'

Philippe was staring hard at the painting. Then he raised his round eyes to Aliénor, and I knew he was as troubled as I by the changed designs and what that could mean. Luckily Philippe keeps secrets – he is almost as quiet as Aliénor. 'I don't remember,' he said. 'Not enough to change them back.'

'All right, then,' Georges said. 'We'll just have to weave them like this and hope no one notices.' He shook his head. 'Damn that painter. I don't need yet another worry.'

Aliénor jerked her head at his words, and for a moment she looked as sad as the Lady in Sight. I bit my lip. Had Nicolas painted her as the Virgin who gets the unicorn only because he desired it, or had it indeed happened?

I began to watch my daughter – watch her the way I should have when Nicolas was here. I studied her with a mother's eye. She seemed no different. She was not sick in her stomach, or more tired than we all were, or having head-aches or tempers. All of these things had happened to me when I carried her and Georges Le Jeune. Nor was her waist thick or her belly round. Perhaps she had managed to escape the trap that men set for women.

In one way she did change – she wasn't as curious about things as she had been. It used to be that she was always asking me to describe something, or to tell her what I or others were doing. Now I'd begun working on her trous-seau at night when we couldn't weave. As the year grew old and the work days shorter, I wasn't so tired by the day's end and could do a bit of sewing after we ate. On nights when I worked on shirts or handkerchiefs or head-scarves to fill her chest, Aliénor didn't ask why I wasn't joining her at the tapestries, or what I was working on instead. Indeed, she seemed happy to sew alone. Some-times I would glance over at her by the wool mill, or in the garden, or helping Madeleine by the fire, or bent over the tapestry, and she was smiling a smile I hadn't seen before – that of a cat who has eaten well and found a place by the fire. Then I felt sick and knew in my heart that the trap had caught her.

It was her blindness that gave her up. Aliénor has never understood how others see her. I was forever pulling leaves from her hair or wiping grease from her chin or straightening her skirt because she didn't think of people seeing these things. So when she did at last begin to thicken, she thought her heavy winter skirt covered it but didn't know that the whole way she stood and moved had changed.

There wasn't one moment when I knew for certain she was with child. It crept over me as twilight does, so that one day in November when I saw her in the garden stepping awkwardly among the cabbages she must gather before the snows began, I simply wondered when I should tell Georges. I should've told him weeks before, of course, back when he was fretting about Aliénor's bed. Every dowry must have one, and he had been to see a carpenter, returning to worry over its cost. 'There's not a *sou* to pay him,' he told me, 'unless I use the money meant for Jacques for the last lot of wool. Jacques will be furious as it is when I tell him she can't go to him until February.'

'When will you tell her?' I asked. Aliénor still didn't know of what was planned for her.

Georges shrugged. He is no coward, but he didn't relish seeing his daughter so unhappy.

I was no coward either, but I didn't tell him what I suspected, and I didn't ask her. Of course I should have, but I didn't want to disturb what peace we had in the workshop. During those many months of weaving, Georges and I had put off problems, to see to them after the tapestries were done. Everything halted – the house was dirty, Aliénor's garden was shabby, Georges wasn't looking for new work for the next year, I wasn't going to market or keeping up with the goings-on. I am ashamed to say even our prayers were cut short, and we neglected feast days. We worked on the afternoons of All Saints' and All Souls' when we should have remained in church.

But Aliénor's problem could not wait. A baby cannot be put off to another day.

It was Thomas who spotted it. Of all the weavers his were the eyes that roamed the most, that could not stay fastened on the work under his fingers. If anyone moved about the workshop – especially Aliénor or Madeleine – his eyes followed them. One morning Aliénor stood at the side of one of the looms, handing across a bobbin of white wool to Georges, who was just beginning the Lady's face in Sight. Joseph and Thomas were on either side. As she leaned against the loom the shape of her belly was revealed to anyone who wanted to see it. No one did – save Thomas, who was sitting close to her and looking for an excuse to stop his work.

'So, Mistress of the Wool,' he said, copying Nicolas, though without the charm, 'I see you're fattening up nicely. When is the harvest?'

I pressed the pedals of the shed hard so that the whole loom clattered, but the noise couldn't cover his words. When my loom went silent the workshop was as well.

Aliénor dropped the bobbin onto the warp threads and stepped back. She pressed her hands to her sides, but that movement caught her skirt and pulled it tight across her belly so that if anyone hadn't understood Thomas before, they did now.

It seemed my husband was the longest in taking it in. When Georges weaves he's lost in his work, and doesn't leave it quickly. He stared at Aliénor but didn't seem to see her, though she stood facing him, hands clenched at her sides, head bowed. When at last he did understand, Georges looked at me, confirming his thoughts in the grim line of my mouth. He stood up, the bench creaking, Joseph and Thomas shifting away to give him room.

'Do you have something to say to me, Aliénor?' he said quietly.

'No.' Aliénor was even quieter.

'Who is the man?'

Silence.

'Who is he?'

She didn't move or speak. Her face looked broken.

Georges stepped over the bench and knocked her to the ground with one heavy blow. Like any mother, Aliénor protected her child, wrapping her arms around her belly as she fell. She struck her head against the loom bench. I stood up from my bench and went to step between them.

'No, Christine,' Georges said. I stopped. There are times when a mother cannot protect her child.

There was a movement in the doorway. Madeleine had been peeking out, and now disappeared. A moment later I saw her run past the workshop windows.

Aliénor sat up. Blood was running from her nose. Perhaps the sight of that vivid red stopped Georges' hand.

She got up unsteadily, then turned and limped across the workshop and out to the garden.

Georges looked around, at Joseph and Thomas and Georges Le Jeune and Luc all sitting in a line like judges, staring up at him. 'Go back to work,' he said.

They did, one by one bowing their heads over the tapestries.

Georges looked at me and his face was desperate. I jerked my head towards the house, and he followed me there. We stood side by side at the fire, staring down into it. Until I felt its heat I hadn't realized how cold I'd been in the workshop.

'Who do you think the father is?' Georges said. He hadn't made the connection between what the Lady in Sight was doing and what Aliénor had done. In a way I hoped he never would.

'I don't know,' I lied.

'Perhaps it's Jacques Le Bœuf himself.' Georges was trying to be hopeful.

'You know it's not. She would never do that with him.'

'What will we do, Christine? Jacques will never take her now. He'll probably never dye wool for us again. And there's the bed money I've already paid that is his.'

I thought of Aliénor shuddering in the Sablon when she spoke of Jacques Le Bœuf, and a part of me was glad she was spared sharing a bed with him, though of course I couldn't say so.

Before I could respond there were footsteps outside again, and Madeleine came in, with Philippe de la Tour behind her. I sighed – one more outsider to witness our shame and Aliénor's misery.

'Go away,' Georges said before Philippe had opened his mouth. 'We're busy.'

Philippe ignored his rude words. 'I wanted to speak to you,' he said. Then he seemed to lose his nerve. Madeleine gave him a shove. 'About – about Aliénor,' he continued.

Georges closed his eyes briefly and grunted. 'So you're busy telling everyone already, are you, girl?' he said to Madeleine. 'Why don't you go and shout it in the market? Or get Jacques Le Bœuf and lead him here by the hand, so he can see for himself what folly has gone on.'

Madeleine scowled at him. 'You are all blind,' she said. 'You never see how he loves her.' We stared at her – Madeleine never talks back. And could she be talking of Jacques Le Bœuf? He was not the kind of man who loved anyone.

'Leave her be, Georges – Madeleine means well,' Philippe said, his voice full of fear. 'I've not come to mock. It's just –' He stopped, as if terror were choking him.

'What is it, then? What use can you be to us now?'

'I – I am the father.'

'You?'

Philippe looked at me wildly. In a flash I understood. I held his eyes and nodded slightly so that he would take courage and go on. Madeleine must be right – Philippe loved Aliénor. Now he was going to help her – her and us too.

Philippe gulped and kept his eyes on my face to steady him. 'I am the father, and I would take Aliénor for my wife, if she'll have me.'

PHILIPPE DE LA TOUR

My wife is a quiet woman. That is no bad thing – quiet women don't gossip and aren't as likely to be gossiped about.

Nonetheless, I wished she would talk more to me.

She said nothing when we married except to answer the priest. She never spoke of the baby she carried, nor of Nicolas. She never thanked me. Once I told her I was glad to have saved her. 'I saved myself,' she answered, and turned her back.

We weren't living with my parents yet, and wouldn't until the tapestries were done. They needed her to sew at night, not to lie with me. Though we'd knelt before the priest at the Sablon, we hadn't lain together yet, to do the things I learned from the whore in the summer. Aliénor was too big, and not yet willing. All in time, I hoped.

When Georges and Christine went to see Jacques Le Bœuf, they told me to stay with neighbours until it was safe. I refused – I can't hide from him all my life. They never said what it was like to tell him Aliénor was to be my wife, but a few days later I saw him for myself. He spotted me across the market on the Place de la Chapelle as I was buying walnuts, and bellowed. There was time for me to run but I stood still and watched him charge towards me like a bull. I should have been scared but all I could think of was Aliénor's crooked smile. She smiled little enough for me, and she never would have done for this smelly brute. Even with him coming for me now, I was glad I'd saved her.

Everything went black after he knocked me flat. When I woke I was lying in the snow – the first of the winter – with walnuts scattered about and Jacques Le Bœuf standing over me. I gazed at the tall filigreed windows of the Chapelle that loomed behind him and wondered if he would kill me. But in truth he is a simple man, with simple needs. Flattening me was enough. He leaned over and growled, 'Take her, then. What use is a wife with no eyes? I'll marry my cousin and she'll be more help to me.'

I wasn't going to argue with him. I couldn't, anyway – the smell of him made everything go black again. When I next woke he was gone and they were carrying me along the rue Haute to Georges' house. Aliénor herself washed my bruises, holding my head against the bulge in her lap. She said nothing when I asked what had happened. Only when I asked what the plant in the water was did she speak. 'Vervain,' she said. It was only one word, but the sound of it was like music.

Jacques Le Bœuf left me alone after that, but insisted that Georges pay him immediately for the last lot of blue wool or he'd not supply it. Georges had already given the money meant for Jacques to a carpenter for Aliénor's dowry bed. There I was able to help him – my first useful act as his son-in-law. I had a cousin soon to marry and I convinced her parents to buy the chestnut bed, and so Georges got his money back from them. Aliénor and I could wait for a bed.

Helping him with that made things a little less awkward with Georges – though I still caught him glaring at me sometimes. Or he would look puzzled, wondering how I could've been with Aliénor without him knowing, and why I would do it. He had trusted me once, but now he didn't know what to think. He had to accept me as his son-in-law, but instead of welcoming me into the family he was offhand and uneasy.

Georges Le Jeune too was funny with me, and less friendly than before, even though we were now brothers. Thomas and Luc liked to snigger and tease me – that was no surprise. At least they left Aliénor alone. No one said anything to her about it.

It was all easier to bear because Christine was kind to me. She was clear in accepting me as family, and that made the others hold in check whatever they were feeling. No one seemed to guess what had really happened, even as a clue pointing to it sat in the threads right under their noses. Good weavers as they all are, perhaps they were too close to their work to see it properly. They never thought of Nicolas – they assumed the unicorn was me. It was easier that way.

But then, there was little time to ponder such things, for there was little time left to finish Sight and Touch. The days were short and dark. Sometimes it felt as if the bells of the Chapelle had only just rung to start the day when they rang again to end it, with little to show for it in the weaving. The cold didn't help. Tapestry workshops are especially cold because the windows and doors must be left open for the light and there are no fires for fear of sparks. Many workshops close or cut down on work during the coldest months, but of course Georges could not. Although it was only the Advent, already it was as cold as if the Epiphany were long gone. Madeleine put buckets of coals from the fire at the weavers' feet but they made little difference. Nor could the weavers wear heavy clothes around their arms or shoulders, for that got in the way of their work. They did wear fingerless gloves Christine had knitted out of extra bits of wool, but they still got chilblains on the tips of their fingers.

Georges took the short days especially hard. The months of worry over the work had marked him. Dark rings grew under his eyes, themselves crisscrossed with red. Overnight it seemed his hair turned completely grey. He hunched his shoulders and did not speak much or with cheer. Christine wouldn't let him work on Sundays, but he was so tired that he slept as he sat during Mass at the Sablon. No one tried to wake him, even when he was meant to stand or kneel. The priest said nothing. He along with everyone else knew the workshop was in trouble.

I came most days to the workshop to help. There were no cartoons for me to draw elsewhere – *lissiers* rarely get new commissions in the winter, when no one travels up from Paris and elsewhere. Besides, I wanted to be there, even just to be near my wife. Aliénor helped Madeleine, or sewed the tapestries when there was space for her. But much of the time she and I were like cats roaming through alleys in search of scraps to keep us busy. It was painful to watch others work so hard and not be able to do so as well. I envied Christine's industry, though it was still a shock to see her weaving tapestries that were meant to be passed by the Guild. Of course I said nothing. I was family now, and kept family secrets.

There was little celebration over Christmastide. We had the Eve feast at least, though food was scarce and dull, with no money for meat or cakes or wine. Only Joseph and Thomas did not work on the Feast of St Stephen. Christine did go to Mass for the Holy Innocents, and insisted everyone go to the Sablon for the Epiphany, but afterwards we worked rather than feasted. By then even Joseph and Thomas weren't joining the merriment in the streets, for they were close to finishing Touch and wanted the work done at last.

They pulled ahead of the other weavers – though it was no game, and no winners – because of a problem with Sight. One day Georges looked over the tapestry and frowned at the leaves of an oak tree Christine had been weaving. 'You've left out a bit of branch. See, it ends there and begins again there, with leaves where there should be wood.'

Christine stared at her work. The other weavers were silent. Georges Le Jeune came over to look. 'Does it matter?' he said, peering at the leaves. 'No one will even notice.'

Georges gave him a look, then said, 'Move, Christine.' She

went to stand by Aliénor at the wool mill, and wept as he began to unpick her weaving. I had never seen her cry.

'*Bonjour*!' We all turned to look at the head poking through the workshop window. It was another *lissier*, Rogier Le Brun, come to check on the workshop for the Guild. Georges had made such unexpected visits himself to other workshops – that way the Guild assured its members kept to its rules, *lissiers* didn't cheat, and the quality of Brussels tapestries remained high.

I didn't know how long Rogier Le Brun had been there watching us. If he had seen Christine weaving there could be trouble. Certainly he had seen her crying and would wonder why. We were all thinking that as Christine wiped her eyes on her sleeve and hurried to join her husband in greeting the *lissier*. 'Of course you will take some beer, and there are some spiced cakes left from the Epiphany. Madeleine!' she called as she stepped towards the house, Rogier Le Brun protesting feebly at the food and drink. He must know how hard up the workshop was. Those cakes were a gift from a pitying neighbour.

'Madeleine is out,' I whispered to Aliénor, who quickly handed me the wool she'd been winding and went to help her mother. Rogier Le Brun's eyes followed her as she crossed the workshop, belly straining at her dress. When she was gone he looked at me for a moment, as if trying to guess how a shy man like me could have managed such a thing. My face went hot with shame.

'Ripping out work, eh?' Rogier Le Brun said, turning to the oak Georges had been unpicking in the tapestry. 'The apprentice make a mess of things as usual, hmm?' He

tapped Luc's head lightly. Luc glared up at him but merci-
fully did not deny it. He is a bright boy and knows when
to keep quiet. Rogier Le Brun narrowed his eyes and turned
back to Georges. 'I sympathize, Georges. There is nothing
worse for a *lissier* than pulling out work. But for tapestries
like these, every bead must be good, eh? It won't do to
have weavers who can't weave well work on it. The Guild
wouldn't pass the work, would they?'

The room was silent. 'Luc has made very few mistakes,'
Georges mumbled.

'Of course not – I'm sure you've trained him well. But
this will put you back, *n'est-ce pas*, just when you need the
time most. When must the tapestries be done?'

'Candlemas.'

'Candlemas? How can you finish by then?'

Before Georges could answer, Christine had reappeared
with mugs of beer. 'Don't you worry about us, Rogier,'
she interrupted. 'We'll manage. Look, the other tapestry is
almost done, and then the weavers can move across to
this one.'

Thomas snorted. 'For more pay, perhaps.'

Rogier Le Brun was barely listening. I could see him
considering the work left to do, the number of weavers –
would he count Christine among them? – and the time
there was left to do it in. We all watched him do his
figuring. The bench the weavers sat on creaked as they
shifted about. I shuffled my feet. Despite the cold, Georges'
brow dripped with sweat.

Christine folded her arms across her chest. 'We will
manage,' she repeated, 'as I expect you will manage when

Georges pays you a visit on the Guild's behalf.' She smiled at him.

There was a short silence as Rogier Le Brun took in her reminder of how Guild men help each other. He gazed at her, and I could see his Adam's apple move as he swallowed.

Aliénor came out then and stepped lightly to his side. 'Please, Monsieur, try one,' she said, and held a plate of cakes in front of him.

With that Rogier Le Brun laughed. 'Georges,' he said, biting into a cake, 'you may have problems in the workshop but your women make up for it!'

When he had gone Georges and Christine looked at each other. 'Georges, I think St Maurice must be watching over us,' she declared, shaking her head. 'If I hadn't woven that oak poorly, I'd still have been weaving when Rogier came. And if he had caught me at it outright, he could not have turned a blind eye.'

Georges smiled for the first time in many weeks. It was like ice cracking on a pond after a long winter, an evil spell breaking. The boys laughed and began mimicking Rogier, and Christine went for more beer. Myself, I stepped over to Aliénor and kissed her brow. She did not lift her head, but she did smile.

Two weeks before Candlemas, the weavers finished Touch. The cutting-off from the loom was not the drawn-out ceremony Georges Le Jeune, Joseph and Thomas might have liked, but quick and cursory. When the tapestry was unwound and turned over, Georges nodded and praised the work, but his thoughts were in his fingers, and his fingers wanted to be weaving. Christine saw their dis- appointment, however, and after her nudge Georges gave them his last *sous* to drink away at the tavern.

Georges Le Jeune moved over to join his father and Luc at the loom of Sight, and Christine left it to make the hem of Touch. She and Aliénor folded the ends of the warp threads under, then began to sew a piece of woven brown wool around the edges to finish it. As I sat near Aliénor, watching her and Christine sew, I said suddenly, 'Show me how to do that.'

Christine chuckled and Aliénor wrinkled her brow. 'Why? You're a painter, not a woman.'

'I want to help.' You're my wife – I would sit with you, I wanted to say.

'Why don't you find your own work?'

Then I had an idea. 'If you teach me I can help you with the hemming and Christine will be free to work with the others.'

Christine looked at Georges. After a moment he nodded.

'All right,' she said, poking her needle through the wool and getting up. 'Aliénor will show you how to do it.'

'Maman,' Aliénor said then. She sounded annoyed.

Christine turned to look at her. 'He's your husband, girl. You'd best get used to that and be grateful for it. Think of the alternative.'

Aliénor bowed her head. Christine gave me a little smile and I thanked her with my eyes.

Aliénor wouldn't let me sew the hem straight away, but

made me practise on a scrap of cloth. It was simple enough sewing, yet I couldn't get the stitches as even as hers, and kept pricking my fingers till Aliénor laughed. 'Maman, we'll never finish this if you let Philippe work on it. I'll be always ripping out his work and starting again. Or he'll bleed all over it!'

'Give him a chance,' Christine said without looking up. 'He may surprise you.'

After a day of errors I began to improve, and at last Aliénor allowed me to work on the hem, though I sewed much more slowly than she. We didn't speak much at first as we worked, but sitting together for so many hours seemed to make things easier between us. Silence is always a tonic for her. Then, gradually, we began to talk – of the cold, or the hem we sewed, or the pickled walnuts we'd had at dinner. Little things.

We were almost done with the hem when I got up the courage to ask about something bigger. I looked over at the enormous bump in her lap that she rested her hands upon like a table, with the tapestry pulled over it. 'What will we name the baby?' I said quietly so the others wouldn't hear.

Aliénor stopped sewing, her needle paused over the cloth. Because her eyes are dead it's hard to know what she's thinking by looking at her face. You have to listen for her voice. I waited a long time. When she answered her tone was not as sad as I'd expected. 'Etienne, for your father. Or Tiennette if it's a girl.'

I smiled. '*Merci*, Aliénor.'

My wife shrugged. She did not begin sewing again,

though. She threaded the needle through the seam and left it there. Then she turned to me. 'I would like to feel your face, so that I will know what my husband is like.'

I leaned over and put her hands on my cheeks. She began rubbing and squeezing my face all over. 'Your chin is pointed like my cat's!' she cried. She likes her cat – I have seen her sit with it in her lap and stroke it for hours.

'Yes,' I said. 'Like your cat.'

A week before Candlemas Georges finished the last curve of the lion's tail. Three days before Candlemas first Christine, then Luc reached the edge of the tapestry. Georges was still working on a rabbit – his signature, of a rabbit holding its paw to its cheek – while Georges Le Jeune finished a dog's tail. Aliénor joined her father and brother on the bench to sew slits then, though her belly was so huge it kept her far from the tapestry. As I watched, she stopped for a moment, hands pressed against her belly, her brow furrowed. Then she began to sew again. Several minutes later she did the same thing and I knew the birth was beginning.

Unless she said something herself she would not want me to say anything about it. Instead I drew Christine aside and quietly showed her. 'We weren't expecting this for a few weeks yet – she's early,' Christine commented.

'Shouldn't she be in bed?' I said.

Christine shook her head. 'Not yet. There'll be plenty of that later. It could be days yet. Let her work if she wants – it'll take her mind off the pain.'

And so Aliénor sewed for many hours that day, long after it was dark and the weavers had stopped. Even when everyone was asleep she kept sewing. I stayed awake, lying on a pallet and listening to her shift and tense on the bench. At last, very late in the night she moaned, 'Philippe, get Maman.'

They put her in bed in the house, and Georges came to sleep in the workshop. In the morning Christine sent Luc for the midwife. Soon he burst back into the workshop. 'Jean Le Viste's soldiers are here!' he cried. 'I heard when I was out. They've gone to the Guild in the Grand-Place to ask after you.'

Georges and Georges Le Jeune looked up from their work. 'It's not Candlemas for two days yet,' Georges said. He looked down at their hands. 'We'll be done today but there's the hemming yet to do and the women are busy.' He glanced at the house – from inside came a long groan ending in a shout.

'I can hem it,' I said quickly, pleased to be of use at last.

Georges looked at me. '*Bon*,' he said. For the first time since Aliénor and I married I felt I was a useful part of the workshop.

'Don't fret, lad,' Georges added to Luc, who was hopping from one foot to the other. 'The soldiers will wait. *Tiens*, go and tell Joseph and Thomas to come this afternoon for the cutting-off – they'll want to be here. We can't wait on the women.' Another moan from inside made him and Georges Le Jeune duck their heads over their work and Luc run from the workshop.

She was screaming by the time we cut Sight from its

loom. A cutting-off is meant to be joyful, but her screams drove us to cut as fast as we could. Only when we'd turned over the tapestry and seen it whole for the first time was I distracted from Aliénor's cries.

Georges looked at it and began to laugh. It was as if he had been holding his breath for months and suddenly could let it out. While Georges Le Jeune and Luc and Thomas began thumping each other on the back, Georges laughed and laughed, Joseph joining him. They laughed so hard they had to prop each other up, tears pouring from their eyes. It was a strange response to a long journey, but I too found myself laughing. We had indeed been travelling a long way.

Aliénor screamed again, and everyone stopped. Georges wiped his eyes, looked at me and said, 'We'll be at Le Vieux Chien. Let me know when the baby comes, or the soldiers – whichever is first.' Then, after almost two years of work that gave him a head of grey hair, a stoop and a squint, the *lissier* walked away from the tapestry without even looking back. I think he was glad not to.

When they were gone I studied Sight for a long time. The Lady is sitting, and the unicorn lies in her lap. You might think that they love each other. Perhaps they do. But the Lady holds up a mirror and the unicorn may well be looking at itself with eyes of love rather than at the Lady. Her eyes are crooked in her face, her lids heavy. Her smile is full of woe. It may be that she does not even see him.

That is what I think.

I was pleased that Georges trusted me with the hem.

I got out the brown wool and a needle and thread, and carefully folded the warp threads under as I'd seen Aliénor and Christine do. Then I sat by the window and made a stitch, then another. I sewed as slowly as if I were counting the hairs on a sleeping baby's head. Each time Aliénor screamed I gritted my teeth and quelled my shaking hands.

I'd sewed half of one side of the tapestry when the screaming stopped. I stopped too, and simply sat and waited. Though I should have prayed, I was too frightened to do even that.

At last Christine appeared in the doorway with a bundle of soft linen in her arms. She smiled at me.

'Aliénor?' I said.

Christine laughed at the look on my face. 'Your wife is fine. All women scream like that. That's what birth is. But don't you want to know? We have a new weaver here.' She held up her grandson. His face was squashed and red, and he had no hair.

I cleared my throat and held out my arms for Etienne. 'You've forgotten who his father is,' I said. 'He will be a painter.'

V

PARIS

Septuagesima 1492 ·

NICOLAS DES INNOCENTS

I have never liked the weeks leading up to Lent. It's cold – a cold gone on far too long, a cold that has entered every part of my body. I am tired of the chilblains and the bones that creak, and the way I hold my body tight because if I let go I grow even colder. There is little food, and what is left is dull – pickled and salted and dried and hard. I long for fresh lettuce, for fresh game, for a plum or a strawberry.

I don't work much during Septuagesima – my hands are stiff with the cold and can't hold a brush. Nor do I find women to please me then. I am waiting. I prefer Lent, even with its rigours. At least it grows warmer and lighter with each day, even if there is still little to eat.

One bitter morning, when I was shivering under many blankets and wondering whether I should bother getting up, I had a message to meet Léon Le Vieux at Saint-Germain-des-Prés. I didn't go there now, for fear of seeing Geneviève de Nanterre. I had little fear, and no hope, of seeing her daughter there. A friend who kept an ear out for me on the rue du Four – where I dared not show my face – said that Claude had been sent away the previous summer, none of the servants knew where. Béatrice too had disappeared.

I wrapped myself in all my clothes and hurried south, crossing the frozen Seine over the Ponts au Change and St Michel. I didn't stop in at Notre Dame – it was too cold even for that. When I got to Saint-Germain-des-Prés I looked around inside the church cautiously, wondering if I might find Geneviève de Nanterre on her knees there. But no one was about – it was between masses and too cold for lingering.

At last I found Léon out in the withered cloisters garden. Little was growing at that time of year, though there were a few snowdrops, and other shoots pushing through the mud. I didn't know what they would grow into. Aliénor had tried to teach me about plants, but I needed more than a green nub to tell me what it would become.

Léon Le Vieux walks with a stick in winter to help him over the snow and ice. He was using it now to poke at the lavender and rosemary bushes. He looked up. 'I'm always surprised how hardy these are in winter, even when everything else is dead.' He reached over and plucked some leaves from each, then squeezed them and put his fingers to his nose. 'Of course they don't smell so sweet now – that comes with sun and warmth.'

'Then too it depends on the gardener, *non*?'

'Perhaps.' Léon Le Vieux dropped the leaves and turned to me. 'Jean Le Viste's tapestries have arrived.'

At the news I felt an unexpected surge of joy. 'So Georges did finish them by Candlemas! Did you see him?'

Léon Le Vieux shook his head. 'I refuse to travel on such roads in winter, even if the King himself asked me. At my age I should be sitting by the fire, not riding all night through snow and muck to bring tapestries back to Paris in time. I want to die in my own bed, not in a filthy inn on the road. No, I sent a message with the soldiers and had a Brussels merchant I know check on the work. And of course the weavers' guild there approved them – that is the important thing.'

'Have you seen them yet? How do they look?'

Léon Le Vieux gestured with his stick and began to walk towards the archway leading out. 'Come along to the rue du Four and you can see for yourself.'

'Am I welcome?'

'Monseigneur Le Viste has had them hung, and wants you to check them to make sure the height is right.' He looked back at me and added, '*Écoute*, behave yourself there.' Then he laughed.

Even in my drunkest fantasies during sessions at Le Coq d'Or, I'd never dreamed I would be invited to pass easily through the door of Claude Le Viste's house. There I was, though, with the sour-faced steward letting us in. If I had not been with Léon Le Vieux I would have gone for him, to pay him back for the beating he'd given me. Instead I had to follow meekly in his footsteps as he led us to the Grande Salle, then left us there to fetch his master.

I stood in the middle of the room, with Léon Le Vieux at my side, and looked back and forth from one Lady to another, my eyes darting about the room, trying to take them in all at once. I looked for longer than I have ever looked at anything. Léon too was very still and silent. It was as if we were frozen in a dream. I was not sure I wanted to be woken.

When at last Léon shifted his feet, I opened my mouth to say something and laughter came out instead. It was not the response I'd expected to have. Yet I kept thinking, How could I ever have worried about dog-like lions and fat unicorns and oranges that looked like walnuts when these Ladies were here? They were all of them beautiful, peaceful, content. To stand among them was to be part of their magical, blessed lives. What unicorn would not be seduced by them?

It was not just the Ladies who made the tapestries so powerful, but the *millefleurs* as well. Whatever faults there were in the designs got lost in that blue and red field filled with thousands of flowers. I felt as if I were standing in a summer field even in the midst of a cold dark day in Paris. It was those *millefleurs* that made the room whole, pulling together the Ladies and their unicorns, the lions and servants, and me too. I felt I was with them.

'What do you think?' Léon asked.

'Glorious. They are even better than I ever dreamed I could make them.'

Léon chuckled. 'I see your pride has not lessened. Remember, you were only one part of their making. Georges and his workshop deserve the highest praise.' It was the sort of thing Léon Le Vieux liked to say.

'Georges will do very well from them.'

Léon shook his head. 'They won't make him a rich man – Jean Le Viste is stingy with his purse. And from what I heard, Georges may not be so quick to take on more work. My Brussels merchant said he only saw Georges either drunk or asleep, and he squints now. Indeed, it was the cartoonist who had to help Christine sew the hem of the last tapestry – Georges was drunk and the daughter was abed with a baby.' He narrowed his eyes at me. 'Did you know of this?'

I shrugged, though I did smile to myself – Aliénor had got what she wanted from me. 'I haven't been to Brussels since last May – how could I know?'

'Not been to Brussels for nine months, eh?' Léon Le Vieux shook his head. 'Never mind – she has married the cartoonist.'

'Ah.' I was more surprised than I let on. Philippe was not as shy with women as I'd thought. It had helped introducing him to that whore, certainly. Still, I was glad for Aliénor. Philippe was a good man, and he was not Jacques Le Bœuf.

'You haven't said what you think of the tapestries,' I said. 'You who want your women to be real. Have I – have we changed your mind, me and Georges, and Philippe too?'

Léon looked around the room again, then shrugged with a little smile. 'There is something about them I have not seen before, nor felt before. You've created a whole world for them to live in, though it is not like our world.'

'Are you tempted?'

'By them? *Non*.'

I chuckled. 'So we have not converted you after all. The Ladies are not as powerful as I thought.'

There was a noise outside the door, and Jean Le Viste and Geneviève de Nanterre entered the Grande Salle. I quickly bowed to hide my surprise, for I had not expected to see her. When I raised my head she was smiling at me as she had the day I'd met her, when I'd first flirted with Claude – smiling as if she already knew what was in my head.

'So, painter, what do you think of them?' Jean Le Viste asked. I wondered if he had forgotten my name. Before I could speak he added, 'Are they hung at the right height? I thought they should be another arm's length off the floor, but Léon says they look fine as they are.'

It was just as well that I hadn't spoken, for now I grasped that he didn't want to talk of the tapestries' beauty or the weavers' skill, but rather of how they graced his room. I studied the tapestries for a moment. They came to within a hand's length of the floor. That put the Ladies just a little above us. Any higher and they would tower over us.

I turned to Geneviève de Nanterre. 'What do you think, Madame? Should the Lady be higher?'

'No,' she said. 'That is not necessary.'

I nodded. 'I think, Monseigneur, we are agreed that the room looks very impressive as it is.'

Jean Le Viste shrugged. 'It will suit the occasion.' He turned to go.

I couldn't resist. 'Please, Monseigneur, which tapestry do you like best?'

Jean Le Viste stopped and gazed about him as if he had only just realized the tapestries were to be looked at. He frowned. 'This one,' he said, gesturing at Sound. 'The flag is very fine, and the lion noble. Come,' he said to Léon Le Vieux.

'I'm staying a moment to have a word with Nicolas des Innocents,' Geneviève de Nanterre announced. Jean Le Viste hardly seemed to hear, but strode to the door with Léon Le Vieux at his heels. The old man glanced at me before he left, as if to remind me of his earlier warning to behave. I smiled at the thought. I was with the wrong woman for making mischief.

When they were gone Geneviève de Nanterre chuckled softly. 'My husband has no favourite. He chose the tapestry nearest to hand – did you see? And it's not the finest – the Lady's hands are awkward, and the pattern of the tablecloth is too square and harsh.'

Clearly she had studied the tapestries carefully. At least she hadn't said that the unicorn was fat.

'Which tapestry do you like best, Madame?'

She pointed. 'That one.' I was surprised that she chose Touch – I had expected her to prefer À Mon Seul Désir. After all, she was the Lady.

'Why that one, Madame?'

'She is very clear, that Lady – clear in her soul. She's standing in a doorway, on the threshold between one life and another, and she's looking forward with happy eyes. She knows what will happen to her.'

I thought of what had inspired me to paint the Lady that way – of Christine standing in the doorway to the workshop, pleased that she would be weaving. It was so different from what Geneviève de Nanterre had just described that I had to suppress the urge to correct her.

277

'What about the Lady here, Madame?' I pointed to the Lady in À Mon Seul Désir. 'Doesn't she also leave one world for another?'

Geneviève de Nanterre was silent.

'I painted her especially for you, Madame, so that the tapestries aren't just about a seduction, but about the soul too. Do you see – you can start with this tapestry, of the Lady putting on her necklace, and go around the room to follow her seduction of the unicorn. Or you can go the other way, with the Lady bidding farewell to each different sense, and end with this tapestry, where she takes off her necklace to put it away – to let go of the physical life. Do you see that I've done that for you, Madame? When the Lady holds her jewels as she does, we don't know if she is putting them on or taking them off. It can be either. That is the secret I've made for you in the tapestries.'

Geneviève de Nanterre shook her head. 'The Lady looks as if she hasn't decided which she prefers – the seduction or the soul. I know which I prefer, and I would like to see her choice clearly made. *Tiens*, it's better that the tapestries are of the seduction of the unicorn – they will go to my daughter eventually. The seduction will please her.' She gazed at me and I blushed.

'I'm sorry you don't like them, Madame.' I was indeed sorry. I thought I'd been very clever, but my cleverness had tripped me up.

Geneviève de Nanterre turned around, taking in all of the tapestries once more. 'They are very beautiful, and that is enough. Certainly Jean is pleased, even if he doesn't show it, and Claude will love them. To thank you for them

278

I would like you to join us tomorrow night for the feast here.'

'Tomorrow?'

'Yes, the Feast of St Valentine. The day birds choose their mates.'

'So they say.'

'We shall see you here, then.' She gave me a look before turning from me.

I bowed to her back. One of her ladies peeked around the doorway, and joined her mistress as they left.

I was alone with the tapestries then. I stood for a long time in the room, looking and wondering why they now made me melancholy.

I had not been to a nobleman's feast before. Painters aren't usually invited to such things. Indeed, I wasn't sure why Geneviève de Nanterre had asked me to come. Quickly and at great expense I had a new tunic made – black velvet with yellow trim – and a cap to match. I cleaned my boots and washed myself, though the water was icy. At least when I arrived at the torch-lit house on the rue du Four, squires let me in without blinking, as if I were a noble among others. In my room I'd thought my new tunic and cap very smart – and had been cheered by the men and women in Le Coq d'Or – but as I walked towards the Grande Salle among the rich dresses of the ladies and men around me, I felt like a peasant.

Three girls ran in and out of the crowd. The eldest was Claude's sister Jeanne, who had been looking into the well in the courtyard the day I first met Claude. The second resembled her and must be the youngest Le Viste girl. The smallest came up only to my knee and looked nothing like a Le Viste, though she was pretty in her way, with dark red ringlets all in a mess at her neck. In the crowd she got tangled in my legs and as I set her straight she scowled up at me under a heavy brow in a way that seemed familiar. She ran off before I could ask her name.

The room was crowded with guests, with *jongleurs* playing and dancing and tumbling, with squires bringing around wine and titbits – pickled quails' eggs, pork cutlets, meatballs decorated with dried flowers, even raspberries usually impossible to find in winter.

Jean Le Viste stood at one end of the room, by the tapestry of Smell, dressed in a red fur-trimmed gown among other men wearing the same. They would be discussing King and Court, matters I was never much concerned with. I preferred Geneviève de Nanterre's end of the room, where I could watch the ladies in their brocades and their furs of mink and fox and rabbit. The mistress of the house herself was dressed quite simply in sky-blue silk and grey rabbit fur, and stood beside À Mon Seul Désir.

The tapestries were much admired, but though they made the room warm and softened the sound of so many people, they were not so striking in loud company as when I had been alone with them. I could see now that a battle with its clamour of horses and men would have better suited a feast room, whereas these ought to be hung in a lady's chamber. Jean Le Viste had been right after all.

I tried not to think about this too much, but drank as

much spiced wine as the men pouring it would serve me. At first I stood alone and watched the tumblers and the ladies dancing, and ate a roasted fig. Then a noblewoman I'd once painted called me to her. After that it was easier, to talk and laugh and drink as I would if I were at the tavern.

When Claude entered wearing red velvet, surrounded by ladies – Béatrice among them – I felt my shoulders loosen and my arms flap at my sides like pieces of twine. Of course I had been waiting for her to appear – even as I drank and flirted and ate my fig and even danced a galliard with a merry lady. Of course she would come. That was why I was here.

The room was crowded and I didn't think she saw me. At least she gave no sign. She was thinner and bonier than when I'd seen her last. Her eyes were still like quinces but they were not as lively as they had been. They fastened onto her ladies rather than following the dancers, or she looked at something distant – perhaps at one of the *millefleurs* in Smell or in Taste across the room from her, though not at the Lady herself.

Béatrice did see me, and looked boldly with her dark eyes. She too was thinner. She didn't lean over to her mistress and whisper and point, but stared at me until I looked away.

I didn't try to go up to Claude. I knew it would be futile – someone would get in my way, the steward would be called to march me away and throw me into the street, perhaps with another beating. I knew this without being told. Now I knew why Geneviève de Nanterre had invited me – I had been brought here to be punished.

281

Soon the music and dancing stopped, and trumpets sounded for the meal to begin. Claude joined her parents and some others at the high table – the oak table I had once stood on to measure the walls. The rest of the guests sat along trestle tables down the sides of the room. I found myself at the very end – the lowest place, furthest from Claude. Just behind me hung Taste. Across from me hung Sight with Aliénor's sweet, sad face keeping me company.

A priest from Saint-Germain-des-Prés came to lead us in prayer. Then Jean Le Viste stood and held up his hand. He did not honey his words but spoke bluntly, so that when I heard it the wound was clean and deep. 'We are gathered here to announce my eldest daughter Claude's betrothal to Geoffroy de Balzac, valet de chambre of the King. We will be proud to call a member of such an honourable family our son.' He held out his hand and a young man with a brown beard stood up from the high table and bowed slightly to Jean Le Viste and to Claude, who kept her eyes fixed on the table before her. Geneviève de Nanterre did not bow her head, but looked down along the trestle table to me perched at the end. Now you are having your punishment, her look said. I dropped my eyes to my trencher, and saw that the bread had been carved with the initials CLV and GDB intertwined. Birds finding their mates indeed.

After that I did not listen to what Jean Le Viste said, though I raised my cup when everyone else did in toasts that I didn't hear. When the trumpets sounded the squires brought in the roast fowl – a peacock fanning his tail before the female, a pair of pheasants with their wings arranged as if they were about to fly away, two swans with their necks entwined. I took in these sights without pleasure, and didn't reach with my knife for a taste. My neighbours must have thought me dull company indeed.

As a boar covered with gold leaf was brought in, I knew I wouldn't stay to see the many courses announced, the drink and the food and the spectacle going on and on all night and into the next day. I had no taste for the feast. I stood and after a last glance at the tapestries – for I knew I would not see them again – I slipped away to the door. To get there I had to pass the high table, and as I did a movement caught my eye. Claude had brought her hand down on the table suddenly and her knife clattered to the floor. 'Oh!' she cried. One of her ladies went to fetch it but she stopped her with a laugh – the first merriment I had seen in her all evening. 'I'll get it,' she said and dived under the table. I couldn't see her – the white tablecloth painted with Le Viste coats of arms fell to the floor, shielding everything behind it.

I waited a moment. No one seemed to notice me. Béatrice was standing behind her mistress's chair, talking to a man who was serving Geoffroy de Balzac. Geneviève de Nanterre was speaking to her future son-in-law. Jean Le Viste was looking my way but seemed to see straight through me. Already he didn't remember who I was. When he called over his shoulder for more wine I pulled my cap from my head and let it fall, then went on my knees to retrieve it. In a second I had hiked up the cloth and was under the table.

Claude was sitting in a ball, arms around her legs, chin on her knees. She smiled at me.

'Do you always have your *rendezvous* under tables, Mademoiselle?' I asked as I put my cap back on.

'Tables are very handy for hiding under.'

'Is that where you've hidden all this time, beauty? Under a table?'

Claude stopped smiling. 'You know where I've been. You never came for me.' She turned her cheek to her knee so that her face was hidden. All I could see was her red velvet head-dress, beaded with pearls, her hair carefully tucked away under it.

'I didn't know where you were. How could I?'

Claude turned her face back to me. 'Yes, you did. Marie-Céleste said – ' she stopped, doubt spreading over her brow.

'Marie-Céleste? I haven't seen her since the day I last saw you – when I was being beaten. Did you send a message with her?'

Claude nodded.

'I never got it. She lied to you if she said I got it.'

'Oh.'

'Damn her. Why would she lie?'

Claude rested her head on her knees. 'She has her reasons. I was not so kind to her before.'

A greyhound strayed under the table, rooting around for scraps, and Claude reached over to pat it. When her sleeve fell back from her wrist I saw that it had been scraped raw, as if by angry fingernails that wanted cutting. I reached over and gently clasped her wrist. 'What has happened here, beauty? Have you hurt yourself?'

Claude pulled her wrist away. 'Sometimes it is the only thing that makes me feel. Well,' she continued, scratching at the wounds, 'it doesn't matter, really. You couldn't have got me out.'

'Where were you?'

'In a place that is a paradise to Maman and a prison to me. But that is what a lady's life is, I've found.'

'Don't say that. You're not imprisoned now. Come with me. Run away from your *fiancé*.'

For a moment Claude's face lit up like the sun on the Seine, but as she thought about it more her face went dark again, like the river's normal muddy colour. Wherever she had been had changed her spirit. It was a sad thing to see.

'What about *mon seul désir*?' I asked softly. 'Have you forgotten that?'

Claude sighed. 'I have no desire now. That was Maman's.' The dog sniffed at her lap and she cupped her hands around its face. 'Thank you for the tapestries,' she added, gazing into the dog's eyes. 'Has anyone thanked you? They're beautiful, though they make me sad.'

'Why, beauty?'

She looked at me. 'They remind me of what I was like before, all light and happy and free. Only the one where the unicorn lies in her lap is like me now – that Lady is sad and knows something of the world. I prefer her to the others.'

I sighed. I seemed to have got all the Ladies wrong.

The tablecloth rippled then and the tiny red-haired girl crawled under the table. She had found the dog's tail and followed it back to its source. She showed no interest in us but patted the dog's back with both hands, squeezing its ribs. The dog didn't seem to notice – it had found a lamb bone and was gnawing on it.

'Mind you, I did find one good thing in the prison.' Claude nodded at the girl. 'I brought her back with me. Nicolette, take the dog away. Béatrice will find him a bigger bone. Go, now.' She gave the dog's rump a shove.

The girl and dog ignored her.

'She will be one of my ladies-in-waiting when she's grown,' Claude added. 'Of course she'll need training, but that's a long time away yet. She's still a baby, really.'

I stared at the girl. 'Her name is Nicolette?'

Claude laughed as she had once done – a girlish laugh full of promise. 'I renamed her. We couldn't have two Claudes at the convent, could we?'

She laughed again when I jerked my head so hard I banged it against the top of the table. I looked at the girl who was my daughter and then at Claude, who gazed at me with her clear eyes. For a moment I felt the old surge of desire push me towards her, and reached across to her.

I never found out if Claude would have let me touch her. Once more – as she had the last time Claude and I were under a table together – Béatrice poked her head into our hiding place. It was her role to come between us. She didn't even look surprised to see me. She'd probably been listening the whole time, as ladies-in-waiting do. 'Mademoiselle, your mother wants you,' she said.

Claude made a face but got to her knees. '*Adieu*, Nicolas,' she said with a small smile. Then she nodded at Nicolette. 'And don't worry – I'll keep her with me always. Won't I, *ma petite?'* She scrambled out from the table, Nicolette and the dog following her.

Béatrice was looking at me. 'I've got you,' she said. 'I had to live nine months in Hell because of you. I made messages go astray because of you. I'm not going to let you go now.' She pulled her head away and disappeared.

I remained on my knees under the table, puzzling over her words. At last, though, I too crawled out from my hiding place and stood up. No one noticed me. Jean Le Viste had left the table and was talking to Geoffroy de Balzac, his back to me. Geneviève de Nanterre was standing with Claude at the other end of the table. Béatrice was whispering in her ear.

Geneviève de Nanterre looked over at me. *'Bien sûr,'* she cried brightly, holding out a hand and stepping over so that she stood between me and Béatrice. 'Nicolas des Innocents, how could I have forgotten you? Béatrice has told me she's tired of service and would prefer the life of an artist's wife. Wouldn't you, Béatrice?'

Béatrice nodded.

'Of course it's not for me to arrange, as Béatrice is my daughter's lady now. She must decide. What do you think, Claude – will you release Béatrice from service to you so that she may marry Nicolas des Innocents?'

Claude looked at her mother and then at me, her eyes bright with tears. We were both of us being punished.

'Claude and I will be sorry to lose you, Béatrice,' Geneviève de Nanterre added. 'But my daughter will give her permission, won't you, Claude?'

After a moment Claude gave a little shrug. 'I will,

Maman. As you wish.' She did not look at me as her mother took Béatrice's hand and slipped it into mine, but fastened her eyes on the tapestry of Taste.

Myself, I did not look at the tapestries with the Ladies gazing down from their walls, nor at the nobles eating and drinking and laughing and dancing. I did not need to look at them to know that they would all be smiling.

EPILOGUE

Nicolas des Innocents was commissioned to design a stained glass window for Notre Dame de Paris. He had three more children, none of them with Béatrice.

Claude Le Viste and Geoffroy de Balzac had no children. After he died in 1510 she married Jean de Chabannes. They also had no children. After her death the Lady and the Unicorn tapestries passed on to the family of her second husband.

Nicolette was Claude Le Viste's lady-in-waiting all her life.

Jean Le Viste died in 1501. After his death Geneviève de Nanterre entered the convent at Chelles.

Philippe and Aliénor had three more boys. The first son, Etienne, and the youngest became painters, while the other two became weavers.

Georges was offered several other commissions to weave unicorns. He turned them down. 'Too much trouble,' he said to Christine.

Christine wove a small *millefleur* tapestry for her daughter's belated trousseau. She did not weave for the workshop again.

Léon Le Vieux died in his own bed, his wife and children at his side.

NOTES AND ACKNOWLEDGMENTS

This story is fiction, yet based on sensible suppositions concerning the Lady and the Unicorn tapestries. It is not certain which member of the Le Viste family the tapestries were actually commissioned by, nor why they were made, nor exactly when – though the Ladies' clothes and the weaving techniques indicate they were probably woven towards the end of the fifteenth century. Jean Le Viste was the only male who had the right to display the family coat of arms at that time. Nor do we know who made them, though the skill and techniques displayed indicate the workshop would have been northern, possibly in Brussels, where *millefleurs* were a speciality at that time.

For all their expense and their glorification of the Le Viste coat of arms, the tapestries did not remain in the Le Viste family for long – on Claude's death (some time before 1544) they probably passed to another branch of the Le Viste family. By 1660 they had been hung in a château at Boussac in central France. They were rediscovered there in 1841 by Prosper Mérimée, inspector of historical monuments. He found them in poor condition, for they had been gnawed at by rats and in some places cut up – apparently people in neighbouring villages used parts of them as tablecloths and curtains. The writer Georges Sand soon became their champion, writing about them in articles, novels and her journal. In 1882 the French government bought the tapestries for the Musée de Cluny (now the Musée National du Moyen Âge) in Paris – where they still hang, restored and in a specially appointed room.

I have tried to be faithful to what little is known about the tapestries, but on more general matters I have taken liberties here and there, as novelists always do – in using modern French throughout, and perhaps most of all in having the Brussels folk speak French when they quite likely would have spoken Flemish among themselves, if not to visitors.

There are many sources on late medieval/Renaissance France, and on medieval life in general. One of the most entertaining is *Life on a Mediaeval Barony* by William S. Davis (1923). Books that helped me on more specific topics include: *La Tapisserie au Moyen Âge* by Fabienne Joubert (2000); *Tapestry in the Renaissance: Art and Magnificence*, edited by Thomas P. Campbell (2002); *The Lady and the Unicorn* by Alain Erlande-Brandenburg (1991); *The Unicorn Tapestries* by Margaret B. Freeman (1976); *Medieval Tapestries in the Metropolitan Museum of Art* by Adolfo Salvatore Cavallo (1993); *The Oak King, the Holly King, and the Unicorn: The Myths and Symbolism of the Unicorn Tapestries* by John Williamson (1986); *Sur la terre comme au ciel: Jardins d'Occident à la fin du Moyen Âge*, edited by Élisabeth

Antoine (2002); *Le Château d'Arcy et ses seigneurs* by A. et C.-M. Fleury (1917).

In addition, I would like to thank Élisabeth Antoine at the Musée National du Moyen Âge in Paris; Philip Sanderson, Katharine Swailes, and especially Caron Penney in the Tapestry Studio at West Dean College in Sussex – they are recreating another famous unicorn tapestry and showed me first hand how medieval tapestries were woven; Lindsey Young; Sally Dormer; Katie Espiner; also Susan Watt and Carole Baron, Jonny Geller and Deborah Schneider.

More great reads from Tracy Chevalier . . .

'Tracy Chevalier gives the gift of life to the historical novel.'
Independent

At your reading service

How would you like to have news of the latest releases by your favourite authors brought directly to you? Well, now you can. Author Tracker is a unique tailor-made service that keeps you updated with news, offers, previews and much more without you moving a muscle. All you have to do is tell us which authors you love, and we'll do the rest.

RSVP today